FORGED IN DECEPTION

FORGE BROTHERS SECURITY
BOOK 3

KENDRA WARDEN

Fearless Faith Press

CHAPTER
ONE

THE WOMAN

BEFORE

The woman looked down at the palm of her hand. The sound of drums and chanting voices were getting louder.

They seemed to brush up against her ears as though they were real things, as solid as the hard-packed sandy floor where she sat. Smoke filled her nostrils, the smell shifting from rich and pleasant to sour and sweet. A bonfire danced in the center of the room, sparks escaping only to extinguish themselves against the rough stone walls.

She tried to ball her hands into fists, but she could no longer figure out which muscles to use.

Her limbs had been working just fine. She was still quite sure of that. She had gripped a rough clay mug, lifting it to her lips and imbibing the herbal brew within.

1

But her fingers were shifting now, growing longer before twisting, warping, crawling upward toward the top of the hut.

They no longer looked like hands at all.

They were slithering flesh, like pale snakes coiled together, waiting for an unlucky soul to tread upon them in the dark.

She tried to swallow the sudden sick feeling that pooled in her gut.

This was wrong.

All of this was horribly, terribly wrong.

The world she had known was washed away, replaced by something different altogether. Something vast. A sky with stars and black holes in equal measure, a fickle place where a thousand doors waited to be opened.

And there was no way out.

There were no fingers now, no sturdy stone walls, no shifting smells, no fire.

People had been there moments before, she remembered. At least ten of them, casting their dark shadows in the firelight, chanting together, their voices blending as one. Now, they were gone, replaced with waves of light that seemed to undulate through the air like smoke, a spectacle of a thousand colors.

She didn't know if she was chanting or not.

She heard her voice, meek and high-pitched amid the bellows of the others, but she couldn't make her mouth open or close. Her tongue felt dry and thick.

She couldn't make herself scream.

Her breathing felt fast.

Sputtering exhales followed rough inhales as smoke choked at her throat. She couldn't look down at her chest, but it was expanding and shrinking again, in and out, fast and ruthless.

It felt real. Breathing still felt real.

It was something. Something to hold on to.

She closed her eyes, trying to hold on to the sensation of air rushing into and out of her lungs. Even the wrongness of the smoke was welcome. It was unpleasant and blessedly real.

"You don't need to be afraid."

A voice was there now.

It seemed to be beside her.

It was *his* voice.

But no longer could she open her eyes and see her beloved Professor.

"You're doing just fine for your first time. I promise. Don't fight it. Just surrender. Trust me."

She breathed again and again, grasping for her thoughts in the frenetic show of color and thundering sound.

Two words entered her mind before leaving it again, carried on the smoke and the waves of light.

"I'm scared."

She hadn't spoken them aloud, but she knew that he heard her. Some part of herself, a part that felt very far away now, was certain of it. She could trust him, just as she always had.

She felt herself beginning to relax at last.

The Professor was there beside her in the hut, and everything would be all right.

He was there.

He was still holding tightly to her hand.

3

CHAPTER
TWO

ASHER

"We can still fix this. This is not an emergency."

"The bridal shop canceled! That is the *ultimate* wedding emergency."

"I'd say throwing up on your dress is a little bit worse. Or being left at the altar–"

"Ladies, can we focus, please? We'll just find new bridesmaid dresses. It'll be fine."

"Ooh, now that we have the chance to change things up, have you considered doing orange? I look so gross in green. And orange is the hottest color for weddings this season. I read it in, like, ten bridal magazines."

"Orange-orange, or pastel orange?"

"Either one. But not, like, orange soda orange. Obviously. Gross."

"But orange is the hottest color for *fall*. It's going to be almost Christmas!"

"So what? This is San Antonio! It's not like it's going to snow. Probably."

"Okay, hold on. How about this? We keep it simple and just do black. It'll be classy. And everyone looks good in black."

"Black? Bristol, you can't have your bridesmaids wear black! I know you're stuck marrying Cam and therefore cleaning a house he lives in, but this isn't a funeral."

"Um, ouch! You do realize I'm sitting right here?"

"She's right. You're the messiest person on earth!"

Asher Forge stifled a laugh as his youngest brother, Cameron, glared over at the group of women gathered around the large dining room table. Just when he thought he'd die of boredom from all this wedding talk, things were finally starting to get interesting.

Cameron and his fiancée, Bristol, were due to be married in two months, and they seemed to be feeling the crunch. The father of the groom, Gabriel Forge Sr., had suggested that a family Sunday dinner and wedding planning session at his home in the country would be just the thing, considering that the reception would be taking place under a huge marquee in the backyard.

Apparently, it was going about as well as Asher had expected.

"You want my advice, Cam?" their cousin, Reilly, chimed in from the adjoining living room. "Just let the women handle the wedding. Just let them do whatever they want. It's the most painless option."

"He's right, you know," Gabriel Forge Sr. called out in agreement, sitting up straighter in his favorite armchair that rested in the corner of the living room. "Mary chose everything for our wedding, God rest her. I was happy to make her mine. That was all that mattered to me."

5

"Mom would have loved this chaos," Asher's twin brother, Benjamin, declared in his rumbling timbre from his place at the far end of the table. "Can't say I share that particular trait."

Cameron shot Bristol a wink.

"Guys, guys, guys. You don't have to tell me twice. I'm just here for the first kiss and the cake."

He paused, allowing Bristol an opening to give him a playful swat on the arm.

"And the whole binding-our-souls-before-God part, of course," he added.

Grace Hinton, Ben's girlfriend and the office manager of their company, Forge Brothers Security, got to her feet and pointed at the back door.

"As maid of honor, I am officially declaring this meeting to be women only until Gabe gets here with dinner. Go take the twins out to the yard. Show them a chicken or something. You, too, Reilly. Gabe Sr. can stay if he wants, but only because it's his house."

Ben shot out of his seat before Grace had even finished her sentence, and Asher, Cameron, and their old man followed without hesitation. Reilly paused for a moment to sweep his eight-month-old twin girls, Clara and Josefina, off of the dining room floor.

His wife, Lauren, leaned over and pressed her lips to each of their foreheads in turn, cooing something to them in Spanish that Asher didn't quite hear.

"No kiss for me?" Reilly joked. "Is our marriage getting boring already?"

Lauren rolled her dark brown eyes and gave him a quick peck on the lips.

"Seriously, out!" Grace admonished, shooing them toward the door.

The late afternoon breeze was refreshing as Asher followed the others out into the backyard of the spacious farmhouse. The men sank into the grass and watched as Clara and Josefina each found a crisp fall leaf and proceeded to stick them directly into their mouths.

"So, Benjamin," Gabe Sr. said, swatting a fly that had landed directly on top of his balding head, "when are you and Gracie getting married?"

Ben paused to pick up Josefina, who was happily poking her sister's tanned forearm with a stick.

"Soon enough," he grumbled. "I've been waiting for the right moment, but this wedding excitement is sending Grace into hyperdrive."

"Don't wait too long, son," Gabe Sr. replied.

"I agree," Cameron said. "Honestly, I kind of wish I'd asked Bristol sooner."

"You guys know that Lauren and I wasted no time," Reilly added. "No regrets. I love being married. And being a dad."

Ben narrowed his eyes. "At least I have a girlfriend. Why don't you guys hound Asher for once? He isn't even trying to find anybody. He's getting way too comfortable sitting around listening to music and playing video games until two in the morning."

Asher put a hand to his chest in mock indignation. "In case you missed it, dear brother, I've also been focusing on getting closer to the Lord for the last few years. I'd say that counts for something."

It was true. Though the Forge boys had all been raised Christian, they hadn't all stayed on the narrow path as they grew up. Asher certainly hadn't. Neither had their brother Jacob, who was currently halfway across the world

7

aiding persecuted Christians in an attempt to atone for the sins of his youth.

"It does," Gabe Sr. acknowledged. "Our relationship with Jesus comes first. But that doesn't mean you–"

Before the lecture could continue, however, the men were interrupted by the sound of a truck rumbling along the quiet dirt road.

The men went quiet for a couple of minutes as Gabriel Forge Jr. pulled his black Ford into the driveway and cut the engine, but the babies kept up a running commentary of adorable babbling.

"You're hungry too, huh?" Cameron said to the girls, ruffling the nearest twin's dark hair with his fingers. Lauren had dressed them in the same outfit today, and though they weren't identical, Asher had already lost track of which one was which at a glance.

"Good to see you here, bud," Gabe Sr. said, getting to his feet along with the others as Gabe Jr. stepped out of his truck. Asher and the rest of the boys shot glances back and forth as the two men embraced one another.

Though they were all generally on good terms, there was still some tension yet to be resolved between the Forge family's patriarch and his oldest son.

Even after more than eight years, it was clear that Gabe Sr. still held some resentment toward Gabe Jr. for leaving the original family agriculture business, Forge & Sons, in order to found a private security firm.

"Sorry I'm late," Gabe Jr. said, handing several paper bags of still-steaming food to Reilly, Cameron, and Ben.

Asher couldn't help but notice he wasn't entrusted with any of the Screaming Peach Cafe's delicacies. Fair enough, he supposed. He probably wouldn't have been able to resist digging in right then and there. The local coffee shop mostly served breakfast food, but Iris was always willing to adapt the menu for some of her most loyal customers.

"Don't worry about it," Gabe Sr. said easily, pulling back to look his son up and down as though he hadn't seen him in years. "I'm just glad to see you stepping foot on the property. Especially with Iris's catering in hand."

"But please make sure you're on time for the actual wedding," Cameron joked.

Gabe Jr. smiled, but Asher could see that his blue eyes were troubled. "In my defense, I was stuck at the office trying to finish up some paperwork for the Fairman file. It's due tomorrow, but honestly, I think I'm going to have to admit defeat and break the news to our lawyers that we'll need an extension."

Gabe shot Asher a brief glance that filled his stomach with lead.

He looked down at the twins playing in the grass, surprised that his oldest brother hadn't yelled at him in front of the others, which he probably deserved. He was supposed to have had that paperwork done by Friday, but instead he'd forgotten about it completely.

And then proceeded to spend most of the weekend at a music festival, having also forgotten his phone back at the house he shared with Ben.

Oops.

"Don't worry about the paperwork," he said quietly to Gabe as the men began to file into the house. "I'll eat fast and go finish it. I was gonna be up too late tonight, anyway."

"I appreciate it, bro," Gabe said as he followed the others. "At least dad will be ticked at you for leaving early instead of being mad at me for... everything he's always mad at me for."

Asher wanted to say more, but Gabe had already slipped into the house and let the screen door fall shut behind him.

KARLIN

Karlin McKenna fiddled with the photograph in the pocket of her white lab coat as she walked, turning the worn paper over and over between her fingers.

She'd started carrying the photo of her older brother, John, a few years ago. Now, the picture felt like it had become a part of her. During her most difficult hours at work, it was a reminder of why she kept pushing, no matter how much she wanted to give up.

Fighting back the nervous urge to stare down at her feet, she kept her chin high and gave a curt nod as she passed a group of interns, who scurried out of her way immediately.

So far, she hadn't seen anyone else down here on the lowest lab floor of Senera Pharmaceuticals.

It was getting late, and most of her colleagues who had gotten stuck working on a Sunday had long since gone home for the night. Still, she couldn't shake the feeling of guilt that bubbled up every time she took even the shortest break. Despite the fact that she was now a senior research scientist, a small part of her still felt like the terrified newbie she'd been a decade ago.

Karlin pushed through a set of swinging doors, wincing at the sudden glow of artificial light in the wide hallway beyond. Finding the space empty as well, she brushed a stray wisp of red hair behind a freckled ear and stood a little taller.

Maybe she owed her past self a little bit of self-confidence now. If she hadn't been so terrified to do what was right back then, perhaps she wouldn't be carrying so many regrets.

She nodded to another passing scientist, an Asian man she didn't know very well, and picked up her pace. There was no point in dwelling on her mistakes.

She had to get outside and call John. Surely he was out of the insurance office by now and, hopefully, he had good news.

She headed for the elevator at last, pausing for a moment to glance over at the nondescript but heavy door that led toward the most secure area in the entire facility.

She could almost see the small room in her mind, lined with tall refrigerators, cryo freezers, warming trays, and room-temperature cabinets, all filled with little vials of DX8.

She'd been in and out of the high-tech storage space what felt like a million times, retrieving sample after sample in pill, liquid, and powder form. She had spent countless hours recording data, analyzing and refining chemical properties, and every now and then, procuring doses of DX8 for research on animal and human test subjects.

Years and years of research, pools of sweat and tears, all for a powerful psychedelic that would revolutionize the treatment of mental health disorders.

A familiar shiver of unease wound its way up her spine as she continued on her way, instinctively quieting the clicking of her heels on the cold tile as though someone was waiting to jump out of the storage room and grab her.

Ever since Senera Pharmaceuticals had hired Dr. Daman Bajwa as head of research and development, he'd been running her and her colleagues ragged. Their hours had never been so long, but, to the man's credit, Senera had never made so much progress on so many medical products.

But there was nothing that Dr. Bajwa cared about more than DX8. When it came to that drug in particular, he was single-minded. Sometimes even to the point of cruelty. Nothing else mattered. Not his employees' personal lives, not labor laws, not his reputation as a boss, none of it.

On the other hand, his enthusiasm for DX8 was often inspiring. It was easy for most of Karlin's colleagues to forgive his eccentricities. They never doubted that Dr. Bajwa was genuine in his belief that the drug was deeply important to the future of humanity. He wanted to see DX8 being widely prescribed as soon as possible.

Sometimes, Karlin believed his hype, but she often found his eager speeches in the lab to feel a little too forced, his beaming smile a little too wide. It set her teeth on edge, and it kept her from ever feeling comfortable in her role.

Some part of her was always wondering about what it would be like to be somewhere else. Somewhere she could breathe.

But however she felt about the direction Bajwa was taking, she knew one thing better than almost anyone else working at Senera.

At the cutting edge of mental health research, errors in judgment could be deadly.

And they could also get her fired, sued, or thrown in jail.

CHAPTER
THREE

ASHER

The halls of Forge Brothers Security were quiet, even for a Sunday.

Though official company policy was to observe the traditional day of rest and worship, it was rare to find the place truly empty. As Asher made his way to his oldest brother's fifth floor office to retrieve the files he needed, he knocked on the edge of the doorframe out of habit before entering.

The expansive windows looked out at the busy streets of downtown San Antonio, though thanks to the thick glass, Asher could hear nothing but the gentle buzz of the air conditioning.

Even though he was supposed to be there, he couldn't help but feel slightly ill at ease in the oppressive silence. The sterile tidiness of Gabe's office wasn't exactly inviting. Everything in it was white, gray, or black–not that there was any clutter to speak of. Honestly, the place reminded him more than a little of the San Antonio morgue.

Asher crossed the short distance to the large metal filing cabinet along the side wall, taking all of five seconds to locate the correct file before making a beeline back toward the door.

Had it been anyone else, he would have stopped to snoop a little in search of a late afternoon snack. With Gabe, though, he knew he'd probably find nothing but plain water, plain chicken, and salad greens in the mini fridge. Certainly there would be nothing worth spending another two minutes in the cold, lonely corner office looking for.

As he waited for the elevator to bring him back to the first floor, he heard his phone buzzing in the pocket of his jeans. When he looked down at the caller ID, however, he couldn't help but to curl the side of his lip in disgust.

He silenced the call and stepped out into the lobby of FBS, watching as a dozen or so people filed past the front windows in the fading sunlight, couples laughing and pausing for kisses as they rushed to catch their dinner reservations along the famous River Walk.

He rolled his eyes good-naturedly as he turned down the hall that led toward his office. Between Reilly and Lauren, Cameron and Bristol, and Ben and Grace, he had seen enough PDA to make him V-O-M-I-T.

He was happy for his brothers, but after the experiences he'd had with women–most of them embarrassingly regrettable–he was in no hurry to follow in their footsteps.

Just then, he felt the annoying buzz of his cell phone again.

Sure enough, it was the Veteran's Freedom Society continuing to pester him.

Nowhere to be found when his fellow soldiers were

desperate for help, but pathologically unable to leave him alone.

He settled down in his worn leather office chair, swiped several random papers out of the way, and plunked the Fairman file down on his desk.

The voicemail notification pinged.

With another, less good-natured eye roll, Asher hit speaker and let the message play.

Hello Mr. Forge, I'm sorry we missed you! We apologize for calling on a Sunday, but we wanted to make sure you knew about our virtual town hall meeting. It will be a good opportunity for you to voice your concerns as well as to connect with others who share a similar background. We want to know how we can better serve those suffering from combat-related trauma. Please get back to us at–

Asher hung up the phone and sat in silence for a moment, fiddling with the smooth metal of the dog tag necklace he still wore, considering not for the first time if he should toss it out the window.

He didn't need to talk about his feelings with some pencil-pusher who had never stepped foot on Afghan sand. That was all in the past. He was fine now.

And he'd be even more fine if they would just leave him alone.

KARLIN

Even after a decade of living in Amarillo, the chill of desert evenings in autumn still managed to take Karlin by surprise. She pulled her lab coat more tightly around herself and drew out her phone, trying to read what was on the screen as the wind whipped strands of auburn hair into her eyes. It was almost seven o'clock, and her brother's meeting had ended at least half an hour ago.

"Hello?"

"Hey, John," she said. "I can't talk long. It's super windy here and I have to get back to the lab, but I wanted to hear the verdict."

The line was quiet for several long seconds.

She listened to the howl of a coyote from across the expanse of reddish sand, tufts of dry grass, and the occasional prickly pear cactus.

Still, John said nothing.

"Can you hear me? Should I try and go back inside?"

A sigh cut through the rustling wind.

"It's not that, sis."

"Then what?"

"I don't like having to give you bad news."

Karlin's heart sank.

"Just spit it out."

"I've been praying hard for this service dog. I really thought it was going to go through this time. But no. The Veteran's Freedom Society won't cover the cost. That was my last stop for finding funding. Maybe I read the signs wrong. Maybe it's not God's plan right now."

Karlin gritted her teeth before she told her little brother what she thought of God's opinion. Namely, that He should have intervened back in Afghanistan.

"Forget the VFS, the VA, all the rest. I'm gonna figure out a way to get that dog if it's the last thing I do," she said instead.

"Chill, Karl. It's fine. I've managed this long without one."

His words made her feel sick. He had not *managed*. Not at all. But she didn't think reminding him of his lowest point would do him any good. Not to mention that it would only drag up yet another unpleasant memory that she was desperate to forget.

"I thought you'd agreed that nickname was dead at last," she said breezily, hoping he couldn't sense the hidden sadness and anger beneath her words. "You need to let me help you. You've been doing better. You haven't drunk in what, five months? You've even been going to the gym again! I don't want you to stop making progress."

"I won't. But a dog trained to assist with PTSD costs thousands of dollars. Therapy is expensive enough, not to mention the loony bin bill–"

"Don't call it that."

"Whatever I call it, you're still paying for it, sis. Honestly, it makes me feel like a pathetic loser working part-time. I need to find a better job and pay my own way again."

The wind was picking up, and this time, Karlin was thankful for the noise. They'd had this fight too many times already. John was trying to battle his demons, but mental health improvement took time, and it also took energy. Energy he wouldn't have if he pushed himself harder at work than he was capable of right now.

"I gotta go, sorry, I can't hear you," Karlin nearly shouted into the phone as another helpful gust of wind whipped dust along the side of the building. "I'll talk to you later! Bye!"

Without waiting for a reply, she hung up and shoved the phone back into her pocket before turning to head back inside.

If she could focus for another forty-five minutes, she could let herself call it a night. She'd gotten a lot done today, anyway. Maybe she could lay out the lab prep for tomorrow, that would give her a–

She stopped just short of the doorway.

"Ms. McKenna," Dr. Daman Bajwa said mildly, pushing the glass door open for her with seemingly no effort. "Why are you out here in the cold? I need to talk to you."

CHAPTER
FOUR

KARLIN

Karlin tried without success to calm her racing heart as she followed Dr. Bajwa through the lobby of Senera Pharmaceuticals. The fact that she hadn't actually broken any rules and had actually volunteered to work overtime on a Sunday was irrelevant. She knew that the man's temper was easy to kindle, and his good graces were easier to lose than to regain.

"Ah," Dr. Bajwa said, gesturing toward a random, empty conference room. "Good enough. I just want to make sure no one is listening in the halls."

She nodded noncommittally and followed him in, sitting down in one of the modern, uncomfortable chrome and leather chairs.

"I'm sorry for making a call while I was on the clock," she said quickly. "I had to talk to my brother. It was important, but I should have waited another hour until I was off."

He looked over at her, his brown-skinned forehead wrinkling in a moment of brief puzzlement.

"Ms. McKenna, focus, please," he said, clapping his hands together as his face broke into a smile.

She released a breath. She wasn't in trouble. Actually, the man seemed to be in an absolutely stellar mood.

"What can I do for you?" she asked.

"I wanted you to be first to hear the good news," he said, leaning forward over the table while somehow managing to keep his wrinkle-less shirt perfectly tucked in. "We did it, Karlin."

Now it was her turn to look puzzled.

"Did…what?"

"We got a sixty-five-year-old for the next research retreat. Sixty-five! And it's a male subject!"

Karlin was taken aback, and for a moment, her mouth seemed to cease operating properly.

"Do you not realize the significance of this?" Dr. Bajwa continued, waving his hands in the general direction of the walls.

She nodded. She did. Testing any new drug was difficult, but a psychedelic like DX8 posed additional challenges, especially when it came to finding patients to volunteer for clinical trials. Young people were significantly more likely to be willing to ingest it—sometimes too willing—which could skew the trial results.

"I understand we've been in dire need of older patients for more than a decade, so yes, that's excellent news," she said carefully. "I'm just not sure why you would be willing to spend time on a Sunday to come into the office to tell me personally."

An almost imperceptible look of disdain crossed Dr. Bajwa's face, only to be replaced by excitement once again. The man was practically bouncing out of his chair.

"You didn't even let me finish. I just got off the phone with my guy at the FDA. We're officially moving into Phase II. Efficacy tests. Patients with actual, diagnosable mental disorders to treat. Lives that DX8 will change."

Karlin took a moment to let his words sink in.

She wanted to share in her boss's excitement, but she couldn't shake off her nerves.

Senera had been conducting Phase I safety and dosage tests on the drug that was now known as DX8 for a decade, and had spent untold millions doing so. Things were moving slowly, and in the pharmaceutical industry, if you didn't innovate, you'd be stomped by someone else who did.

Karlin wanted to move forward, too. But she couldn't just ignore the red flags.

Especially not when she considered the DX8-related incident that followed her like a ghost.

"Are you sure we're ready?" she asked. She tried to sound nonchalant, but Dr. Bajwa could sense what lay beneath her light tone at once.

"Of course. Our research retreats this year have been a huge success."

"What about the blood test results for two of the younger guys back in July? They both had elevated hematocrit levels at the end of the retreat."

"Barely elevated, Karlin. Those results could be–shall we say–interpreted as a rounding error."

He gave her a pointed look.

"The FDA has already been informed of the amended report stating as much."

"You signed off on this?" Karlin said incredulously.

Dr. Bajwa shook his head. "It's your file. I need your signature."

"You're asking me to fudge research data so that we can give a psychedelic drug to mentally ill patients?"

Her voice seemed to echo against the sleek walls of the conference room.

"Please keep your voice down," Dr. Bajwa said firmly. "Think about the big picture, Karlin. Medical research isn't for the faint of heart. We can't let miniscule anomalies get in the way. It's *slightly* elevated hematocrit in two patients who have just spent two weeks in the North Texas desert. In summer. Think about it."

She gripped the edge of her chair. He did have a point. Dehydration was by far the most likely explanation for the test results, especially in two healthy young men. But that didn't justify lying to regulators.

"I can't do that," she said, forcing her voice to lower. "We need to account for every potential risk factor that comes up. We can't just pick and choose because the executives are getting impatient."

"You think I care about the executives?" he snapped. "You think it's about a nice bonus and a bigger office?"

"I didn't say that, I–"

"Good. Because that's nonsense, and you know it. No. This is about this life changing, life saving, incredible medicine. It's about making the world a better place. I thought you believed in the work we're doing here."

Karlin swallowed hard. "I do. But we've had safety issues a lot worse than elevated hematocrit."

"We have had one death connected to DX8," Dr. Bajwa replied slowly, his voice low and dangerous. "One. A decade ago. It was a tragedy, but we have no idea what role, if any, DX8 played."

Easy for him to say. He hadn't been working at Senera then. He hadn't met the victim. He hadn't seen pictures of the husband and the little girl that she had left behind.

"I just want to make sure nothing like that comes close to happening again. That's all."

"Good. We're in agreement. When I interviewed for this job, I demanded to see Amira's file," Dr. Bajwa said, his eyes softening as he leaned against the conference table. "I examined it thoroughly. I agree that her suicide was a tragedy. But you should know better than anyone else here that tough decisions must be made when it comes to furthering the greater good."

He paused, allowing his words to hang in the silence.

Suddenly, the conference room felt cold.

All at once, Karlin was the terrified junior researcher she'd been ten years ago. Back then, she'd been scared of not being able to pay back her student loans. Now, she had John to take care of.

She had personally signed off on allowing Amira to enter that Phase I trial despite the woman's history of severe depression. Whether or not she'd been manipulated into doing it was irrelevant. She had blood on her hands.

And Senera—and apparently, Dr. Bajwa—knew it.

If she refused to fiddle with the research data, would they punish her for crossing them?

They could blacklist her in the medical research field. Senera was powerful. All they had to do was spread a rumor or two, and she'd never work in a research lab again.

And that was far from the worst thing that could happen to her.

After Amira's death, Senera had managed to success-fully argue in court that a lightning strike had damaged their computer servers, creating a ripple effect that had led to the destruction of much of their trial data.

Karlin had never believed them, especially considering the company's penchant for keeping what she considered an excess of paper records. She suspected there was evidence that implicated her, hidden away somewhere in case they ever needed someone to sacrifice.

She was trapped.

But still, every so often, a small ray of hope flickered in the back of her mind.

The slightest possibility of a way out, always there in the background, waiting for her, just in case the time came when she really needed it.

Maybe that time was now.

The thought filled her with dread, but she forced herself to ignore her feelings. If she could keep her emotions in check, she could think. She could at least get an idea of what her options were.

All she had to do was make a call.

"I'll let you know tomorrow what I decide," she said at last, catching Dr. Bajwa's dark, brooding eyes and daring him to argue with her. "Now if you'll excuse me, I think I'm going to head home."

Without waiting for permission, she strode out of the building and into the biting cold of the desert night.

She had another phone call to make.

And if there really was some God out there beyond the twinkling stars, she hoped he was looking down on her now.

Because if this didn't work, she was officially out of options.

And John would be the one to pay the price.

CHAPTER
FIVE

ASHER

A sher turned on his computer monitor, clicked open his music player, and hit shuffle on his enormous library. He stretched his arms over his head, closing his eyes for several long seconds and soaking in the upbeat vocals of Third Eye Blind. They were currently battling for a coveted spot on his top ten playlist, and with the whole office to himself, he could turn up the volume to his satisfaction without the company's head of security, a slightly scary woman named Dolly, wandering in to yell at him.

Unfortunately, the song ended all too soon, and the Fairman file lay open on his desk, beckoning him to make some actual progress. At least Gabe was enjoying dinner with the family, for once. It made Asher feel a little better about volunteering to come into work on a Sunday night.

He turned down the volume on his state-of-the-art sound system and clicked over to a mellow neoclassical playlist before picking up the file.

He skimmed its contents, refreshing his memory of the case, which had taken place a few months prior. A young woman named Katie Fairman had gone missing on spring break, and he, Ben, and Grace had traveled to sunny South Padre Island to find her.

He spent several minutes brushing up on the details, all while trying to avoid remembering too much about the part where he had almost killed someone. He didn't need that guilt floating around in his brain right now.

Just as he was about to start signing the legal records, however, his phone buzzed in his pocket again.

Why couldn't the Veterans Freedom Society just leave him alone?

He reached over and slammed his finger down on the space bar with too much force, silencing the piano track before answering the call.

"If I wanted to talk about the war, I would have answered the first eight times," he snapped.

The line was silent.

Oops.

He had sounded exactly like his twin brother, Ben, when someone woke him up too early.

"Sorry," he added quickly. "I'll still make a donation at Christmas, I promise. But I'm not interested in this town hall thing, okay?"

"Is this Asher Forge? From Forge Brothers Security?"

The voice on the other end was female, and probably not from VFS. Whoever it was, she sounded annoyed.

Which, he supposed, was fair enough, considering his greeting.

"Yep," he said. "This is my personal line, actually, so if this is about a private security gig, our office opens at–"

"I work at Senera Pharmaceuticals and I need help," the woman said, cutting him off.

She was clearly trying to sound assertive, but Asher could hear the shaking in her voice. He sat up straighter in his chair. He supposed he could give her a few moments to make her point.

"I did some digging and saw that you were one of the operatives that our competitors hired when Senera was accused of corporate espionage."

"That was me, yes."

Asher remembered the case well.

He and Reilly had spent many extremely boring hours digging up dirt on the company, only for the whole thing to eventually be settled out of court earlier this year. As far as he could tell, Senera's reputation seemed to be a lot better these days. He'd even heard the buzz in the media about some new drug they had that was supposedly going to revolutionize mental health treatment.

"I saw your number on file and figured that contacting someone directly was my best shot at actually being taken seriously."

Asher's frustration was beginning to rise.

He didn't appreciate the fact that his number was floating around somewhere at Senera Pharmaceuticals, and in any case, who did this woman think she was? Was her case really too urgent to wait until tomorrow morning?

"We take all of our case applications seriously," he retorted.

"Not ones where the client's identity has to be kept secret. And certainly not ones where she has no money to pay you for your services," the woman said, her snappy tone matching his own.

Well, that complicated things.

27

"Now that I have your attention, I can explain," the woman said.

Asher had to admit it: he kind of admired her audacity.

"Uh…go ahead, I guess," he managed, grabbing a pen and hunting around his desk for a notebook before settling on the back of a takeout menu.

"Not over the *phone*," the woman hissed. "We need to be discreet. Senera can't know. Surely you have a procedure for handling sensitive meetings."

Okay, now he was annoyed.

"I'm afraid the trench coat and prosthetic nose shop closes early on Sunday, so if you can't tell me anything, I have a lot of work to do tonight, and I'd appreciate it if you stopped wasting my time."

He heard the woman huff with annoyance, but no retort came.

He considered apologizing, but bit back his words. This woman was being completely unreasonable. She was totally in the wrong. He didn't owe her anything. If she wanted Forge Brothers Security to help her, she could get in line.

"Maybe this was a mistake," she said finally, her voice cracking as she swallowed back a sob. "Just forget it."

Oh no.

He couldn't handle the thought that he'd made a woman cry. Especially one who clearly needed his help. No matter how rude and entitled she might be.

"Wait, wait, wait," he said quickly, gripping the phone more tightly as though he could physically prevent her from hanging up. "I'm sorry. I want to help. We'll figure something out, just…don't hang up."

KARLIN

Karlin opened her mouth to speak, but no words made it through her sobs.

She was officially crying to a stranger on the phone.

The warm air wafting out of her car's dashboard did little to dry her tears. Instead, she managed to smear black mascara stains all over the edge of her lab coat as she attempted to swipe them away.

"Hey, are you still there? Hello? Look, I'm sorry, okay?"

Asher Forge's voice was gentle now, the picture of kindness and concern now that she was crying like an idiot.

And it seriously ticked her off.

What was wrong with her?

Dr. Bajwa made other women cry at work. Heck, sometimes he made the men cry. But never her. Ever. Not until she was safe at home in her little apartment in Amarillo, at least.

Meanwhile, this guy held her future in his hands just as much as Dr. Bajwa did, and she was losing it.

It had been a long day at the lab, and between John's bad news and Dr. Bajwa's demands that she sell her soul, she must have stepped right over the edge of her personal limit.

Not that it excused whatever this pathetic breakdown was.

"Hey, mystery lady, seriously, are you okay over there?"

His pitying tone had lasted all of five seconds. Now he just sounded happy to be alive, and she couldn't decide if that made her more or less annoyed with him.

She settled on more.

The Forge family were millionaires. He couldn't possibly understand the stress she was under.

"I'm here," she said, swallowing the last of her sobs.

"Are you planning to tell me your name, or should I just put 'Mystery Lady' in my contacts?"

"I told you, I need to be careful. I don't know who might be listening."

"Where are you calling from?" Asher said.

"My cell phone," she said, casting a glance around the interior of her hatchback as though she might spot a microphone hidden behind the rearview mirror.

"You do realize that if 'they' have your cell phone bugged, they'll have your name, right?"

She could almost hear the smirk on his face.

"Fine," she said, digging her fingernails hard into her palm before she could snap at him. "My name is Karlin. Karlin McKenna."

"It's so lovely to meet you too, Karlin. I'm Asher. Asher Forge."

His cheerful tone was vaguely sincere enough that she'd sound like a jerk if she called him out for sarcasm.

She settled on ignoring him.

"So, how are we doing this?"

"Well, if you give me an hour to finish up with this paperwork, I can meet you at this great taco place down-town. They've got a Sunday special. I'll pay. So long as you don't eat as much as my brothers. They could bankrupt me on dollar tacos. Seriously. And they're not those little scrawny tacos with, like, a teaspoon of ground beef and two shreds of wilted lettuce, either. They're the best. Legit, authentic Mexican in the heart of San Antonio."

Karlin stared at her reflection in the sun visor's mirror.

Maybe there was a hidden camera along with the

hidden microphones she'd imagined lurking around her Kia Rio. Had she accidentally stumbled on to some weird reality show?

"I'm–I'm in Amarillo right now," she managed.

The line was blessedly quiet for several seconds.

And then Asher started to laugh.

"What?" she snapped. "What is so hilarious about this situation?"

"Sorry. Sorry, I shouldn't laugh. I just assumed–I mean, did you think I was going to fly my private jet over real quick?"

Her fingernails bit harder into her palms as she willed herself not to yell at him.

"Obviously not," she said coldly. "But I figured you'd have some kind of, I don't know, *procedure* for handling sensitive cases. Not a casual chit chat at Taco Cabana."

Asher let out an audible gasp.

"They have Taco Cabana in Amarillo now? Sick! Last time I had to work up north, my only chain option was–"

"Can we stay on topic, please?"

"Right," Asher said, laughing again. "The *procedure.*"

"Exactly."

"The one where my clone living in some canyon sneaks off to Amarillo and meets you in a dark alley. Or behind a cactus."

"That's not what I meant," she snapped again. So much for trying to control her temper. Her heart rate felt like it had doubled. The man was infuriating.

"Ah, so you're talking about our *actual* procedure? You know, the one where you make an appointment during business hours and we handle things professionally, which may include one of us flying out to meet with you, at your expense, in two to three weeks when we can slot you in. That procedure?"

Karlin pressed her mouth into a firm line. Suddenly, the Kia felt uncomfortably hot, and it took all of her resolve to avoid hanging up the phone, jumping out the door, and running off into the cold desert night.

ASHER

Silence filled the line.

Asher cradled the phone between his neck and shoulder, gathering up the loose Fairman file papers and trying to corral them into some semblance of order. This conversation was fascinating, but that didn't mean he wanted to stick around until midnight.

"Okay, fine, you're right," Karlin said at last, sighing heavily into his ear. "I know I'm asking a lot here already. But I'm desperate. I'm sorry."

"Why?" he pressed.

"You've dealt with Senera before. You know how powerful they are. And I've managed to find myself in the middle of one of their schemes. I'm–I'm scared."

Asher felt his playful smirk falling away in an instant. He could tell by the woman's voice that she really was afraid, whatever it was she'd gotten herself into. And even though Senera's rivals had never been able to prove it in court, Asher had little doubt that the pharmaceutical giant would resort even to violence if someone got in their way.

"I believe you, Karlin. But I need more than that if I'm going to help you. I can't even begin making a plan if I don't know what I'm dealing with."

Karlin drew a deep breath as silence once again rested

between them. For a moment, he thought she was going to hang up.

Instead, he had apparently opened the floodgates.

Asher listened for the next forty-five minutes as Karlin told him about her time at Senera, their experimental psychedelic drug, and her recent impromptu meeting with her crazy-sounding boss and his insistence on stretching the truth to get the results he wanted. Asher had said very little and managed to sign a few of the Fairman documents as she talked.

At last, she paused for air, but despite all the information she'd given him, a couple unanswered questions nagged at him.

"So if they're as sketchy as you say they are–and from my own experience, I have no reason to doubt you–why have you stuck around this long?" he asked. "I don't get it."

"I have my own reasons," Karlin said firmly. "Can we please just leave it at that?"

He paused. He was curious, but he was getting the distinct feeling that he'd pushed her hard enough. In any case, she'd given him plenty to chew on.

"So the Phase II trial is in two weeks, correct?" he said.

"Yes. I know it's not a lot of notice, but–"

"Let me worry about that part. Just prepare for a new trial participant, and I'll let you in on more details about the plan when we get there."

"You're joining the trial?" Karlin half-yelled into his ear. "How on earth is that supposed to work? Won't someone recognize you? What if I get caught? This is–"

"If this is gonna work, you're going to have to trust me," he said, unable to keep the edge from his voice. Goodness, this woman was impossible. "I know what I'm doing. If you can't accept that, you're going to need to find someone else to pull off a last-minute miracle. Good luck to you. I'll even give you some numbers of other private security agencies. Got a pen?"

That did it.

"No," Karlin said quickly. "No, no, that's fine. I called you guys for a reason. I guess I'll see you in Amarillo."

"Looking forward to it."

Asher only paid half attention as they said their good-byes, already getting lost in his thoughts about the challenge that lay ahead. He'd done everything he could to sound confident, but the truth was, he wasn't sure he felt it. Gabe was almost certainly going to flip out on him for accepting a case without going through the proper channels or even asking him about it first, but he supposed he'd find a way to deal with that.

Still, his big brother would probably be the least of his problems. Taking on Senera wasn't going to be easy, and this wasn't going to be the sort of case that lent itself well to mistakes. He'd made enough of them during his time in private security, including a fairly massive one during the Fairman case.

His confidence wasn't high at the moment.

Every day, he considered telling Gabe the whole truth about just how nervous he felt about his own abilities to hold himself together in the field. And every day, he decided to push through, hoping everything would just get better on its own.

He fiddled with the dog tag at his neck, sliding it back and forth along the chain as his thoughts wandered to places he did not want them to go.

Asher Forge had been part of plenty of screwups. But

all of them paled in comparison to what had happened back in Afghanistan.

CHAPTER
SIX

ASHER

TWO WEEKS LATER

"I'm sorry, Mr. Forge. It appears your suitcase is on a flight to Honolulu at the moment, but we will recover it as soon as possible."

Asher looked down at the diminutive woman manning the Amarillo Airport's lost luggage desk, forcing a somewhat pleasant look onto his face. This particular airline had already lost his luggage on three different occasions. Once, they'd sent his suitcase to Malaysia, never to be seen again. But it wasn't like this woman had anything to do with it. And at least he still had his gun case and his carry-on.

"I see," he said instead, glancing over his shoulder in the general direction of the exit. "I'm in a bit of a hurry, but I'll call with the address of where I'm staying."

After spending a good thirty minutes sifting through

several baggage carousels and another twenty in line to report his missing luggage, he was already extremely late. Great first impression.

"Very good, sir," the woman said, typing something into her computer. "Again, I apologize for the inconvenience."

"No problem," he said, hefting his army green duffel bag up higher on his shoulder. "Thanks."

He gave the woman a quick wave and followed the exit signs, weaving between other passengers who seemed determined to take up as much of the hallway as possible.

This case was not getting off to a great start.

Just as he'd feared, Gabe had been angry at him for neglecting to follow his beloved procedures. What he hadn't expected, however, was his brother's refusal to take on the case in an official capacity. They handled pro-bono cases from time to time, but apparently when such a case involved Senera, it was too much of a risk.

Ben and Grace had been willing to help him work on a plan on his own, and he'd even gotten hold of his brother, Jacob, who encouraged him to help a woman in need despite the possibility that it could backfire.

Still, Gabe had made it crystal clear that Asher would be acting as a private citizen, and not an official representative of Forge Brothers Security.

No pressure.

Asher finally managed to weave past the throng of people, quickening his pace as he saw the automatic doors up ahead. Karlin was waiting here somewhere, and he had a feeling that she wasn't going to be pleased with his tardiness.

He'd spoken to her exactly once within the last two weeks, and their conversation had quickly devolved into bickering. He'd told her the fake last name he planned to use, only for her to insist on a fake first name as well, which was total overkill.

A few steps ahead, he spotted a square piece of poster-board with "Axel Bishop" written neatly on it in black Sharpie.

Yeah, he'd lost that argument.

He didn't have the chance to rekindle his annoyance, however.

The woman holding the sign was so gorgeous that he just about let his jaw fall open.

She was dressed simply, in black shoes, a pencil skirt, and a white blouse, but the simple office-casual look did nothing to tamper her good looks.

"Uh, hi," he said quickly, extending his hand as his gun case bashed painfully against his hip bone. "Axel. Axel Bishop."

He winked, but the woman in front of him only narrowed her eyes at him, her red ponytail swinging as she took a step closer.

"Karlin McKenna," she said, shaking his hand. "It's nice to meet you in person."

She gave him a faint smile before promptly turning on her heel and gesturing toward the parking garage. "You're late. Let's get moving."

Yep. This case was definitely going to be a challenge.

Maybe his biggest one yet.

KARLIN

Karlin's neat black flats clacked against the smooth floor of the airport as she headed toward her car. She could hear

Axel's Converse-clad steps behind her, but she didn't turn.

She was already referring to him as Axel in her head. She liked the name Asher much better, but she didn't want even the slightest chance of anyone at the trial figuring out who he was.

Who knew how much Bajwa had read about Senera's past legal woes? It wasn't worth the risk. Axel would do.

She had to admit, the man did not look anything like she had been expecting, and it had thrown her for a bit of a loop. Even if he was dressed like an unemployed bass player in a garage band, she couldn't deny he was handsome, with dark blonde hair, slight facial scruff, and an expression of mischief in his blue eyes.

And she hadn't been around a cute boy in about ten years. She much preferred the silence of her lab, and all the better when she got to work completely on her own. Other people had a way of throwing off her focus, and that had never been something she'd been able to afford.

"So," Axel said, half-scurrying to keep up with her brisk pace. "How are we feeling about the plan so far?"

She slowed as an older man carrying a chihuahua in a purse waddled past them, allowing Axel to catch up with her. He smelled faintly of cologne, and not the bad kind.

"Wouldn't it be smarter to stay in character?" she hissed under her breath.

"What, the whole time?" he replied, laughing and seemingly unconcerned with anyone else in the busy airport hearing them.

"I'm just trying to be careful. If someone figures out who you are, this will all be for nothing."

"Karlin, no one is going to find out anything."

"They might."

"But they won't. Trust me. Most people are just going about their lives, not trying to figure out some undercover plot. You need to chill," Axel said, wincing as he stepped out into the breezy night. "Goodness, it's freezing. I think I have a hoodie in my duffel bag, at least. They lost my suitcase. It's in Hawaii, and I'm kind of jealous of how warm it probably is right now. The weather, I mean. Not the, er, suitcase. The suitcase doesn't care if it's warm."

She couldn't help but to smile a little as he tried to make up for her silence. He actually sounded nervous, which wasn't the reaction she expected to elicit from a member of the opposite sex.

Then again, it was probably because she'd been acting like kind of a jerk, not because he'd been stunned by the beauty of her plain face and burning red hair.

"My car is by that light at the end there," she said, pointing. "The silver Kia. Do you need to pick up any essentials before we head to the retreat site?"

Axel shook his head. "I think I'll be okay, though I will need an address to tell the airline where to mail my suitcase when they find it."

"Sure."

An awkward silence fell as they piled into the small vehicle, and Karlin quickly found herself wishing that he'd continue to ramble on about the weather on Oahu. The traffic was weirdly busy, however, and she quickly became absorbed in navigating her way out of the airport.

"So," Axel said as they finally pulled onto the highway, "do you usually pick up patients at the airport yourself? Will that be suspicious?"

She shook her head. "No one will think anything of it. I've actually done it before. So has Dr. Bajwa. We aren't given much of a staff budget for our retreats. We bring in people part-time as we need them, but it's usually just me, Dr. Bajwa, and our camp cook who stays on-site overnight."

"Right, that makes sense. Good thinking."

The car went quiet again, but this time, it didn't feel quite so awkward. She felt herself relaxing as they left Amarillo proper and drove deeper into the dark desert.

She wished it were morning. Right now, there wasn't much to look at to distract herself from the bizarre two weeks that lay before her.

Still, as her headlights lit up the edges of the highway, she could see cacti and late-blooming flowers, and overhead, the clear sky was dotted with stars. Despite the unpredictable weather, she couldn't help but to love the beauty of northern Texas.

"Why do you call it a retreat, anyway? I thought you said you were testing DX8?" Axel asked.

"Sorry, habit. I know it's kind of dumb," she said, cracking a small smile. "Totally one of those annoying newspeak terminology things that Senera wants us to use."

Axel smiled back at her, waiting for her to say more.

"Language matters. Calling it a 'trial' makes the important task of our patients sound impersonal and sterile," Karlin said in a mocking tone. "Likewise, we prefer to use the term 'patients' rather than 'subjects'. After all, we don't want to make our patients feel like lab rats!"

"Right. The outdated term 'subject' would indeed evoke ideas of animal testing in the eyes of the public," Axel said gravely. "And we at the Senera Pharmaceuticals Public Relations department know how well animal testing does in focus groups."

She couldn't help but to laugh, and as she did, she realized with a sinking feeling just how long it had been.

Axel actually seemed pretty fun to be around. Even if he was bossy and seemed to take way too much pleasure in stressing her out.

Either way, fun or not, she was going to have to trust him if they were going to hold Senera accountable, and that wasn't going to be easy.

Her whole life, it had been basically just her and John. Their parents were still alive, but they weren't any help. John had found Jesus in the military and tried his best to lean on his faith when times were tough. But Karlin didn't trust his God.

She didn't really trust anybody. She had been carrying everything on her shoulders for so many years, she'd sort of gotten used to it.

And now, it was all she knew.

CHAPTER
SEVEN

THE WOMAN

BEFORE

T he floor of the hut felt familiar now. The whole room was, from the curved walls to the wooden spines that held up the thatched ceiling, piercing outward to form a perfect circle.

She knew many of the faces that shared the space with her, and she offered a serene smile to the new ones, the scared ones.

The mug in the woman's hand seemed to fit her fingers perfectly, and the taste of its contents sliding down her throat no longer made her choke.

The Professor had told her that this would happen if she kept coming back, if she persevered.

Of course, he was gone now.

He was no longer beside her, no longer holding her hand, but that was all right.

She was ready.

The woman leaned back against the wall, feeling the coolness of the uneven stone pressing against the back of her head. Her eyes were closed now, but she could see more clearly than ever before.

She could see the molecules that made up the air, bobbing into her, dancing in a twisting show of a thousand colors. She reached out to touch one, but it was gone already, replaced with a smokey blackness.

The woman thought this was interesting. She wasn't afraid anymore. The journey was safe, she could trust it now.

She had been waiting for what came next, though she didn't know what exactly her prize was until it materialized from the dark.

It was a snake, green and smooth, with scales that sparkled with an inward light. Its eyes were white, and the woman looked into them without fear.

"Who are you?"

The woman's mind spoke the question. She knew her lips would not move. No one else would see. This creature had come for her and her alone. The snake had come to touch her soul.

The Professor had promised, and his word was true. The woman had never doubted it.

When the snake spoke, its voice was gentle, feminine. It floated on clouds of color, filling the woman's mind from all directions, driving out all else.

"I am an interdimensional being. The people of your earth might refer to me as an alien or something else. I have one true name, but I am known by many. You may call me Mother."

"Thank you," the woman said. She realized that tears

were rolling down her cheeks. The beauty of the snake was too much to be contained within her heart. Her joy was spilling over.

"I have chosen you, dear one," the snake said. It was the softest, kindest voice that the woman had ever heard. "I have chosen you for great things."

CHAPTER
EIGHT

ASHER

"Shush! It's officially way too early for you to be squawking like that," Asher said, eyeing the black, crow-like bird that had planted itself directly in the middle of the path to the dining hall. "Though I have to admit, it is pretty out here."

Asher and Karlin had arrived at the retreat site late the night before, and he hadn't been able to see much aside from his comfortable cabin. Karlin had parked her Kia at the main Senera research compound on their way in, exchanging it for a more rugged Jeep, but it had been too dark and quiet to get a look at much aside from the parking lot.

With little to do but read the single book he had in his carry-on, he'd gone to bed early and managed to wake up around dawn. Gabe would be so proud. And in the bright morning sun, the beauty of the property was undeniable.

Several buildings dotted the reddish desert landscape, most of them made with local materials that made them almost disappear into the scenery. Despite the lateness of the season, flowers bloomed all over, and several towering cacti cast cool shadows. From the looks of it, no expense had been spared in designing the area to look more like a Pinterest-worthy resort than a site to conduct medical trials.

When the bird finally meandered off the path–shooting Asher a final threatening glare–he pulled open the door to the dining hall and stepped inside.

It took his eyes a moment to adjust to the gentle lighting as he scanned the large space. It was far and away the largest building he'd seen so far, with a single, massively long table and dark tile flooring that reminded him a little of being inside a cave. Though the decor was simple, it followed the same luxurious-yet-natural style as the exterior.

Along a narrower table on the far side of the room, stacked with breakfast options, he spotted Karlin pouring a steaming beverage into a mug.

"Good morning," he said pleasantly as he began to walk over, his sneakers squeaking slightly on the floor. With no one else but the two of them here, his steps were almost loud enough to echo.

"Good morning, Axel," Karlin said flatly, looking up at him for less than a second before ripping open a pale green packet of stevia and tossing it into her mug.

Guess she was back to treating him like a barely-tolerable annoyance.

Oh well. He'd win her over eventually. And if he couldn't, well, at least annoying her was fun.

"This is quite the spread," he said, gesturing broadly to the piles of fresh fruit, warming trays filled with thick oatmeal, dark brown toast, fresh-squeezed juices, and various other Gabe-approved healthy breakfast options. "But, uh, I don't see any coffee. Or bacon."

That got a smile out of her, along with a single raised eyebrow.

"I thought you would have done enough research to know that the food on this retreat is caffeine free, sugar free, vegetarian, and exclusively organic."

"I was a little more focused on researching other things," he said, taking an instinctive glance toward the ceiling in search of security cameras. He wasn't about to accuse Senera of criminal activity out loud, but Karlin seemed to get the gist.

"Well, there is actually a reason for the diet restrictions," Karlin said, still smirking. "We've studied this question heavily. As it turns out, the traditional diets that shamans prescribe with other psychedelics have some scientific backing, so we follow a lot of the same advice when we give our patients DX8."

"Are you sure it's not just because it makes this place look more like a fancy celebrity rehab?"

"Oh, that's definitely part of it."

"Great," Asher said, grabbing a mug and plucking a bag of herbal tea from the table at random. "If I die of scurvy, I'm suing."

Karlin laughed, and once again, Asher found himself struck with just how different she looked when she loosened up. He could only imagine the gorgeousness that would ensue if she actually removed her ponytail and let her red hair fall to her shoulders.

"You do realize scurvy is the one where you *don't* eat vegetables, right? It's a severe vitamin C deficiency."

Asher picked up a slice of lemon and held it over his

right eye. "Right. Scurvy is the pirate one. Arr, matey! Walk the plank!"

Just then, another man walked over to the buffet table, carrying a metal tray of scrambled eggs.

"Hey, Ned," Karlin said, giving Asher a look until he dropped the offending lemon slice into his mug. "This is Axel, one of our new patients. He got in late last night."

The man placed the tray on the table and shook Asher's hand without meeting his eyes.

"Hi. Ned Anderson. I'm the camp cook. If you need anything, let me know."

"Great. Will do. Oh, and thanks for breakfast."

Ned gave a slight nod, his expression unreadable, and promptly retreated back through the swinging metal doors that presumably led to the kitchen.

"He's the quiet one around here, isn't he?" Asher said when he was gone. There was something about Ned that felt suspicious, but he'd just have to keep an eye on him. It was hardly a crime to be shy.

"Yep," Karlin said, piling a bowl of oatmeal, a banana, and a scoop of egg onto a plate. "Total opposite of you."

Before he could realize that her comment was probably intended to be a jab, Karlin had already turned on her heel and was headed for a table.

"Hey!" Asher retorted, quickling grabbing a plate of his own and loading it with three slices of toast, almond butter, and two massive scoops of scrambled egg. He balanced a cup of orange juice in his other hand as he scurried after her.

KARLIN

Karlin raised her mug of tea to her lips as Axel plunked himself down at the long table across from her, nearly spilling his orange juice in the process. She gave him a tight smile, but inside, she was feeling on edge. She wasn't used to having someone else around who cared about what she was doing. It had become her habit to get up early while working at the retreat site, ensuring she'd get at least twenty minutes to enjoy breakfast solo before everyone else arrived. Ned was even more of a loner than she was, so his presence never bothered her. Axel, however, was a different story.

"So," he said, swallowing a mouthful of toast. "I hope I'll get a chance to see some of the tourist traps while I'm here. I definitely have to check out the canyon and the Cadillac Ranch, minimum. Oh, and the Second Amendment Cowboy."

He paused, glancing over at her eagerly as he swallowed a sip of orange juice.

She suppressed a sigh.

She wasn't going to be able to get out of his endless cheerful small talk. And anyway, she'd already resigned herself to the idea that Axel might be fun to hang out with. She guessed she'd just have to really try and give him a chance.

"I hear that the Palo Duro Canyon is amazing," she replied. "And that the Cadillac Ranch and the big cowboy are totally overrated. So is that restaurant where people try to eat that huge dinner in one hour."

"Woah, woah, woah. You mean to tell me you've never visited these hallowed sites yourself? You've never even tried to eat the legendary seventy-two ounce steak?"

"No. I've been working since I moved here. Guess I just never got around to it. I mean, I've been to museums–"

"Wait. How long have you lived ·here?" Axel interrupted, holding up a forkful of his eggs in mid-air.

Karlin felt a blush rising on her lightly freckled cheeks.

"A while. About a decade now."

Axel looked like he might fall off his chair. "No one is that busy for ten years! That's insane. Girl, you seriously need to get out more."

Karlin rolled her eyes. "Gee, thanks."

"Where did you move here from?"

She let his question hang in the air as she scooped up a bite of oatmeal. It was already starting to get cold as they talked. Somehow, Axel both ate and talked incredibly quickly, and seemingly at the same time. It was actually kind of impressive.

"I grew up in Michigan," she said.

"Oh, whereabouts?"

"Ann Arbor."

She took several bites of oatmeal, hoping that would be the end of this subject.

"Did you go to college there?"

Apparently, Axel's curiosity was not going to be easily satisfied.

"Yes. It was cheaper to live at home."

"That makes sense. Only one of my brothers, Cameron, went to college, but he stayed local and lived at home, too."

"How many brothers do you have?" she asked.

"Technically I'm one of five, but our cousin Reilly is basically considered an honorary brother. He grew up with us."

Axel leaned forward over the table to scoop up the last

of his eggs, and Karlin caught a glimpse of a small wooden cross around his neck.

He was probably a Christian, just like the rest of his big, happy, perfect family.

"I just have one brother, John. But we've always been close. I miss him a lot."

As soon as the words left her mouth, she found herself regretting them. She didn't need to be Axel's best friend in order to help him investigate Senera. The fact that she had a brother was hardly a secret, but their shared past wasn't exactly something she felt like discussing.

"Oh, nice. Where is he?" Axel asked.

"Just a couple hours away, in Lubbock."

"Close enough to visit, at least," Axel said, giving an approving nod. "My one brother, Jacob, is a missionary. Well, kinda. Anyway, he has been living all over the place and hasn't been home in years. I miss him so much."

Karlin was about to ask how someone could be 'kind of' a missionary, but Axel interrupted her train of thought.

"But never mind me. I'm curious about you. Why'd you leave Michigan? You stayed for college, but now you live on the other side of the continent. Bit of a change of heart?"

Her stomach clenched as she tried to formulate an answer he'd accept without actually lying to his face. Her story wasn't the sort one could casually tell in five minutes over a cup of herbal tea.

She decided to settle on something simple. Less words, less of a chance of putting her foot in her mouth and humiliating herself.

"Something like that," she said, forcing her eyes to meet his.

Fortunately, despite his class-clownish demeanor, Axel

seemed pretty good at reading people. He simply smiled and changed the subject.

"I'm still pretty scandalized that I've come all the way to Amarillo, and you can't even give me a personal review of a single tourist trap."

"Not fair! I told you I've been to museums. The RV one and the American Quarter Horse one are both way cooler than they sound."

Axel snorted. "I hope so, because they sound super lame. I've never been a museum guy."

"Why? Too educational?"

Karlin was surprised at the teasing tone her voice had taken. It sounded almost flirtatious, and that absolutely was not going to become a thing.

"Actually, yes," Axel said. "My oldest brother, Gabe, had this weird phase as a kid where he became obsessed with the Alamo, and he forced us all to participate in his geekery. I have spent a scary amount of time there. I swear I have every sign in the visitor's center memorized, and the staff there knows my entire family by name to this day. Once, he made me, all of my brothers, and Reilly dress up and go to this historical reenactment event–"

"To be fair, that sounds like so much fun," she said, interrupting his tirade.

"He made me be a girl! Only me! I even had to wear a wig!"

Karlin couldn't help but to laugh out loud at that.

"Growing up in a big family sounds amazing," she said, still grinning. "I'm kind of jealous."

"Well, I can't fix your dark and mysterious childhood, but I can totally embarrass you at the tourist activity of your choice when this retreat is over. I'll even accept going to a boring museum if you insist."

She glared at him, and in return, he gave a dramatic wink.

Seriously? The man was impossible.

"You're supposed to be undercover," she hissed under her breath.

"It can be part of my cover. And it would be fun."

"We still have to be professional," she argued.

Axel crossed his arms over his chest and grinned. "Fine, fine. Professional. Have it your way."

"Good. I will."

She tried to sound confident, but she felt herself blushing once again.

What was the matter with her?

Fine, he was cute. She could admit that much. Especially his muscled forearms, his blue eyes, and his just-disheveled-enough-to-look-unintentional facial scruff.

But that didn't change the reality of the situation she was currently in.

Even if she was willing to try and enjoy his company, she absolutely had to keep him at arm's length. Even if she didn't need to be professional, she was not interested in getting too close to him or to anyone else. She had an important career to focus on, and that would be even more true if she managed to successfully take down her current employer. Getting involved with some guy who wore wrinkled band shirts and hated museums didn't exactly fit into her plans.

Before she could attempt to steer the conversation toward a safer topic, however, she heard the door to the dining hall fling open across the room. To her relief, Dr. Bajwa and several of the other attendees began to file in.

CHAPTER
NINE

ASHER

Asher watched with interest as his fellow retreat attendees piled into the large dining hall, chatting casually with one another as they lined up to grab breakfast. Aside from himself, Karlin, and Ned, there were five others who would be staying on-site.

"How well do you know these people?" he asked Karlin, keeping his voice low.

"Aside from Bajwa? About as well as you do."

He nodded, watching as the others filled their plates with food and began making their way toward the table one by one. He had done as much research as he could with just their names, but he hadn't gotten very far on most of them. No criminal records, no crazy news articles, no sex offenders. It was likely that they were all what they claimed to be: a completely random group of individuals who had reasons to want to try an experimental psychedelic. But that didn't mean he wouldn't be surprised later.

A short, somewhat stocky man cleared his throat loudly and remained standing as the last of the guests settled down in their chairs near Asher and Karlin. Doc Bajwa, he assumed.

"Good morning, everyone," the man said brightly, a chunky gold ring flashing on his finger as he clapped his hands together. "As most of you know, I'm Dr. Daman Bajwa, and I am so thrilled that this exciting day has finally arrived! Before we eat, let us give ourselves a quick round of applause!"

The others began to clap and Asher joined in, stealing a glance in Karlin's direction. She was clapping, too, but the grin on her face was clearly plastered on.

Not for the first time, he felt a pang of pity for her. She had a lot on her shoulders. The outcome of the next two weeks would affect her life irrevocably, even if it went well.

"I would like everyone to stand up, one at a time, and introduce yourselves. Keep it brief, please–I'm sure you will forget a name or two, but by the end of our two weeks together, I'm sure you will all have become dear friends. Experiencing the magic of DX8 together has a way of bringing people together at a deeper level, so I hope your hearts are open! And remember: teamwork makes the dream work!"

Though the man was clearly a huge nerd, Asher had to admit that Bajwa's enthusiasm was pretty infectious. He found himself returning the man's beaming smile without needing to fake it.

Karlin had told him that Bajwa lived, slept, and breathed DX8, but he hadn't expected the man to have such childlike excitement about the whole project.

From what research he'd managed to do into the man,

Asher had assumed his goals were simple: successfully research groundbreaking drug, make a ton of money, live happily ever after.

He didn't doubt that it was indeed Bajwa's plan to do just that.

But now, seeing the man in person, he understood how Karlin and many others had continued to work beneath him for so long despite his tyrannical management style, not to mention his willingness to take dangerous risks with their patients' health. If the man was faking his passion for his area of research, he was one heck of an actor.

"Now, let's begin with my lovely colleague and partner in crime," Bajwa continued, gesturing in Karlin's direction. She raised her hand and gave an awkward wave across the table.

"Thank you, Dr. Bajwa," she said, smiling sweetly, though Asher noticed that she had flinched at his particular choice of words. "I'm Karlin McKenna, senior research scientist. You're welcome to call me Karlin. At least until I finally get my PhD, then Dr. McKenna it is," she joked. "I've been pretty busy in the lab lately, but we'll get there eventually."

Everyone chuckled appreciatively, including Asher, though he was mainly focused on the sadness he could see hidden behind her pretty blue eyes. He had no doubt she'd been dreaming of a PhD for a very long time, and now, thanks to her courage, she was risking her entire future in an industry that she clearly loved.

And even though he doubted she'd believe him if he told her as much, he had become utterly determined to do everything within his power to make sure she came out of this situation stronger than before.

He wasn't going to fail this time. Not the other innocent patients, and definitely not Karlin.

An older man with a silver moustache and an actual cowboy hat was up next, and he introduced himself as Paul Durant, age sixty-five. To no one's surprise, he was a rancher in Montana.

Asher was next. He introduced himself as Axel Bishop, age thirty-two, and told everyone that he was a drummer for an indie grunge band in Austin.

It was the perfect cover, as far as he was concerned. He could wear all of his old band tees, colorful Converse sneakers, and well-worn jeans that Gabe periodically tried to ban from the Forge Brothers Security office. And, more practically, no one was going to produce a drum set he couldn't play at the evening bonfire.

Asher paid polite attention to the final three patient introductions—a middle-aged woman named Lily, and two younger women named Cora and Destiny—but he was already beginning to feel he'd been sitting still for way too long. He wanted to get to know everyone, but like Bajwa said, that wasn't going to happen over a single breakfast, anyway. And for the moment, he was eager to see what their first day on a drug research trial was going to be like.

"Now, I want to give you all a recap of our rules," Bajwa said, looking over the cluster of patients with the air of a proud mother duckling as he drew a folded piece of paper from the breast pocket of his shirt. "We have a bit of a list here, I know, but this is serious business. We will be saving lives with the results of this trial, and you're all going to be a part of it."

Asher tried to listen, but by about rule number eight he'd begun to zone out Bajwa's cheery speech. Everything the man said had been basic common sense, and in any case, he listened to enough rules and lectures from Gabe to last him three lifetimes. He was going to take full advantage of his time away from the office and loosen up just a little.

At long last, Bajwa decided to take a breath and gestured toward Karlin. "Now, if you're all finished with breakfast, Karlin is going to take over our little tour. Follow us, please."

"Don't worry about the plates," Ned chimed in from somewhere behind them, almost making Asher jump. Where had he even come from? The man was definitely at least a little bit creepy.

"Thanks, Ned," Asher said quickly, handing over his well-scraped plate as he got out of his seat. "Appreciate it."

The cook nodded and seemed pleased, but Asher was already switching his focus in Karlin's direction as she, Bajwa, and the others began filing slowly toward the door.

He hurried his pace a little, not wanting to wind up at the back of the pack. Karlin gave him a pointed look as she opened the door of the dining hall and gestured for the others to pass her and head outside.

"Pay attention," she mouthed at him as he followed.

He gave her a silent salute. Yes, ma'am. He'd definitely be paying attention.

He wanted to get a feel for where the off-limits areas of the retreat site were. But he also doubted he'd be able to peel his eyes away from Karlin for long, even if he wanted to.

CHAPTER
TEN

KARLIN

Karlin looked into the crackling firepit, not wanting to take her eyes off of the dancing orange flames. For the first time since that morning, she felt like she could finally relax a little.

The others, including Axel and Bajwa, were lost in conversion for the moment, and no one seemed to mind her silence. Overhead, the sky was inky blue and filled with stars, and the bonfire gave off the perfect amount of heat to cut through the chill of the desert in autumn.

The day had managed to feel both long and short at the same time. She and Bajwa had shown the guests the cabins, the small gym, the yoga huts, the sauna, and everything else the modern retreat compound had to offer. She had also made sure to point out the direction of the main Senera research compound and gave everyone a brief rundown of the work they did there.

Finally, she'd given everyone a tour of her on-site lab. She dreaded that part of introduction day, but Bajwa always insisted on it. He thought that giving the patients a glimpse at the scientific side of what they did would help them to feel more at ease, but for Karlin, it was the opposite.

Having a bunch of strangers in the small room made her feel like her most private sanctuary was being invaded. Even at the main compound where she often worked with other people, she could usually grab a couple hours a day of solitude. The lab was her happy place, where everything in her life actually made sense.

Still, she always tried her best not to let on to the patients how uncomfortable she felt. She did enjoy teaching on some level, and most of the group seemed to enjoy asking her questions and engaging with the subject, so she had tried to see the bright side of the forced tour.

By the time they'd enjoyed a long, relaxed dinner, it was cold enough that everyone had leapt at the possibility of building a fire in the pit behind the dining hall.

All day, she'd found herself on edge, reading into everything Bajwa did or said, constantly afraid that he suspected something.

Axel, on the other hand, was the picture of calm and serenity.

He'd sauntered along near the middle of the pack, asking just the right amount of questions and offering the occasional witty comment. She had to admit, she was impressed, though the cross she'd seen hanging around his neck earlier nagged at her.

Did his confidence come from practice and being good at his job? Or did he experience the same sort of deeper peace that her brother, John, always claimed to have?

She wasn't going to ask, though that didn't stop her from feeling nervous about talking to him alone tonight.

On the drive up to the retreat site, they'd agreed to meet up and debrief each day, at least when they were able to without arousing suspicion. It made sense, and as they dug deeper into investigating Senera, it would be essential.

But it was still terrifying. Something about him seemed to pull at her, and the fact that she couldn't put her finger on it was driving her crazy.

"Karlin? Hello, earth to Karlin?"

Bajwa's singsong voice jolted into her brain.

She snapped to attention, blinking away the glow of the flame that had imprinted upon the backs of her eyelids. "Sorry, Dr. Bajwa, yes? What?"

He chuckled. "Relax, Karlin. Destiny here was just wondering if you enjoyed your time at college up in Michigan. Her sister is considering studying classical literature at Hillsdale."

"Oh," Karlin said, forcing a smile as she shook off her scattered thoughts. "I've heard Hillsdale is really nice, though I confess that my knowledge of the classics pretty much ended with reading Hamlet in high school."

"I read that one!" Axel chimed in. "Well, okay, I forget most of it, but the witches were pretty cool. Bad, obviously. But cool."

Karlin stared at him as Destiny started to laugh.

"The one with the witches is definitely Macbeth," Destiny said, plucking away a piece of floating ash that had landed on her tight black curls. "Anyway, Karlin, I was more thinking about the Michigan weather than anything. My sister and I were born and raised in Dallas. But going to a college that will support her faith means a lot to her."

"That's wise, young lady," Paul chimed in from his

place across the fire, giving an approving nod from beneath his ten-gallon hat. "Puttin' the Lord first will always pay off."

"If Hillsdale aligns with her values, it might be worth braving the cold," Karlin said politely. Was everyone here aside from her and Bajwa some kind of Jesus freak? "But I would definitely warn her that it's going to suck until she gets used to it."

Cora gave a dramatic shudder as she tossed her sleek brown waves over her shoulder. "Sounds terrible. Give me the beach back home in Los Angeles any day of the week. If I go my entire life without ever having to shovel snow, I'll be happy."

"West coast men are too soft," Axel scoffed. "Destiny's sister will find a good guy in Michigan, and *he'll* shovel the snow."

Cora crossed her arms over her oversized t-shirt and stuck out her tongue at him. "I don't need a guy anyway. Not right now. I'll enjoy my tanning time in peace, by myself, thank you very much."

"I'm with you, sister," Lily said with a chuckle. "I'm from Vegas, though. I wish I'd had a beach to miss."

Karlin smiled. It was good to see the group beginning to open up a little, and so far, everyone seemed to be getting along.

She watched as Lily leaned back in her camping chair, holding her water bottle out in one hand. "If I close my eyes, I can almost imagine this is a cute little cocktail with an umbrella and everything. Don't worry, I would spare you all having to see my bikini."

Even Bajwa chuckled at that. "Well, Ms. Moonchild, it would be pretty cold for that tonight."

Karlin watched as the others chatted with the older

woman, who had begun to jokingly beckon for a towel boy to bring her a robe. Something about Lily looked slightly familiar, but she couldn't put her finger on it.

In any case, she wasn't in the mood for investigating anything or anyone at the moment.

She leaned back in her own foldable camp chair and stretched her toes out toward the warm fire, closing her eyes as the others continued their conversations. Soon enough, everyone but her and Axel would go to bed, and there would be plenty of time to talk, whether she was ready for it or not.

ASHER

A rock slipped under Asher's sneaker as he approached the final stretch of the steep path, and he found himself flailing through the air for what seemed like a comically long amount of time. When he finally landed, his hand was burning, and even worse, Karlin was smirking at him from the door of the small cabin where he was supposed to meet her.

Awesome.

"I'm fine!" he called out across the remaining distance. "This cactus broke my fall."

He got to his feet, pulling a couple of stray spines from where they had embedded themselves in his hoodie's sleeve before walking toward her.

Steep red stone walls rose all around the small valley, blocking off some of the cold wind, though it was still chilly without the fire. The place reminded Asher of being on the inside of a giant bowl.

"Fortunately for you, that was barely a cactus," Karlin

said with a laugh, beckoning him forward. "But seriously, you're good?"

He nodded, accepting her invitation to enter the shadowy structure. Unlike the modern guest cabin he was staying in, this one looked old and decrepit, with a slightly crooked roof and several missing roof tiles.

As his eyes adjusted, he realized that the dim interior wasn't any nicer than the outside. Two rickety wooden chairs sat around a small log table with an empty bookshelf behind it. The only other furniture was a short stretch of cabinets on the opposite wall, a threadbare futon, and a black pot-bellied woodstove that had been left unlit. A single candle was burning in the middle of the table, giving just enough light to see by.

"Is there really nowhere else that we can meet?" he asked, plunking himself into one of the chairs as Karlin did the same. "That hike on the way in was rough, especially that last hill. And can we at least start a fire? It's dark. And freezing."

"Apparently it's not just those west coast men who are soft," Karlin joked.

"Ha-ha. Seriously, what is this place? It's kind of a dump. No offense."

"I'm actually not sure. I'm guessing it came with the land when Senera bought the place," she said, casting a glance at the small window near the front door. "Anyway. Never mind that. We need to get to the important stuff. We don't have all night."

Asher nodded, picking at a hole on the edge of his chair's armrest where decades-old stuffing was beginning to spill out. Now that he was actually alone with Karlin, he was beginning to feel a little bit nervous. Her personality was a bit of a roller coaster to navigate. Two minutes ago she'd been smiling and teasing him, and now she was all business. It made him feel like he was constantly losing his balance.

Still, he knew he could help her come around. He'd only known her for a couple of days, and building trust took time.

"Allow me to give you today's briefing, ma'am," he said, matching her serious tone. "To begin, I was awoken around 0600 with the help of the Samsung alarm clock your organization so kindly provided. Following that, I went to acquire breakfast in the dining hall, wherein I found a near-total dearth of protein–"

"Axel," Karlin warned, rolling her eyes. "Be serious."

"I am!"

She glanced at the table between them, and then at the bookshelf.

"Looking for something to chuck at my head?" he added, giving her a wink. "Karlin, come on. I'll stop being a butthead. But you really need to relax a little. No one has any reason to suspect we're in here."

"That's why we're not lighting a fire. There would be smoke from the chimney."

"So? Karlin, it's past midnight! Everyone is asleep or almost asleep," he said, trying to decide if it was amusement or frustration he was trying to keep out of his voice. "You need to accept that we are going to need to take some small risks if we're going to pull this off. Not communicating during this investigation is not an option."

He had kept his tone light, but to his horror, she looked like she might actually burst into tears. When she finally spoke, her voice shook.

"Today was scary for me, okay?" she said meekly. "My stomach still feels like it's in knots, I'm beyond exhausted, and now I don't think I'm going to get any sleep, so I'm gonna be a wreck tomorrow, too. So yeah, I need to relax, but it's not that easy."

Asher felt guilt twisting in his gut.

"Hey, hey," he said softly, shaking his head. He leaned forward slightly in his chair and rested a hand on her shoulder. "You're right. I'm sorry for goofing around so much. I do stuff like this all the time. It's easy to forget that this is new for you."

Though Karlin hadn't moved to shake off his hand, he could feel her bristling a little beneath his touch, and further pity shot through him. This woman clearly struggled with trust, and he had no doubt she had her reasons. He pulled away and leaned back in his chair.

"It's not even just that," Karlin said. "I mean, it is nerve-wracking having an undercover private security operative walking around. But it's more than that. I feel so guilty."

"Why? It's a necessary omission of the truth in order to get the job done."

"Not because of that. I'm worried for my patients. I know that the risks of taking DX8 are greater than Bajwa and I are letting on, especially in patients with comorbidities."

"Which I'm guessing your patients have?"

Karlin nodded. "This is the first Phase II trial, which permits us to actually use the drug to treat mental health orders like we would be doing once it's on the market. But DX8 isn't ready. I'm so worried for my patients. They're my responsibility, and here I am, letting this retreat continue. I just feel so slimy."

Okay, now that made a lot more sense.

Karlin knew things that her patients didn't. Would they

have agreed to this trial if they knew the real risks they were taking?

"I understand why you feel that way," Asher said, choosing his words carefully. "But I never want to hear you call yourself 'slimy' again. You want to take care of these patients, and that makes it clear you have a good heart. For the record, that was obvious to me from the beginning. Your courage is why I took the case."

Karlin's face went bright red, and for a moment, he thought she was going to interrupt him and argue with his compliments.

"This is about more than Paul, Lily, Cora, and Destiny, though," he continued. "I need to get the evidence against Senera so that you can protect people for years to come."

"I know. But I wish there were another way."

"Me, too. Believe me, I've laid awake quite a few nights, contemplating how to handle this case without crossing any moral boundaries."

Asher paused, turning over his thoughts in his mind. She wasn't going to agree with what he said next, but he figured he owed it to her to be honest. "You should know that I have serious concerns about the ethics of taking psychedelics at all, let alone actively giving them to vulnerable patients. As a Christian, I don't think that's something I could participate in directly, so it's fortunate I'm here as a fake patient rather than as a fake researcher."

Karlin's expression was stoic. "I can understand that. I've dedicated years of my career to this area of medicine, but that doesn't mean I think it's perfect. And this whole situation has really brought the ethical concerns into focus."

"I'm here because I know that you've run many successful trials in the past where no obvious patient harm has been observed," Asher said carefully. "And while I may have remaining theological, moral, and ethical concerns about the so-called 'safe' use of psychedelics, what Senera is doing is clearly much worse. And if one more trial is what it takes to stop them, I've decided that I can accept that. I truly do not see another way. If we tried to go after Senera now, based on what we already have, we'd lose, and they'd continue hurting people. It's as simple as that."

"So, basically, I just need to suck it up?" Karlin asked, her voice sounding small. She shivered a little, pulling her arms around herself as she sank deeper into her chair.

"Basically," Asher said, giving her a quick smile. "Like I said, chances are good that nothing will go wrong. Do the best job that you possibly can to keep everyone safe. I'm going to handle the rest. I promise you that, Karlin. I can do this. Everything is going to be okay."

Asher felt his heart twisting in his chest as soon as the words escaped him. He had made the same promises to protect the people he cared about before, and he'd utterly failed to keep them.

He offered a silent prayer, begging God to help him keep his promise to Karlin.

He would not fail again. Not this time.

CHAPTER
ELEVEN

KARLIN

Karlin bolted upright in bed, her brain taking a couple of seconds to catch up with her body.

It was still dark outside her staff cabin, and somewhere in the distance, she heard a strange sound carried on the wind. She couldn't quite place what it was, but it had been different enough from the usual sounds of the desert to set her heart racing.

She reached over to her nightstand and glanced at her alarm clock, blinking away sleep. Already, the sound had faded away. Perhaps she had imagined it entirely, stuck somewhere halfway between dream and waking. But in any case, despite her exhaustion from being up so late the night before, it was too late now to bother going back to bed.

As she took a shower and got dressed for the day ahead, she found her mind drifting to thoughts of Axel.

She cringed as she remembered the way she'd reacted

when he had touched her shoulder. It was such an innocent, meaningless touch, and yet she had recoiled as if his fingertips had scalded her.

"Why was I such a jerk?" she muttered under her breath as she tossed a few items into her black leather tote, including the wrinkled photo of John.

She had never been the victim of anything that would provoke such a reaction, and yet, she'd always hated being touched. Something about it signaled a level of trust in others that she almost never felt. She was happy to give her brother a big hug when they saw each other, but that was about it.

Not that anyone else wanted to hug her anyway.

As she stepped through the door, she could see that the sun had just begun to rise, painting a slim line of pink along the eastern horizon. She shivered as she made her way in the direction of the on-site office and lab, her racing thoughts momentarily cast aside by the chilly breeze.

By the time she slid her keys into the lock and let herself into the lab, however, the nagging thoughts of her and Axel's conversation had returned. Clearly, he was uncomfortable with DX8, and she wasn't surprised. Her brother had developed the same attitude after becoming a Christian. She couldn't entirely disagree with him, either.

Karlin had taken several different psychedelics in the past in order to aid in her research of DX8. She'd even spent a month in Peru on an extended ayahuasca retreat. And yet, she'd never liked the feeling that the drugs gave her.

Frankly, they scared her.

But unlike John and possibly Axel, she didn't think that demons were involved. She understood the science of these compounds better than almost anyone else in the world, and it was clear to her that the effects of psychedelics were caused solely by the brain and within the brain.

People might have used the drugs throughout the ages for various religious purposes, even including terrible ones like ritual sex acts and human sacrifice, but at their core, they were a mere tool based on repeatable science.

Still, she was going to respect Axel's wishes and ensure that he would never take real DX8 during the extent of this retreat. Fortunately, her unpleasant awakening this morning had provided her with the perfect opportunity to prep all of the doses that the patients would take throughout the week, including a placebo for Axel.

As she meandered around the lab, gathering various vials from small fridges and freezers and checking and double-checking measurements, she couldn't help but to feel a flash of nerves prickling along her spine.

This lab was mainly used during the trial retreats, but it also served as extra storage when things got crowded down at the main Senera research lab.

One of the storage fridges that contained larger vials of completed DX8 they often used in non-human mammal testing looked slightly off to her. She could have sworn that when she was last in here to pick some of them up, they'd been lined against the left-hand side of the fridge. Now, apparently, a few were closer to the middle.

She glanced up at the camera overhead and took hold of the glass containers, shuffling them all back into place. She was probably imagining it. Only a handful of people had keys to this lab, anyway, so the most likely explanation was that Bajwa had needed something when she wasn't around to fetch it for him.

Before she could consider the matter any further, she heard her smartwatch beeping loudly from its place on her wrist.

It was later than she'd realized. Ned would be ready with breakfast in about five minutes, and the patients would be arriving soon after. Axel was probably there already, not that she was in a hurry to catch him alone again.

She needed to focus.

For the rest of the retreat, she had to be fully committed to keeping her patients safe, investigation or no investigation. They needed her.

And just like when it came to taking care of John and getting him his service dog, Karlin wasn't going to let anything or anyone get in the way.

ASHER

Asher poured boiling water into his mug, sending the herbal tea bag bobbing along the bottom. For once, he didn't feel like he needed his usual coffee-induced energy boost, even after getting only a few hours of sleep. Was this how Gabe felt all the time? Maybe his early bird of a big brother wasn't as masochistic as he thought.

After his meeting with Karlin last night, he had found it easy to hop out of bed, though unfortunately, she hadn't appeared at the dining hall until half of the guests had already arrived.

He picked up his breakfast plate, once again disproportionately laden with eggs, and began to saunter over to where she was sitting. Before he could get any closer, however, she shot him a look which wasn't difficult to read. She was sitting with Bajwa and Ned, and the three were lost in their own conversation. Apparently, the staff were sitting alone today.

"Sup, everyone?" he said, sliding into a chair at the far end of the table next to Destiny and Paul. Lily and Cora sat down shortly after, both carrying heaping plates of fruit salad.

"Morning!" Lily said cheerfully, stabbing at a large strawberry with her fork.

Soon the group was buzzing with conversation, but Asher found his eyes drifting to the other end of the table as he wondered what Karlin, Bajwa, and Ned were discussing. Hopefully something boring. In any case, Karlin would fill him in on anything important, and in the meantime, he might learn something from his fellow guests.

"So, has anyone here tried DX8 before?" Cora was asking, her dark eyes wide with excitement. "I've tried shrooms a few times, and totally wimped out on taking salvia once. That's it, though."

"Definitely not me," Paul said, shaking his head. "I've never touched anything stronger than a beer. My nephew is an addict, and I've seen where it leads."

"I was an only child, with super strict parents, so I got a little wild with the Mary Jane in college, I'll admit," Lily said, offering Paul a wink. "But I'm looking forward to my first psychedelic journey!"

Asher glanced between the two oldest retreat attendees.

Sometimes, judging people by how they looked made a whole lot of sense.

Absolutely nothing about Paul's down-home attire or demeanor indicated that he'd be interested in this sort of retreat. Asher wondered what his story was, but he supposed he had to have a reason for being here.

Lily, on the other hand, looked like she'd never left the flower-child era, even though she looked too young to have actually been part of the original hippie movement. Today, she was wearing an actual tie-dye scarf to hold her long silver hair back, paired with a bright red tunic over loose acid-wash jeans. It was hardly a surprise to Asher that she'd wound up here.

"I've never even had alcohol before," Destiny chimed in. "This is going to be a big step."

She fingered the cross necklace she wore absentmindedly, but Asher certainly noticed. He felt a pang of worry for the soft-spoken woman. Did she share his concerns about DX8 based on her own faith? But if she did, why would she be here?

"No alcohol? Ever?" Cora asked, leaning over the table until the ends of her wavy hair nearly ended up in her empty oatmeal bowl.

Destiny smiled and shook her head, her curls bouncing. "I grew up in a church that really emphasized staying away from drinking. I'm not sure what I think about that these days, to be honest, but I've kind of just kept up the habit."

Cora's expression moved from horror to fascination. "Woah. That's intense. I mean, my grandmother goes to church sometimes, but I don't think I know anyone that intense."

"Admittedly, you are from Los Angeles," Destiny teased. "Things are different in Dallas."

"Amen to that," Asher added, raising his empty tea mug into the air.

He couldn't help but to feel a little pity for Cora. She was clearly the youngest in the group by quite a few years, and he knew that thanks to TikTok and all the rest, the broader culture she had grown up in was a lot different than his own.

He stole a glance in Karlin's direction, noticing the fake smile she'd slapped on as Bajwa said something to her and Ned. He doubted Karlin could tell him very much about the backgrounds of the other guests unless he had a good reason to ask, but he was definitely curious about how much she knew.

"So, how about you, Axel?" Cora asked, raising her own tea mug and clinking it against his own. "I gotta admit, you look kind of like a guy who has tried it all."

Touché.

Judging a book by its cover worked, but not always.

"Nah, not me," he said, offering her a breezy smile. "I like a cold Bud after band practice once in a while, but I'm not into anything else."

Paul said nothing, but gave him an approving nod from his place across the table. Well, if name dropping cheap beer was all that was required to get into the man's good graces, he'd happily take it.

The others began to chat more about their feelings on alcohol or the lack thereof, and Asher once again found both his eyes and his thoughts drifting in Karlin's direction.

He wondered what the day ahead would hold when breakfast was finished, but already he knew he was looking forward to hiking to that crummy cabin again tonight so he could let his guard down a little.

Being undercover, even using mostly his real personality, was exhausting.

And that was the only reason he was going to let himself get excited about seeing Karlin alone.

He'd been so focused on the Lord, his work, and his family for the last couple of years. It had been good for him, and he had to stay the course.

Even if everything about the beautiful researcher had a way of drawing him in.

KARLIN

Karlin stole a glance at her watch as the hour hand ticked slowly toward eight o'clock. She'd finished her breakfast twenty minutes ago, but unfortunately she and Ned had been stuck listening to Bajwa for what felt like forever. Ned barely said anything, either, so she had mostly been responsible for keeping up some semblance of a back and forth conversation.

Maybe Ned could be friends with Paul, who didn't seem to be opening up very much to Axel, either.

Not that she was keeping tabs on their end of the table or anything.

She knew that the trial needed Paul for demographic reasons, but she was beginning to wonder how much useful data she'd be able to get. Despite her asking several times for more medical history on their patients, Bajwa hadn't told her very much about any of them, only that their doctors had signed off on their being here.

It was not how a medical trial was supposed to go, but that was Senera. Bajwa would talk her up to the guests as a colleague, but when it came down to actually doing their jobs, he had no problem treating her like a lowly intern rather than a competent scientist in her own right.

On the other hand, the last time she'd had a large

amount of involvement in patient selection, one of them had ended up dead.

She glanced over at the others again, noticing that the others save Paul were all chatting happily together.

They all looked happy enough.

No, the word she was looking for was innocent.

They all looked innocent, and she was going to be giving them a psychedelic drug that had hurt people in the past and could hurt them, too.

But Axel was right. She had to hope for the best and let the rest of the trial take place. They weren't going to let Senera hurt anyone else in the future. This was the last group of people who would face this risk.

She felt her gut twist as she considered the future that awaited her personally.

If everything went like she and Axel hoped it would, these people would move on with their lives, probably with a large financial settlement courtesy of Senera.

But what would happen to her? Where would she work?

She wasn't concerned about getting a settlement. She would be happy just to have a medical research job that paid enough to support her and to help John.

She was going to get him that dog, and more. He had always been the one person in her life who truly loved her. She couldn't let him down.

Not after what had almost happened to him already.

At last, she heard Bajwa clearing his throat.

"All set?" he asked, gesturing toward her and Ned's empty dishes. Ned nodded, and to her relief, Bajwa finally got to his feet.

"All right, people!" Karlin watched as the others ceased their chatter, letting their attention fall on Bajwa. "I hope you all got a good night's rest and a good morning meal because today's the day we start making history. We need you at the top of your game! Over to you, Karlin."

She resisted the urge to roll her eyes as she got to her feet and tried to look half as excited as her boss. "The reality is maybe a *little* less exciting than Dr. Bajwa's motivational speech would have you believe," she joked. "We're actually not going to be giving you any DX8 until tomorrow."

Axel led the small crowd in a chorus of light-hearted boos, and suddenly Karlin's smile felt a lot more genuine. "But that doesn't mean that today isn't going to be meaningful," she continued. "Like we said yesterday, if we're going to succeed at properly testing out DX8, we need to be a solid team. We need to have each others' backs."

She felt a fresh barb of guilt piercing her stomach. So much for having her patients' backs as she was actively putting them in danger.

She snuck a quick glance at Axel before continuing. Their eyes met for only a moment, but somehow, he seemed to know exactly what she was feeling. He gave her the slightest hint of a nod, but it was the look in his eyes that told her he needed her to keep being brave.

She cleared her throat. "Psychedelic drugs are, in my opinion, more serious than anything else on the market or on the street. They work within the depths of the mind, where there is still so much that we don't understand.

"For years, our team here at Senera has been not only studying DX8 in terms of chemicals and atoms, but holistically, as well. Ancient cultures from all over the world prepare and use various psychedelic plants native to their regions. We've learned a lot from all kinds of different shamans and other traditional healers, and one thing that has come up again and again is the importance of trust. Trust between guide and seeker, and trust between seekers themselves."

She paused again, allowing her words to sink in.

This time, she couldn't force herself to meet Axel's eyes.

Talking about seekers and shamans and ancient drug rituals had always made her feel a little foolish—she was a scientist, after all, and not exactly prone to reveling in the unquantifiable—but this was different.

Now that she knew of his Christian faith, she imagined she could actually feel his judgment radiating from across the room.

John had hated her work with psychedelics ever since he'd become a Christian, but he especially disapproved of her learning from traditional elders or attending their psychedelic ceremonies. He hated these practices not because they were fake or silly, he said, but because they were real, and they were dangerous.

Karlin shook her head, hoping no one had noticed just how far she'd gotten lost in her own thoughts. She wasn't here to worry about demonic portals to the underworld, or whatever else John and Axel and maybe even Destiny thought about. Whatever her emotions wanted her to believe, the facts told her that science was on her side, and that was that.

"Anyway," she continued, giving a little chuckle that sounded fake even to her own ears, "Today we're going to start off with a moderate hike, enjoy a picnic lunch, and do a basic group intake."

Bajwa nodded, cutting in at last to take over. He looked like he was about to jump out of his shoes with excitement.

She was relieved to get out of the spotlight, and even better, Bajwa looked more than pleased with her little speech. So far, nothing he'd done or said gave her any real reason to fear that he knew what she and Axel were up to, and she was going to make sure it stayed that way.

CHAPTER
TWELVE

ASHER

Asher handed his plate to Ned, careful not to let the little wooden knife and fork fall into the sand.

Of course they didn't use plastic cutlery here.

Even their disposable plates looked to be made of some sort of recycled paper pulp.

"Lunch was great, thanks," he said to the quiet camp cook, who looked distinctly uncomfortable to be beyond the walls of the dining hall. Ned offered a nod and a half-smile in return as he turned to grab plates from the others.

Asher had told the man the truth–the salad really was good, as far as vegetarian salads with no cheese or croutons went–but on the whole, he was already excited to grab a nice burger back in San Antonio. Maybe he'd invite Gabe along so he could watch him eat half his weight in salad and bland chicken. This health-obsessed place would have been perfect for him.

Save for the experimental, mind-altering, synthetic drugs.

He caught himself glancing in Karlin's direction, wondering how she'd feel about grabbing a bite with him when all this was over.

The group had spent the last couple of hours enjoying a winding hike through the retreat grounds and surrounding areas, stopping for an early lunch atop a flat, windswept bluff. For most of the day, Karlin had seemed to be avoiding him, always managing to walk and now to sit as far away from him as possible.

Every time he thought he was making some leeway in gaining her trust, she closed herself off again. Even if all it had accomplished was to make him more curious about what lay beneath the surface of her chilly personality and more eager to know why she was so determined to keep him at arm's length.

Though he had to admit that maybe she was just being smart.

It probably would be good for him to learn to keep his distance. He'd spent way too much of his life looking for love in all the places he'd never find it. Deep down, he knew that finding his soulmate while undercover at a medical trial was about as realistic as meeting her in a bar.

"Earth to Axel, earth to Axel," Destiny announced from somewhere on his right, startling him out of his thoughts. She was staring at him like he had three heads, and so were Cora, Paul, and Lily.

"Hi. What?" he said stupidly, shaking a smattering of sand loose from his hair.

"These dear ladies were trying to ask you if you had anyone special waitin' back home," Paul drawled patiently.

Once again, Asher's gaze drifted involuntarily toward Karlin, who was now chatting with Bajwa and Ned as they helped him to finish tidying up.

Stupid. He seriously needed to get a hold of himself if he was going to keep his cover, let alone his dignity.

"Nah, not at the moment," he said quickly. "I'm just focusing on the band right now. Most chicks can't handle all the gigs and the late practices. I don't think they want to share the A-man with any rabid fans, you know?"

Paul raised an eyebrow from beneath his cowboy hat, saying nothing. Lily chuckled to herself.

Asher knew he sounded like a world-class douche, but fortunately, Destiny and Cora seemed satisfied with his answer.

"I mean, that makes sense," Cora said, bobbing her head up and down. "I dated this YouTuber once. He's really big in the ufology world. Anyway, it was *such* a nightmare. Never again."

"Ufology world? What does that even mean?" Destiny asked, wrinkling her nose.

Asher noticed that even out here on a hike in the desert, Destiny was dressed better than the average woman on a Sunday morning back home. She reminded him a little of a black version of Grace, though the latter would have probably opted for a bubblegum-pink skirt instead of the red one that Destiny wore.

"You know, like people who study unidentified craft and interdimensional beings," Cora said, waving her hand as though this was the most normal thing in the world. "It's really fascinating."

Paul retreated further under his hat, though Asher was certain he muttered something under his breath.

"Aliens?" Destiny said, shaking her head. "I don't

know. All the abductions and the…probing? It just sounds like demons to me."

Cora rolled her eyes. "It's science, Destiny. Not invisible horned dudes in the sky tempting us to sin or whatever. What do you think, Axel? Lily?"

Gabe and his friends had let Asher watch Signs with them when he was ten, and the movie had totally freaked him out. He wasn't sure he'd given a whole lot of thought to the existence of aliens since then.

Then again, right now, he was supposed to be fake drummer Axel Bishop.

"I mean, aliens would be pretty awesome," he said with a grin. "The universe is huge, man. So many planets and stars. Why would we be the only intelligent beings out there?"

Lily ran a hand through her silvery hair. "Well now, I'm just not sure one way or another, I suppose, though I've read some interesting things."

"I don't really see how the existence of intelligent life elsewhere in the universe is compatible with the incarnation of Jesus," Paul said at last.

"Right," Destiny agreed. "And the fall. And a whole lot of other things. Did Adam's sin affect little green men on Mars? Do they need a savior? Is Christ crucified again by the aliens? I find the whole idea creates a lot of problems."

Cora made a face. "I'm not going to let ancient superstitions get in the way of scientific progress, but you guys can believe what you want."

Asher pressed his mouth together into a firm line. He couldn't really get into an argument while he was supposed to be undercover, however annoying he found the woman's presuppositions.

"Hey now," Lily said. "I don't think you have to pit

faith against science. Maybe it's more complicated than we think."

"Exactly," Cora said excitedly. "I'm not necessarily saying that aliens are gray men with big eyes who drive spaceships. They might be something else. Something we can't usually see or perceive with our minds under normal circumstances."

"I have heard of people speaking to what they call aliens while under the influence of psychedelics," Lily said, her brow wrinkling. "But I sure hope that doesn't happen to me. No thanks. Sounds way too spooky."

Destiny shuddered visibly at the thought, but Cora looked more bright-eyed than before.

"Speak for yourself! I'd love to chat with another being. Imagine how much we could learn from them. Maybe they know the cure for cancer or how to build a car that runs on water. The way I see it, it's just another reason why studying DX8 is so important."

Alarm bells were ringing in Asher's mind the more that Cora talked.

He didn't know what mental health condition she had claimed to have in order to be accepted into the trial, but it seemed like her real intentions had a lot more to do with some weird UFO contact project.

He glanced over at Karlin, who was off on her own near the edge of the bluff. He wanted to talk to her about Senera's patient selection policies. He doubted the FDA would take kindly to Cora being part of this kind of supposedly scientific trial, and it could be a source of easy evidence for the company's negligence.

Just as he thought he might get the chance to catch her alone, however, Bajwa got to his feet and announced that it was time for a trust building exercise.

Asher could practically see Karlin rolling her eyes from where he stood, but he forced himself to keep his groan an inward one. He had a feeling that whatever the man had in mind was going to be a lot less fun than the annual Forge Brothers Security paintball tournament.

Maybe it wasn't the best activity for building trust, but getting to shoot paint pellets at his brothers once a year just had to be good for his job performance.

"All right, everyone, it's time to pair up!"

Bajwa began ordering people around, and before Asher had a chance to think, Karlin was standing beside him.

He couldn't believe his luck. Except for the fact that she looked like she was ready to shoot *him*, and maybe not with a paintball gun.

"You know, there are worse people than me you could be forced to partner with," Asher said.

"I didn't even say anything," Karlin said, though her expression didn't soften.

"Has anyone ever told you that you have a very expressive face?"

"Gee, thanks."

"It can be a compliment!"

"Okay, was it?"

Asher considered this for a moment while Karlin continued to frown.

Seriously, something had to give with this woman before he lost his mind completely.

"I just don't understand why you insist on being so hostile to such a sweet and handsome gentleman such as myself, Karlin," he said innocently. "It's really quite confusing."

"I'm not hostile," she argued.

"Maybe not on purpose," Asher admitted, giving her a

wicked grin. "I did notice that you made no attempt to deny my sweetness, nor my handsomeness."

"That's not what–"

Before Karlin got a chance to damage his ego any further, Bajwa gave an ear-splitting whistle and told them all to pay attention.

"What are we doing?" Asher whispered.

Karlin just shrugged, looking as confused as the other group members paired up around them.

"Let's start with the classics," Bajwa announced. "It's time for some trust falls!"

KARLIN

Karlin felt her heart beginning to beat a little faster. She seriously hated stuff like this, and Bajwa usually changed things up with each retreat, so it was difficult to know what to expect.

"Now, if my lovely partner would help me demonstrate?"

Bajwa had already directed everyone into forming two neat parallel lines. Karlin shared a quick glance with Ned, who was standing behind Paul and looked even less thrilled than she felt. She couldn't blame him–this totally wasn't his job–but unfortunately such little details rarely stopped Bajwa from making unreasonable demands of his staff.

"Ready?" Bajwa asked his partner, Lily, who was standing about two feet in front of him. She had her eyes pressed firmly shut, but she was smiling.

"Ready."

A second later, she fell straight back, landing promptly in Bajwa's waiting arms.

"Now, you guys give it a try," he ordered.

"You've got me, right?" Cora asked her own partner, Destiny. Destiny assured her that she did, and caught the woman easily. Paul and Ned followed suit, though both of them looked more interested in trust-falling Bajwa right off the bluff.

Karlin's palms felt sweaty. She was confident Axel would have no trouble catching her weight, but that didn't mean she was thrilled about having to let him do it.

She'd managed to avoid him for most of the day, and now Bajwa had forced them together. It was maddening. She knew that she had to work with Axel, but that didn't mean they had to spend every second together. She had enough going on in her head without him poking into her life.

"You got this, Karlin," Axel was saying behind her. She pressed her eyes shut and stood up straight, forcing herself to take a few deep breaths, but Bajwa spoke again before she worked up the nerve to make the fall.

"Now that you have the basic move down, there's a twist," he said. "You knew there had to be a twist, right? I can't have this be too easy. Otherwise, how are we really going to learn to rely on one another?"

He paused, as though waiting for someone to actually answer. Of course, no one did.

"Anyway," he continued, "we're going to have a little competition. The catcher who can step back the furthest and still catch their partner wins."

Now Karlin's heart was really racing.

This sounded like an absolute nightmare. Falling a foot with Axel standing right there was bad enough, but this?

"Are you ready for real this time?" Asher asked, positioning himself a couple of feet behind her and extending his arms outward. Despite his compact build, she could see the wiry muscles that covered his arms, and she had to admit, it made her feel a little better.

She nodded, unable to form words as she once again positioned herself to get ready to fall.

She closed her eyes and let herself tip backwards. She didn't even get the chance to realize she was in the air before Axel caught her.

"Okay," she said, letting out a breath. "I can do this. It's not that bad."

"Heck yeah you can do it!" Axel crowed. "We need to win this thing!"

She made a face. "I mean, do we?"

"Why not? It's a competition."

"What does that matter?"

Axel lowered his voice and leaned close enough to her that she felt his warm breath against her ear. "Do you really want to get smoked by a bunch of old people and two women?"

"You do realize I'm a woman myself?" she pointed out, trying to sound more stern than she felt.

"Yeah, but you're not the one doing the catching. We have an advantage!"

"So you can't lose to a girl?" she asked, getting in position for another fall. This time, she allowed Axel to step a few inches back. "Are you twelve?"

"You know, my brothers ask me that like once a week," he said. "It's not really an effective insult any more. The sting is gone from overuse."

She let herself fall, and once again, he caught her with seemingly no effort.

"I guess I'll need to think of some more creative insults."

"You could," he agreed. "Or you could just accept that I'm a pretty great guy. Then you wouldn't need to insult me at all."

She said nothing, instead getting herself ready as he set up for another fall. She glanced over her shoulder and felt instantly sick. He was much further back now, easily several feet.

This time, she was certain she'd feel the fall. She'd have a split second in mid-air to imagine herself crashing backward onto the hard ground.

Too late. She was already imagining it.

Her legs felt shaky, and suddenly she felt desperate to sit down and have a drink of water. Maybe she could tell Bajwa as much and get out of participating any further. She certainly didn't care about winning some stupid–

"Karlin, come on!" Axel was calling out to her. He had to speak more loudly than before, as everyone else was shouting encouragement to their own partners. Her throat felt thick.

"I don't feel good," she said.

"Okay, so let's finish, and then you can take a break," he said without skipping a beat. "Come on."

"I–I can't," she stammered, turning around. The distance was just as terrifying as it had been a second before. Some part of her logical mind knew that it was just the ground, but it may as well have been a gaping chasm. She absolutely did not want to play this stupid game anymore. "This is stupid. I can't. I can't, Axel. I don't want to. Just stop. Why are we even doing this!"

She was sure Bajwa heard her, but she didn't care. He was insane if he thought this was actually doing anything to build trust. If anything, it had made her trust her boss even less than before.

"Karlin?" Asher asked, his voice gentle. "Can you look at me?"

She didn't want to do that any more than she wanted to fall into his way-too-far-away waiting arms.

But something within her led her to meet his eyes.

Even though there was a gap between them, she could see the kindness resting within the pools of blue. As much as he made fun of her, joked around constantly, and totally did act like he was twelve, she had hired him for a reason. He was a good man, and she knew it.

"You can trust me," he said. His voice didn't hold any of its usual light tone. He sounded dead serious. "I promise. I promise I won't let you fall. Now turn around."

Something about his command made her obey. She stood there, squinting in the desert sun, trying to force fresh air into and out of her lungs.

Karlin didn't trust anybody.

She didn't trust her parents. She had trusted John for most of her life, but now, after what he'd put her through, she struggled to trust even him completely. And if the God that both John and Axel believed in was even real, she was absolutely certain she didn't trust Him, either.

So why did this total stranger make her feel so safe?

"Karlin," Axel called out again from behind her. "Close your eyes. Let go."

She pressed her eyes shut, blocking out the harsh light. She focused on the sound of the breeze and the call of distant birds. She pushed everything away.

The fear.

The dark memories.

The uncertainty about her future.

And before she could second-guess herself, she fell.

She didn't open her eyes, even as she felt that moment of weightless terror, and before she knew it, it was over.

He'd caught her.

She could hear everyone cheering as Axel pulled her into his chest. She didn't push him away as he hugged her, instead allowing herself a couple of seconds to relax in his warmth.

"You did it!" he said, finally pulling back enough that she could look up at him. "Awesome job. I knew you had it in you."

She caught his eyes for several long seconds, unable to hide the smile that had bubbled out of her.

It was only when she looked around her that she realized how far apart everyone was standing. They had lost horribly. They had come in dead last, even losing to Paul and Ned, who barely seemed willing to participate at all. And she suspected that Axel had known that was going to be the case right away.

Yet still, he had pushed her. He had made her keep going until she'd faced down her fear.

She dusted a few flecks of loose sand off her clothes as Bajwa called for them and the rest of the group to gather back together.

She straightened and walked toward her boss, letting Axel fall behind her, like he was nothing more than a patient she'd teamed up with for a silly exercise.

No matter how much he made her want to let her guard down, she still had to focus.

Because tomorrow, the real danger was going to begin.

CHAPTER
THIRTEEN

THE WOMAN

BEFORE

The woman let her eyes fall gently shut as the liquid magic took her away again.

It was colder tonight, and the hut was not so large or so sturdy as the one where her journey had begun. But she knew that it was worth it.

Everything she had sacrificed, everything she had fought for, would be worth it when the time came.

She felt her thoughts beginning to drift. The cold and the unsettling newness no longer mattered. There were bigger things for her mind to seek.

It took a little while for Mother to come, but at last she did, slinking down through the ceiling of the hut and curling herself up in front of the woman.

There was no longer a floor or walls. Only stars, stars

in all directions, even beneath the woman's body, an infinite glittering pit where she floated without effort.

"Hello, Mother," the woman said. "Our plans are going well."

The snake let out a little hiss, but she did not sound displeased.

"I see that my people have made it to their new home at last," Mother replied, her reptilian lips unmoving.

"Yes. Everyone is well. I have made sure of it. I know it is my duty to take care of them for you."

"Very good."

The snake paused for a moment and then began to move, slithering around the woman and examining her from all sides and angles. The woman could feel her wherever she was. The snake's flicking tongue touched her forehead as she passed, seemingly tasting something that the woman could not understand.

"The time is near," Mother said softly. "Like my beloved tribe of long ago, I will lead my new people to the truth. I will lead them to their home amid the stars."

CHAPTER
FOURTEEN

KARLIN

"Where is it?" Karlin muttered to herself as she rooted around in the cavernous white cabinet. It was at floor level, forcing her to sit in the most ungraceful position humanly possible, and not for the first time, she found herself feeling extremely grateful to be alone in the lab.

At last, she felt her fingers clasping around a small plastic container of the correct shape. She pulled out the green food dye and got to her feet, shoving it into the pocket of her lab coat quickly, though it wasn't like anyone was watching. Unless they were extremely well hidden, she saw nothing that would indicate the lab had security cameras.

She continued her work as normal, making the final preparations for tomorrow night's inaugural psychedelic trip, but found herself continually suppressing yawns. It was late, but she had no choice but to finish her work now, unless she wanted to get up at four in the morning.

Bajwa had been driving her insane all day.

After their group lunch on the bluff, he'd handed Karlin a set of Jeep keys and sent her down to the main office to do some suddenly urgent inventory paperwork. She'd been paranoid for most of the afternoon that he somehow suspected her and Axel, but ultimately, she figured the real reason was a lot more mundane. Bajwa always preferred the more exciting parts of the job and loved to pawn off the most boring work on his inferiors.

Karlin resented it. He may have been her boss, but that didn't entitle him to make her his on-demand administrative assistant.

By the time she'd finally returned to the retreat site and stuffed down some leftover dinner, it was almost client curfew. Before she could attempt to meet Axel at the old cabin like they'd planned, Bajwa had intercepted her and insisted she join him in watching a lecture from the latest Psychedelic Medicine Research Conference that had just taken place a few days prior.

The lecture had been interesting enough, and fortunately, Bajwa wasn't the sort of boss who used alone time with his female employees as an excuse to be creepy, but it had still stressed her out. She couldn't shake the constant sense of paranoia.

Finally, Bajwa had let her escape, but it was late, and she was certain that Axel would have given up waiting for her and gone to bed. Which was a problem, because she had never gotten a chance to explain to him how his fake DX8 dose worked.

Now, as she filled several vials with compounded DX8 for the rest of her patients, she pondered how tomorrow night was going to go.

Her original plan had been to dose Axel with a safe,

non-mind-altering drug that would mimic most of the basic physical symptoms of DX8. This would allow his body to respond normally to any tests that she and Bajwa ran without putting him in a position he wasn't comfortable with.

But of course, she needed his consent for that, or at least to warn him that it was going to be more than just a run of the mill placebo. For now, she had no choice but to set his special doses aside, prepare a simple vial of food coloring and water, and hope that Bajwa wouldn't decide to run any unplanned tests.

Fortunately, it was unlikely. For the first trip or two, they tended to stick to only verbal and visual monitoring, allowing the patients to relax and get used to DX8 before they started taking their blood pressure and prodding them with needles during the experience. But that did little to calm her nerves.

So many things could go wrong, but she had no choice now but to keep moving forward.

She would do everything she could to protect him, even if it was just from taking a medication he didn't want.

But a nagging question lingered in the back of her mind as she printed out the label for the new placebo vial.

Could Axel protect them both if their scheme was uncovered?

ASHER

Asher stretched out in his chair, sticking his sneaker-clad feet up on the dining table. The old cabin's futon might have been slightly more comfortable, but he'd already almost fallen asleep more than once, so he decided it was best not to risk it.

He'd been waiting for Karlin to arrive for the last two and a half hours, and he was slowly going crazy with boredom. He'd found a Tom Clancy novel sitting on top of a case of plastic water bottles, but to his dismay, the first third of it had been rendered unreadable by mold damage.

That left singing to himself, staring at the wall, and wondering if he'd be one of those people who started talking to a volleyball if he got lost on a desert island.

He didn't even have his cell phone with him, not that there was any phone service at the retreat site. If there had been, he would have long since called Karlin and demanded to know what on earth she was doing.

Actually, that was a lie. He probably would have been so relieved to hear that she was safe and sound that all of his annoyance would have melted away in an instant.

She'd opened up to him a little bit when they were doing the trust fall exercise, but man, he'd had to fight for it. And he still wasn't exactly sure why he kept bothering. Sure, she was a client, and he really did want to help her, but he'd be lying to himself if he didn't admit there was more than that. He liked her.

Even if he knew that it was never going to go anywhere.

Even if he knew he never wanted to *let* it go anywhere, even if Karlin suddenly decided that he was worthy of her interest. He had enough to deal with in his life. Flirting was about the limit of his romantic ambition.

He shook his head as he tried to push those thoughts out of his mind, along with his growing sleepiness.

It was getting colder now, and his own guest cabin with its cozy bed sounded like the best thing in the world. But he couldn't leave. Not if there was any chance Karlin would come looking for him here.

Instead, he eyed the old futon and its threadbare blanket. He really was getting chilly.

He jumped up from the chair and strode across the room, giving the old quilt a quick shake to make sure that no bugs or rodents had taken up residence, and made himself comfortable.

Asher woke up suddenly some time later.

There was a strange sound caught in his ears, a long, deepening wail that seemed to pour directly into his head, chilling him straight down to his toes.

He leapt up from the futon, grappling for his M16. "Ambush! Guys, get up, there's an ambush!"

Where was his gun?

He reached under the futon, covering his fingers in dust. He looked to either side of the wooden frame, finding nothing but cobwebs.

"Call it in, Rome! Kent? Guys, let's go! Now!"

No one answered. Suddenly, his own voice sounded very loud.

Where was everybody?

He rushed to the window, peering over the edge of the sill, only to realize he could see nothing but darkness. The noise sounded again, but it was quieter now and harder to make sense of.

His heart was thundering in his chest as realization dawned.

He slid down along the log wall until his butt collided with the hard floor, sending a jolt of pain up his spine that knocked further sense into him.

There was no ambush. He didn't have an M16, only a handgun that was currently locked up under the bed back at his guest cabin. He wasn't in Afghanistan anymore.

He was in a different desert, thousands of miles away, and he was by himself.

None of his friends were getting hurt this time.

No one was dying this time.

He heard the sound once more, but this time, he wasn't scared. It was almost certainly nothing more than the cry of a wolf.

At least that wasn't a dream. Or worse, an auditory hallucination.

It was a real sound, and he wasn't going crazy, even if he had forgotten for a few seconds where he was or what was going on.

He was totally fine.

So why did he still feel so guilty about what had happened halfway across the world?

It was a long time ago now. He wasn't interested in crying to some Veteran's Freedom Society counselor about his feelings. He just wanted to keep moving forward and trusting that if he acted fine, he would be fine. Just fine, fine, fine.

What other choice did he have?

He rubbed a hand over his face and sat back down on the futon, pulling the quilt around himself once more. It was even colder now than it had been when he fell asleep, and as freaked out as he felt being here, he wasn't going out there in the freezing night with the clearly very active coyotes.

Karlin was definitely in bed by now. She had probably just gotten held up somehow. He'd see her in the morning.

He closed his eyes, praying that God would take care of her and that they would be able to succeed in taking Senera down.

At last the strange sounds went completely silent, and after a lot of tossing and turning, he finally managed to fall asleep once more.

CHAPTER
FIFTEEN

KARLIN

Karlin hurried into the dining hall, wishing desperately for a cup of coffee. Maybe even an espresso. She didn't actually like espresso, but it did seem like a more efficient way of getting a lot of caffeine into her body as quickly as possible.

For a brief second, she thought about how she might be able to hide an electric kettle and instant coffee in her staff sleeping cabin next time before remembering that there wouldn't actually be a next time. Not if she and Axel got their way, and not even if they didn't. Soon, she'd be free of this place and free of their draconian anti-caffeine bigotry.

She'd planned to be here early this morning, hoping that Axel would have had the same idea, giving them a chance to catch up alone before the day started. But for the first time in recent memory, she'd overslept. A lot. Ned had actually had to knock on her door and wake her up, no doubt having been dispatched by Bajwa to do so.

She grabbed a cup of tea, a banana, and a bowl of oatmeal before rushing over toward the table where the others sat, including the boss himself, who was calmly sipping herbal tea and looking annoyingly well-rested.

Axel was with the rest of the guests, looking about as exhausted as she felt. He caught her eye as she slid in next to Bajwa, and she could tell by his expression that he was relieved to see that she was okay.

Had he been worrying about her?

She felt a flash of guilt. Maybe he had been waiting for her when she finally went to bed, after all. Not that there was anything she could do about it now.

Bajwa was already talking to her about his plans for the day, but the first moment that he paused and looked away from her, she turned and offered Axel the sweetest smile she could muster. She hoped it was clear to him that 'I'm sorry' was what she meant.

He returned her smile with a wink. She was pretty sure that all was forgiven, and for some reason, it made her feel all warm and giddy inside.

She couldn't deny it.

It was kind of nice having someone worry about her for a change.

Even if it was only because she'd hired him to do it.

Though how that explained his shameless flirting, she had no idea.

She couldn't wait to get away from Senera and find a job in some new lab, where she could find her next scientific breakthrough in peace.

Men were way, way too complicated.

ASHER

Asher tapped his fingertips against the table impatiently as he waited for the others to finish their breakfast. All morning, he'd found himself struggling to sit still. It didn't help that he'd slept terribly after that wolf had woken him up, and it helped even less when he'd had to take a freezing cold hike down here to the main retreat area before sunrise to avoid being seen.

He'd expected Karlin to reach the dining hall early, too, but when he saw her, it became obvious that she'd slept as poorly as he had. Something had kept her awake and away from their meeting. Probably Bajwa.

She had dark circles under her eyes, and for the first time since he'd met her, she had her hair in a slightly crooked messy bun rather than a sleek ponytail. Not that it took anything away from her striking features. He was pretty sure it would take a lot more than being tired to make her look anything less than gorgeous.

He'd stolen several glances in her direction as she ate, but her expression bore few clues to how she was feeling or what she was thinking.

Finally, Bajwa finished his own food and got to his feet, ushering everyone to get up and move in closer. Asher did as he was told, but already he was halfway tuned out. He had heard so many Bajwa rah-rah sessions that they were starting to blend together.

"This morning, I will spare you the preamble," Bajwa said, grinning broadly as the group of patients gathered around him. "At sunset, you will take your first dose of DX8!"

Lily and Cora started cheering, and Asher tried his best to match their enthusiasm. Paul and Destiny clapped

105

along and smiled, but he could see the uncertainty in both of their eyes. He sent up a silent prayer for them both that they would come out of this retreat unscathed, both physically and spiritually. Once again, he found himself curious about what had drawn them here in the first place, despite their obvious misgivings.

"What will we be doing until sunset?" Lily asked as the applause died down. Asher stood up straighter, his interest piqued. There were a lot of hours ahead before the Texan sun slipped below the horizon. Maybe he'd get a chance to slip away and talk to Karlin alone after all.

But when Bajwa spoke, his hopes were immediately dashed.

"We have a guest yoga and meditation instructor visiting us today," he said, looking down at his watch. "She should be here momentarily, actually. Her name is Tourmaline Kelly, and she's going to help you all prepare spiritually for this exciting new experience."

"Her name is *Tourmaline*?" Asher asked, unable to contain the snort that escaped him.

Karlin's gaze in his direction was easy to read this time. Actually, he'd call it more of a glare.

"Yes, and she's very good at what she does, Mr. Bishop," Bajwa said, raising a single eyebrow. He reminded Asher of his high school principal, who he'd gotten to know very well during his four-year sentence.

Before he could say more, Destiny cleared her throat.

"Excuse me, Dr. Bajwa?"

He looked away from Asher and turned to the woman with a smile. "Yes?"

Destiny glanced at the rest of the group before clearing her throat a second time. "I don't want to be a pain, but as a Christian, yoga makes me kind of uncomfortable, and I didn't realize that it was going to be a part of this retreat."

Paul nodded, but said nothing. Bajwa's smile froze on his face, and Karlin's expression, as usual, was impossible for Asher to read.

Cora rolled her eyes and tucked a strand of wavy brown hair behind her ear. "Group unity is important," she said. "No offense, but I don't think your personal religious beliefs should get in the way of that. Not that I'm, like, against Jesus or anything."

Asher noticed Ned standing off near the buffet, seemingly listening in.

As soon as the man caught Asher looking at him, however, he grabbed a couple of empty tea mugs and shuffled into the kitchen. Weird. Was he simply interested in a little drama to brighten up a mundane morning, or was there some other reason he cared what they were doing?

"I'm not interested in trying to preach at anybody or judge anybody," Destiny said, looking slightly pained. "It's just–I didn't know, that's all, and now I'm in a weird position."

Paul finally spoke. "I agree, Doc. I don't like none of this New Age stuff. I came here to take part in scientific medical research, nothing more."

Once again, Asher felt his own personal convictions warring with the demands of his profession. He wanted to speak up in defense of Destiny and Paul, but he also had to stay under the radar as much as possible.

Fortunately, Lily intervened before he was forced to make a decision.

"I don't think there's any reason for this to become a point of conflict," she said, reaching over and patting

Destiny's shoulder. "I don't think anyone here disagrees with Cora that group unity matters–"

She paused for a moment, giving everyone a moment to nod in agreement.

"–but I don't think that pushing anyone to do something they're uncomfortable with is going to do anything but make their DX8 journey more stressful. And if a couple of people in our group are stressed, it's going to rub off on everyone else."

"That's a good point, I guess," Cora said, crossing her arms over her chest. She didn't look entirely convinced.

"I should have made it clear to everyone that yoga and meditation were going to be included," Karlin added. "I apologize. I don't want to force anyone into doing anything they didn't really get a chance to consent to ahead of time."

Bajwa nodded. "We will take everyone's feedback into consideration for the next retreat. In the meantime, it's my job to balance everyone's interests for the good of the whole."

"So what do you suggest?" Cora asked.

Bajwa paused for a moment, scratching at his chin with a fingertip. "I do think everyone should stick together, but anyone who isn't comfortable joining in with the yoga or meditation sessions may simply sit quietly, read, or pray on their own if that would be helpful to them. Any objections?"

Everyone but Cora shook their heads immediately. She rolled her eyes again before finally acquiescing.

Asher was in no place to argue, but he struggled to hide his annoyance at being forced to join in. Sitting in silence for most of the day sounded insanely boring. Furthermore, he was losing what would have been a prime opportunity to snoop around, or better yet, to talk with Karlin before the DX8 session began.

He followed the others as they headed outside. Cora pushed her way to the front of the group and started talking to Bajwa and Karlin. He was curious to know if she was still complaining, but he found himself hemmed in by Lily, Paul, and Destiny before he could find out.

"Thank you for sticking up for us back there," Destiny said, giving the older woman a bright smile. "I really don't like to rock the boat, but I have to listen to my conscience."

"Totally, man," Asher said, nodding. "Follow your heart and all that."

He cringed. He hated that advice, but it had been the first thing that popped into his head.

"I really hope yoga is the last of it," Paul added. "If they try to get me readin' tarot cards or touchin' crystals, I'm going home."

Destiny nodded. "Same here. The idea of taking DX8 has challenged my faith enough. I don't want to worry about anything else."

"I guess I haven't had to think about it in those terms, myself," Lily said with a smile. "I'm not really religious. But I do think a lot of the hippie stuff is kinda silly."

Asher chuckled. "Don't take this the wrong way, Lily, but you kinda look like you'd *love* all the hippie stuff."

She reached over and swatted him playfully on the bicep. "Oh, hush. I like the seventies style. Just not the drug obsession. Or the free love."

Asher made a face. He didn't think Lily was old enough to have been involved in the party scene during that era, but still.

Ew.

Not an image he needed in his head.

At that moment, he noticed that Karlin had hung back a little from Bajwa and Cora. Clearly, he wasn't going to get to speak to her alone before tonight, but he'd take what he could get. Asher sauntered up to her, catching her gaze.

"Hey, Ms. Kenna?"

The rest of the group was still close enough to hear him, so he couldn't say much. "Can I trust you to keep me safe on DX8 tonight?"

She paused for a long moment as a bird cawed overhead, wheeling toward a gnarled tree that stood nearby.

"Yes. I promise."

She held his gaze without faltering.

There was something about the way she looked at him sometimes that he couldn't put his finger on. It was clear that she saw so much more than she let on. That she dug into people, trying to figure out what made them tick, and he was no exception.

It kind of freaked him out.

He grinned at her, offering one of his trademark winks that annoyed women everywhere.

"I trust you," he said.

And despite the fact that she was still little more than a stranger, he did.

CHAPTER
SIXTEEN

KARLIN

Karlin's stomach grumbled as she sat cross-legged on the hard floor, trying to force herself to pay attention to what Tourmaline was saying.

Breakfast had been hours ago, and they'd all skipped lunch. Unlike the others, she and Bajwa didn't need to fast in preparation for DX8, but in his characteristic excitement, Bajwa hadn't thought to actually schedule in time for the staff to have lunch.

She stole a glance at the small clock that hung over Tourmaline's head on the far side of the yoga room.

Apparently, dinner wasn't happening, either. She felt a sudden flash of jealousy that Ned hadn't been forced to participate and had actually gotten to end his work day early.

She was getting seriously hangry.

The only thing keeping her from tossing her yoga mat at Bajwa's head and storming out of here was the fact that she had a granola bar waiting in her bag.

"Now, everyone, come to attention," Tourmaline said. "It is time for the next part of your journey."

Karlin was snapped out of her mildly violent fantasies as the yoga instructor hit the edge of a large bell with a wooden stick. The enormous, sudden ringing sound vibrated through the room, jolting everyone to attention, including Axel. He jumped to his feet and sent the book he'd been reading sailing across the wooden floor.

Cora leaned over on her mat and picked it up. "Hunt For the Skinwalker? Nice. That case is so cool!"

Tourmaline's face was calm, but her eyes looked less than serene. "Please respect the sacred quiet of the room."

Karlin bit down on her tongue. She seriously hated this crap.

Unfortunately, Bajwa didn't share her opinion. If anything, he was just as enthusiastic about the 'holistic' elements of the retreat as he was about DX8 itself.

"Er, right," Cora said, handing the book back to Axel. She pressed her hands together and bowed toward Tourmaline, eliciting a muttered comment from Paul that Karlin couldn't quite make out.

Whatever he'd said, she probably agreed with him. She almost wished she was religious, even if just to have a more legitimate excuse to bow out of yoga than simply thinking it was a waste of time.

Tourmaline stood up and gestured toward everyone in the room before getting to her knees and offering a deep bow in their direction. "I wish you well. Namaste."

Cora, Lily, and Bajwa returned her greeting, and Karlin mouthed the word.

Tourmaline began to gather up her supplies, and Bajwa stepped into her place. "Everyone, after we clean up our things, I'm going to go on ahead of you to the hut where you'll be taking DX8. It's a bit of a hike, so I'll be bringing some supplies we need in the Jeep. Please stay with Ms. McKenna and follow along on foot."

He looked uncharacteristically somber, as though Tourmaline's floaty energy had worn off on him. Not that Karlin was complaining. It was nice not having to fake enthusiasm. She wasn't looking forward to giving these patients DX8, nor was she looking forward to having to conceal the fact that Axel was going to be sober.

Karlin hung back as the others passed her and headed toward the door. After hours of forced silence, the chatter began almost immediately. Paul was telling Destiny that he'd had a good chance to pray and prepare himself. Cora had stopped to chat with Tourmaline as she rolled up her yoga mat. Lily was asking Axel how he was liking the book he was reading.

"Everyone, preserve silence, please!" Bajwa called out loudly. The sharp sound of his voice hurt Karlin's ears in the echo-filled room.

Everyone fell quiet immediately. Satisfied, Bajwa ducked out of the room and out into the darkening evening, followed moments later by Tourmaline.

Karlin waited for the others to pack up the remainder of their things. She watched in horror as Axel rolled his book up and stuffed it in his back pocket before heading over to stand beside her. Unfortunately, Paul was standing too close to them for her to mention her plans for his placebo dose.

"Nervous for tonight?" he whispered.

She narrowed her eyes at him. "Being around a book abuser is a little unsettling, yes."

Axel laughed out loud, eliciting a loud shush from Cora.

"Seriously, are you okay?" Axel asked, barely loud enough to be heard.

Karlin realized then that her hands had begun to shake. She was nervous, but she had to get a grip. Her patients were depending on her to be focused and to keep them safe.

Axel reached out and grasped her hand in his own, giving it a quick squeeze. Paul raised an eyebrow in their direction, but said nothing.

She wanted to yank her hand away before anyone else saw their touch, but she couldn't quite bring herself to do it, not with the way that butterflies had begun dancing around in her stomach.

Everything was going to be fine.

Axel was going to find the evidence that she needed to take Senera down.

And somehow, she'd find another job and she'd be able to get John his PTSD dog and everything else he needed.

She knew what it had felt like to lose him, even momentarily, and it was the worst thing she'd ever gone through.

She would do whatever it took to help him.

No matter what.

ASHER

"Now, everyone, it's time to close your eyes."

Asher obeyed Bajwa's command, pressing his eyelids firmly shut as he listened.

The man was chanting some incomprehensible gibberish, so far as Asher could tell, and it wasn't easy to pay attention. Especially after spending the entire day doing basically the same thing. The only difference was that they were now in a rustic-looking hut instead of a modern yoga studio, and they had high school principal Bajwa instead of hippie fairy Tourmaline guiding them.

Asher let his mind wander to thoughts of Karlin's hand in his and of how nervous she'd looked. He wanted so badly to comfort her and reassure her that everything was going to be okay.

He knew that she'd be awake most of the night monitoring the others–they'd all be sleeping here after taking the drug–and he hoped that they might get even a few minutes alone. He'd just have to stay awake himself rather than dying of boredom.

After what felt like forever, Bajwa finally stopped talking and allowed the group to open their eyes.

Cora looked eager for what was coming next, as did Lily. Paul looked almost lost, and Destiny was visibly praying.

Asher watched as Karlin picked up a tray of small cups filled with a green science-experiment-looking liquid and began handing them out one by one. Each of them had a white prescription sticker stuck to the glass. He felt her fingers brushing against his own as he took his cup and thanked her in a whisper.

She didn't allow her gaze to linger on him before moving on, but he could notice the slight shaking in her hands had begun again.

He glanced down at the contents of the cup. It was obviously some kind of fake dose, but he still felt his own nerves acting up. Sure, he'd be sober instead of tripping on some crazy experimental drug, but he would have to be on full alert if he was going to ensure that no one else realized it. Especially Bajwa, who'd surely be paying close attention.

Finally, everyone had their cups, and Karlin took her seat again next to Bajwa.

"It's time," he said, giving everyone a gentle smile. "Drink up, and close your eyes."

CHAPTER
SEVENTEEN

KARLIN

K arlin felt a held breath escape between her lips as she watched the patients tip back their cups.

She hated this part. Even though she knew it was illogical, she always had a nagging fear that somehow, despite all of her research to the contrary, someone was going to ingest the green liquid and die on the spot.

Of course, no one did, but everyone looked relieved once their cup was empty.

"This tastes way better than it looks," Cora said, poking at the rim of the cup with her finger and licking off the final drops.

"Right?" Axel chimed in. "It's not bad. I was expecting it to be disgusting."

"Let's be quiet now and let the DX8 work," Bajwa said calmly. He stole a glance at Karlin, the relief evident on his face. He hadn't been afraid everyone would suddenly drop dead, of course, but he was always wary that someone would need the bucket left sitting beside their mat.

Despite the spiritual trappings, DX8 was a modern, chemically synthesized drug. Unlike traditional plant-based psychedelics such as ayahuasca, it was unlikely to cause severe nausea or vomiting–though that particular symptom had shown up more often with earlier formulations.

An unwanted memory stirred in Karlin's conscience as she walked around the hut, glancing at each of her patients in turn.

There had been one woman a decade ago who had violently vomited with every single dose she took. Karlin remembered that her name was Dana and that she'd been pleasant enough. The woman's personality hadn't stuck out very much.

But she did remember that she had been in the same retreat group with Amira.

And not long after, Amira had died.

Karlin felt nausea of her own rushing through her as she tried to push the terrible thoughts back down. She couldn't let herself get lost right now.

She was already doing everything she could to bring Amira the justice that she deserved, and in this moment, the other patients needed her even more.

"Karlin, if you could grab a few blankets, please?"

Bajwa was giving her a quizzical look.

"Oh, yes, sorry," she answered in a whisper, gathering up the cotton blankets they'd brought along and passing them out to the others one by one. Only Lily, Paul, and Axel bothered to use them, despite the growing chill of the night. She grabbed one for herself and wrapped it around her shoulders, watching as Bajwa lit several candles and pressed play on a portable CD player they'd brought.

As the room filled with the relaxing sound of rainfall, Lily jolted to her feet, grabbing her bucket and running out into the night.

"Don't worry, everyone," Bajwa said, lifting his voice to a normal volume. "She'll be fine momentarily. No drug is perfect."

Karlin forced a smile, but inside, she couldn't shake the shiver of fear that was coursing through her.

Logically, she knew it was a coincidence.

But it still felt like an omen.

ASHER

It was official.

Asher had never been so bored in his entire life.

At least he'd gotten to read a book when he was stuck listening to Tourmaline the Yoga Lady earlier. This was pure torture.

All he could do was pray, focus on his breathing, or watch the others, the latter being an extremely boring option when all anyone else was doing was sitting there breathing like he was.

He did find a slight hint of gratitude, however, for the fact that he was able to keep his eyes open. He'd half expected everyone else to have theirs pressed shut, but instead, Paul was staring at nothing, Cora was holding her hand up in front of her face, and Destiny was looking at the ceiling. Only Lily's eyes were closed, her expression serene.

Bajwa was fiddling with the CD player, his back to Asher.

Karlin was making the rounds slowly, stopping for a few moments behind each person as she passed. She was definitely the most interesting person to look at, and not simply because of how pretty she was, even wrapped in a blanket with her hair tumbling halfway out of its bun.

Asher could see the genuine care on her face as she monitored her patients, took short notes, and occasionally conferred with Bajwa in a whisper. She was good at her job. And not just the part of it that involved hiding in a lab mixing chemicals.

Despite the generally prickly attitude that she gave off and her obvious preference for solitude, she was unable to hide her underlying kindness. Even in the short time he'd known her, it was clear to Asher that she was a woman who cared deeply for other people. It impressed him.

Bajwa stepped back from the CD player and glanced around the room as the sound of slow drumbeats began to fill the hut.

His eyes lingered for several seconds on Asher.

It wasn't the first time, but he couldn't be sure if it was because he stood out or because Bajwa was analyzing everyone and he was just being paranoid.

Asher used the edge of his blanket to dab at his forehead, and Bajwa looked away at last.

Though everyone looked normal for the most part, there were little things that Asher couldn't easily fake, the profuse sweating being one of them. Hopefully, it wasn't enough of a clue for his deception to be found out.

As Bajwa wandered toward Karlin on the other side of the hut, Asher noticed the sound of the drumbeats was getting much louder and more intense. He adjusted his position on the mat, closed his eyes, and let himself drown in the music. It wasn't exactly Neil Peart, but he was still thankful to have something a little more interesting to listen to than the dulcet birdsong of a fake jungle.

After a few minutes, however, he changed his mind.

The drumbeats had not remained as they were. Instead, they had grown even faster, and they were now interspersed with a discordant ringing noise every few seconds. It was an actively unpleasant sound, and it was all he could do not to press his hands over his ears to try and dampen it.

He opened his eyes again and glanced around the room, a chill creeping up his spine even as he pulled the blanket in more tightly around his shoulders. Everyone else was sitting just as they had been a few moments before, except Cora had gone from carefully examining her hand to staring in fascination at a piece of fiber she'd pulled from her mat.

Asher caught Karlin's eye as she strode by his mat, and to his surprise, she stopped instead of instantly looking away. She knelt down in front of him, notebook at the ready, and looked him over slowly, writing down some scribble he couldn't read.

Her hands still looked a little bit shaky, but it wasn't nearly as bad as before. Asher found himself thanking God for the same boredom he'd been lamenting moments before. It may have sucked for him, but the uneventfulness of the night was better for Karlin, and that was all that he actually needed.

He peered over her shoulder and, finding Bajwa was still looking in the opposite direction, reached out and touched the edge of her forearm. "You're doing an amazing job," he said in a whisper.

She gave him a small smile, and he was pretty sure she actually blushed.

He let his fingertips fall away from her pale skin, but to his surprise, she leaned in closer. He felt a shiver as her breath touched his ear. "Bajwa doesn't suspect a thing. We'll talk later."

The moment passed all too quickly before she was on her feet again.

She walked over to Paul and, to Asher's dismay, whispered in his ear as well. Apparently, their little moment was nothing more than her standard observation procedure.

He watched as she spoke quietly to Lily and Cora in turn, writing down more scribbles on her notepad. Finally, she approached Destiny, whose eyes were pressed firmly shut.

Asher watched as Karlin drew out a hand and gently patted Destiny's shoulder and announced her presence aloud.

Without warning, Destiny let out a guttural, terrified scream.

CHAPTER
EIGHTEEN

KARLIN

Karlin shrank back as Destiny wailed.

Her heart was racing, and once again, she felt like she was going to throw up herself, but she couldn't let it show on her face.

The memories were back again, pressing at her mind, trying to knock her off-balance as the fear coursed through her.

That night was burned into her mind, etched as firmly as a tribal cave painting on stone. Amira had panicked just like this.

And at the time, Karlin had panicked, too.

She'd had no idea what to do or say.

She still didn't.

Instead, she allowed herself five seconds to close her eyes and breathe in and out. Panicking now was out of the question. It wasn't about her, it was about her patients, and she had to be the adult in the room.

God, if you're out there, please help Destiny. Help her to be okay. Help us to help her.

Her ears hurt from the screaming and the drumbeats, but she felt a renewed sense of determination. It wasn't the calm sort of peace that so many Christians seemed to speak of, but it was something to hold on to. It would have to be enough.

Bajwa rushed across the room to help as Destiny got to her feet. She was walking around in place, screaming all the while. "Stop, Destiny! It's okay!"

She ignored the man, and instead began grabbing handfuls of her dark curls and attempting to pull them out of her skull.

The others were in various states of panic now.

Paul had gotten to his feet and was leaning against the wall. Karlin could see from where she stood that he was breathing far too fast. Lily was crying, and Cora had wandered over to her mat, embracing her as she rocked back and forth.

Karlin and Bajwa tried to grab hold of Destiny, but the outburst seemed to have filled her with an almost inhuman sort of strength. She lashed out with her arms and legs, scratching and kicking as hard as she could. Bajwa yelped as her arm collided with his face, sending blood rushing from his nose.

Axel was at her side in an instant. Despite her attempt at calm, alarm bells were ringing in her head. He couldn't break his cover. He couldn't ruin everything. Not after how far they had come.

Everything that came next happened too quickly for Karlin to make sense of it.

Bajwa had pulled away, clutching at his bleeding nose. Destiny took her chance and slipped from Karlin's remaining grasp, but instead of pulling back, her foot slipped on one of the blankets, sending her reeling backward.

Karlin heard Axel swear as he rushed to grab her, but he was a couple of seconds too slow.

Destiny fell backward, her head hitting the hard floor with a sickening thwack.

Everyone was still rocking, crying, panicking. The sound of the drumbeats continued to hammer through the room, adding to the chaos.

Karlin simply stared at Destiny on the ground. Any sense of peace was gone now, pushed out by a relentless, thundering panic that gripped at her insides.

The terrified woman had managed to get into a sitting position, and her screaming had slowed, but her eyes were wild and frantic.

She had to do something.

She had to do something.

She had to help her.

She had to move.

But her body wouldn't cooperate with what her brain was commanding. The fear and guilt of too many swallowed memories threatened to overtake her completely.

"Karlin!" Axel was shouting now, crouching down beside Destiny and examining the back of her head. "She needs an ambulance. She needs something to calm her down. Come on! You need to call 9-1-1. Hurry!"

Bajwa cut in then, his fingers still splayed over his nose as blood dribbled down his chin. "There's nothing they'll be able to do," he argued. "Not without putting her at more risk. There are no known trip killer drugs for DX8 at this time."

Her annoyance at Bajwa's words was enough to snap

her out of her momentary paralysis. She joined Axel on the ground. Destiny had closed her eyes now, and Karlin forced one eyelid open, glancing at her expanded pupils as the woman screamed in her face at the top of her lungs. Fortunately, she seemed to be out of energy for violence, at least for the moment.

Axel's eyes were full of questions, but she'd have to explain later.

Once again, she was faced with the neglect of the company she'd spent years working for. Senera should have prioritized developing effective trip killer drugs for DX8, or at least tried to work out a safe dosage of an existing benzodiazepine or an antipsychotic that could dull the effects of a bad trip in an emergency.

But they hadn't.

Instead, they'd pushed ever forward in their trials, with no regard for their patients. And she'd been complicit.

"Dr. Bajwa, she might have a concussion," Axel argued, not bothering to hide the annoyance that mirrored her own. "We need to get her to a hospital. She may need to be restrained by professionals if she keeps hurting herself."

As if to prove his point, Destiny yanked out several strands of coily black hair and held them in front of her face, staring at them as tears began to roll over her cheeks.

Karlin's heart ached. The poor woman must have been absolutely beyond afraid, completely losing control of her body and mind.

She may have failed John, and she may have failed Amira, but there was no way she was going to fail Destiny now.

As a medical researcher, she had an immediate responsibility to the patient in front of her, however Bajwa felt about it.

"He's right," Karlin said firmly. "She needs more help than we can give her here."

Bajwa looked pained.

He didn't give voice to his concerns, but Karlin could read the truth on his face.

On the one hand, he was clearly worried about his patient, but on the other, taking her to the hospital during an active trial would open up several inconvenient avenues of documentation and inquiry.

"I have to stay with the others," Bajwa protested weakly. "How will you get her down to the main compound? An ambulance will take forever to get up here, if they can make it at all."

"I don't know, I don't know," Karlin said, pressing her palms against her forehead as Destiny let out another piercing scream and the drumbeats continued to hammer at her ears. She couldn't think.

Paul, Cora, and Lily were huddled together now, muttering incomprehensibly. Bajwa was right. He needed to help them, too.

"I'll go. I can help her," Axel said firmly, stepping between Bajwa and Destiny.

Panic bubbled up in Karlin's chest. She wanted to argue with him, to do damage control somehow, but she couldn't think of anything to say. Axel was ruining his cover completely, and the retreat had barely started.

Bajwa narrowed his eyes, but Axel continued before he could say more.

"I don't know, man," he said. "My dose must have been too small or something. I feel totally normal."

"Why didn't you say anything earlier?" Karlin demanded, quickly adapting to his story.

"Sorry. I kept waiting for it to kick in, but I guess nothing is going to happen at this point."

Bajwa considered this for only a second before nodding his head and digging into the pocket of his slacks.

"I'll handle things here," he said, tossing Karlin a set of keys. "Just go. And call me when you know what's going on."

ASHER

Seriously, where was his gym-rat twin Ben when he needed him?

"Careful, don't bump her head," Asher instructed as Karlin yanked open the door of Bajwa's old Jeep. The two of them had only just managed to half-drag, half-carry a frantic Destiny out of the hut and into the cool moonlight. They were both breathing heavily, but the woman had calmed down a little now that she was away from the group and the noise.

"Destiny, you're safe, okay?" Asher said, making his voice as gentle as he could manage as he climbed into the passenger seat and pulled her in after him. "We're getting you help. This is all going to stop soon, I promise."

His heart felt pinched within his chest as she nodded, tears still falling along her umber cheeks. He wanted to help Karlin and stop Senera from hurting people in the future, but at the moment, he couldn't help but to feel that he had only succeeded in letting Destiny down.

He took hold of her seatbelt and pulled it across her chest, shoving the clip in so hard that his knuckles went white.

How many times would he try to help someone else, only to watch them suffer in the end?

Karlin hopped into the driver's seat, and Asher watched as she fumbled with the key in the ignition. Now that she was away from Bajwa and the rest of the group, her panic was evident. Destiny screamed again, smacking her open palm against the window several times in a row.

Asher reached over and took Karlin's hand in his own, gently guiding the key into the ignition and turning it. As the engine sprung to life, Asher watched as she reached up and brushed a few stray tears from her cheeks. "I'm so scared."

"I know. And it's understandable," Asher said. "But we need to focus on getting Destiny's help. I have faith that God will handle the rest."

Karlin's jaw tightened momentarily at the mention of the Lord, but a moment later, she nodded. A look of determination had replaced the fear on her face, even as Destiny continued to cry and shout at invisible bad guys through the window.

"Just drive carefully, okay? It's dark."

Karlin said nothing, but nodded firmly again as she put the Jeep into gear and started down the worn dirt road.

For several minutes, Asher focused on keeping Destiny calm as Karlin drove. When they reached the main retreat site, she stopped, hopping out of the car and racing into the small office building.

While he waited for her to return, he rolled down the driver's side window, letting in some fresh air. Once again, he heard a strange sound in the distance, carried by the breeze. He couldn't quite make out what it was, but he hoped it wasn't anything to do with the other patients or Dr. Bajwa. Hopefully, with Destiny gone, he'd had the good sense to cool it with the jungle drumbeats and let everyone calm down.

Before he could decide what it was, however, the sound abruptly went quiet, leaving only the swishing noise of sand blowing against the ground.

Karlin returned to the Jeep, her hair windswept as she clicked her seatbelt on.

"I called 9-1-1 from the landline and grabbed my cell, just in case I need to get ahold of Bajwa once we have service," she explained, breaking a stretch of silence as they started driving again. Even Destiny had gone quiet now, though she was still breathing hard, her eyes roving in fear.

He took a deep breath, pausing for a moment as Karlin navigated over a particularly treacherous section of rut-filled road. Now was as good a time as he was likely going to get.

Asher steeled himself for Destiny's reaction as he placed a hand on her shoulder. To his relief, she didn't react violently. In fact, she didn't even flinch.

"Look, she's being more docile than you usually are," he joked, glancing over at Karlin.

"Shut up."

She didn't take her eyes from the road, but he could see the smile tugging at the corner of her mouth. He smirked at her before turning back to Destiny.

"I'm going to pray for you, okay?" he said, trying to read the woman's eyes.

It was impossible to know what she was thinking, but he did know that she loved the Lord, and whatever chemical imbalance, or demon, or whatever else had taken up residence in her mind, He was there within her heart.

"Lord Jesus Christ, please have mercy and help your

servant Destiny. Please free her and all others suffering from mental illness or demonic influence. Please help her to regain control over her body and her mind. Please help us to reach the hospital safely. Amen."

He felt self-conscious as he noticed Karlin stealing a couple of glances in his direction. He had never had a particular gift for offering prayer in front of others, but he knew that God was still listening, no matter how clumsy his words might have been.

For several more minutes, the car was quiet.

"Look," Karlin said, interrupting his thoughts. "I think she's falling asleep."

She was right. Destiny's eyes were drooping, and her breathing had slowed significantly.

Thank you, Jesus.

Up ahead, Senera's main compound came into view, along with the flashing lights of an ambulance. Relief filled him, and when he looked over at Karlin, he could see that she was actually smiling.

Maybe he hadn't failed anyone after all. They'd made it, and Destiny was going to get the help she needed. Everything was going to be all right.

CHAPTER
NINETEEN

THE WOMAN

BEFORE

The woman waited.

Tonight, she was especially excited for what was to come. It was special.

She could feel it, even as she drifted away, even now that the hut that surrounded her had been replaced with trees and flowers of a dozen colors. A waterfall tinkled somewhere to her right, the water dancing against gleaming white stone.

She had never expected her life to become so grand. She had never been an important person, but now, here she was, leading others to the truth. Her heart felt like it might burst with pride.

At that moment, Mother arrived.

She felt a stirring in the air around her, a whisper

without words, and then the snake showed herself in all her glory.

Mother greeted her warmly, and the woman did the same.

Silence followed as she tried to think of how to ask what was on her mind. Mother was beautiful, kind, and perfect, but sometimes, she still struck the woman with a sense of dread.

Fortunately, the snake knew this well.

"Don't be afraid, my child," Mother said to the woman gently.

She watched as Mother began to shrink in front of her until her hulking green form had been reduced to something no larger than a snake that she might find in a garden shed.

"I am sorry, Mother," the woman said, feeling a twinge of shame. She should obey Mother and control her emotions. The snake had earned her trust by now.

"What do you want to ask of me?"

"How—how will I know who it is that is chosen?" she stammered out.

Mother was moving now, coming closer to her until she was slithering up the front of her chest. She tried not to flinch as the snake came even closer.

"You will hear my whisper in your heart when the time is right. I am always with you, my child."

All at once, the woman felt a chill rushing through her.

The snake was gone now, but she knew exactly where the being was.

She could feel Mother gleaming within her chest, slipping gently beneath her ribcage and taking hold of her heart.

Everything inside of her was warmth, and light, and happiness.

"Thank you, Mother," the woman breathed, a smile spreading across her face as the trees began to dance. "There is one woman here who I will show to you. She is in deep need of the truth."

"Very good, my child. Very good."

CHAPTER
TWENTY

KARLIN

The waiting room smelled like plastic and rubbing alcohol.

Karlin shifted in her seat. Try as she might, she couldn't manage to get comfortable, nor could she manage to forget about the last time she'd been in a hospital.

She'd been visiting John, and the waiting room had smelled exactly like this one did, right down to the vaguely floral scent of whatever cleaner the staff used.

At least this one led to normal patient rooms rather than a locked psych word. It was a solid step up.

Axel plunked himself in the seat next to her, handing her a vending machine coffee.

"Maybe my next dose of fake DX8 can have caffeine in it," he joked, taking a large gulp from his matching paper cup. "I'm seriously starting to miss it."

She opened her mouth to respond but quickly closed it again. She wanted to joke around with him, and she especially wanted the cheap, crappy coffee after so much deprivation, but she couldn't seem to let go of the night's stress.

Not to mention her own dark memories.

"Karlin, are you okay?" he asked, his expression moving instantly from playful to concerned.

To her horror, she felt her throat choking up with sobs as tears rolled down her cheeks.

What was it with this guy that made her so willing to break down like a delicate flower? It was maddening. But she couldn't seem to help it.

Axel snatched away her coffee and set it with his own on top of a pile of old magazines. She found herself unable to push away as he wrapped his arms around her, even as the armrest of her chair pressed uncomfortably into her ribcage.

"Hey, hey, hey," he said, reaching up to wipe a strand of hair away from her snotty nose.

Lovely.

"You told me the doctor said she was okay," he continued. "Destiny's calm now and she escaped even a minor concussion from falling on that floor. Everything is going to be fine."

Karlin swallowed another sob. "Her head will be fine, but what if her mind isn't?"

Axel seemed to consider his words carefully. "This is partly why I'm not in favor of people taking psychedelic drugs. But she's already acting completely normal. You told me the doctor described it as a bad trip."

"You don't understand."

Axel leaned down until his eyes met hers.

"So help me understand. You can trust me."

She felt small and vulnerable as he searched her face, but she knew that he was right. She couldn't deny the way he was breaking through the walls she'd built around herself, as much as she hated to let it be true.

"Destiny is schizophrenic. She told the doctors readily. Bajwa obviously knows about it. And he let her join this trial anyway."

Axel's eyes flashed with anger. "Even I can figure out that mixing psychosis with drug-induced hallucinations is a terrible idea. How could he allow this?"

"I have no idea, but I feel terrible for letting it happen."

Karlin paused as a fresh wave of sobs threatened to break free. She allowed herself a moment to lean in closer to Axel, even as her snot and tears smeared onto his hoodie. The guilt was too much to handle on her own.

"Bajwa didn't tell you. It's not your fault," Axel said firmly. "And tonight, you did the right thing. You got her help."

"Barely," she spat. "So much could have gone wrong."

"But nothing did."

"But it could have," she argued, not caring how childish she sounded. "Let me guess, you're going to tell me that God was in control the whole time, right?"

Her words came out way more harshly than she'd intended, but she couldn't bring herself to apologize for saying them.

Axel shifted his weight, and she expected him to pull back from her, but he didn't. He was quiet for several long seconds, holding her just as he had before. She could feel the thumping of his heart, and after a few seconds, she felt her anger dissipating.

"I'm sorry," she said at last.

"I'm not," he said. "I do think God was in control, and I think He's in control right now. So, ha."

He pulled away a little, enough for her to see the teasing grin had returned to his face.

"Fair enough," she said, allowing a smile of her own. It felt good, even though her insides were still tangled up in knots. "I still find it hard to believe in any of that."

"You've gone through hard times in your life," he said matter-of-factly.

"Let me guess, you investigated me before you agreed to take this job? Dug into my past? Found out all of my dark secrets?"

She tried to match his light tone, but she knew her bitterness had come through. Every time she thought she might be able to trust somebody, they managed to prove to her why she couldn't.

To her surprise, however, Axel shook his head.

"No, I didn't. I mean, I called our police liaison, Allie, and had her run a criminal record check, but that was about it. I had no reason to pry too much further into your life."

"Oh."

"I assume you've been through hard times because, first of all, who hasn't? And second of all, I mean, you make it pretty obvious that you're dark and twisty."

He grinned, and she scowled at him. "I am not *dark and twisty*."

"So, tell me your secrets. Let me be the judge."

Axel's light tone made it clear that he was teasing.

She didn't have to tell him anything. She could lock it all away just as she always had, and he wouldn't hold it against her.

She knew that, and it was even more clear as she allowed herself a few seconds to get lost in the intensity of his eyes.

She drew a deep breath and leaned back in her chair, glancing around the waiting room, as though any of the other people waiting for their loved ones at four in the morning possibly cared about her messed-up life.

"Okay. I'll tell you."

"Would it help if I held your hand while you confess your dark secrets? Or I could let you use my shirt as a Kleenex again," Axel suggested.

She shook her head.

"In that case, the linoleum floor is yours, madam," he said, making a sweeping gesture.

She chose to grit her teeth and ignore his antics. The closer she got to telling her secrets, the more nervous she felt. She had to spit it out before she lost her nerve.

"I told you I have a brother, right?"

"Yep. John. Both of you guys are from Michigan, but he lives in Lubbock now."

She nodded, impressed. Axel loved to joke around, but when it came to taking in important information, he clearly didn't miss much.

"The truth is, our relationship is a lot more complicated than I let on. I worry about John constantly. I was upset about Destiny tonight, sure, but part of why it hit me so hard is because of the memories it brought back."

"Is John schizophrenic?"

"No, but he has severe PTSD thanks to his time in combat. So does my dad, though his was from fighting in the Gulf War."

"I fought in Afghanistan, too," Axel said. "It's tough. It

139

really is hard to understand for most people who haven't lived through it."

He looked like he might say more, but he didn't, so Karlin continued.

"Neither of us had a good relationship with my dad growing up. I mean, not my mom either, but my dad was worse. He didn't hit us or anything, but he refused to deal with his trauma. He was an alcoholic, my mom was depressed, and they both moved to Florida when John turned eighteen. Left us with a paid off single-wide. Running away from their demons, I guess. From the little I hear from relatives on Facebook, I think they're doing a bit better, so that's something."

She paused to take a breath. Now that she had opened the floodgates, it was difficult to stop talking. She hadn't spoken about her family to anyone other than John for as long as she could remember–and even with him, she rarely brought up her parents.

"How old were you?" Axel asked, his brow furrowing in concern.

"Seventeen," she said. "John and I are Irish twins. Technically, he's the older one, but it didn't make much of a difference when we were both so young to be on our own. It was hard to get by, especially when we were both trying to finish high school. I babysat and John mowed lawns, and we used the food bank a lot. John joined the military the second he graduated. I went to college close by to live as cheaply as possible, but after that, I had no reason to stay in Michigan, so I left, too."

"Not exactly what I pictured when you told me you lived at home during college," Axel chimed in. "You really have been through a lot. You should be so proud of everything you've been able to accomplish. You're...it's amazing, Karlin."

She smiled, but wouldn't allow herself to thank him. She may have beat the odds that were stacked against her, but she didn't like to dwell on it.

"That time in my life was really painful," she conceded, "and just when I thought I had gotten past the worst of it, John was honorably discharged early from his military service. His PTSD was too severe for him to continue as a soldier. As it turns out, it was kind of too severe for him to function in civilian life, either. He spent years self-medicating, mostly with alcohol, but he uses other drugs, too. He's been sober for five months now, and I'm so proud of him, but he still has a long road ahead. He's only able to work part-time, and he isn't earning even close to enough money to pay for the help he needs."

She paused, debating whether or not to tell Axel the source of John's–and therefore, her–biggest medical debt. A part of her wanted to, but she knew that if she did, she'd start crying all over again, and that was not what she needed right now. Not with Destiny in the hospital and a group of other patients back at the retreat site who still needed her.

"You're helping him, aren't you?" Axel asked, breaking the momentary silence. "I know how hard it is dealing with government services, even as a veteran. We're promised the moon, but..."

She nodded. "It's part of why I've stayed with Senera for as long as I have. John is relying on me financially. The therapy, the meds, rent–some of it ends up being covered by his military benefits, but a lot of it doesn't. He's been trying to get funding for a service dog to help with his PTSD, but the Veterans Freedom Society keeps denying his claim. He feels guilty that I have to help him, but I'm all he has."

Axel was about to speak, but before he could, one of the doctors Karlin had met earlier stuck her head out of a doorway.

"Ms. McKenna? Mr. Bishop? Destiny wants to see you."

CHAPTER
TWENTY-ONE

ASHER

"Well, the secret's out," Destiny announced. "I'm a crazy person."

"I don't think 'crazy' is the PC term these days, you know," he joked.

Destiny laughed and raised her eyebrows at him. "I've been reliably informed that 'insane' is also out."

Asher grinned. It was a relief to see her acting like herself, though he had to admit he felt strange being in here with her, especially with Karlin now speaking to the doctor outside in the hall.

He wished that he could go back in time to ten minutes ago and say a few of the things that were on his mind. Though the circumstances were hardly ideal, Karlin had actually been opening up to him, and he found himself even more impressed by her now that he understood more of what she'd been through. He had actually considered telling her more about what he'd been through in

Afghanistan, which was not a topic that just anybody could drag out of him.

"Hey, have you seen anything about this? Check it out."

Asher snapped to attention at Destiny's words. The woman had been through a living nightmare. The least he could do was actually be present with her. He was glad that the hospital allowed him to visit with her at all, considering that sunrise was still a decent way off.

Though he still strongly disagreed with her choice as a Christian to take DX8, he could sympathize with her a lot more now that he understood what she was going through. Even with God's grace, schizophrenia had to be an incredibly heavy cross to carry. He could see why she would be willing to try anything in hopes of being set free from her illness.

Destiny gestured toward the tv that hung over her bed, and he followed her gaze to a report from the previous day's six o'clock news. She picked up the remote control that sat on her nightstand and turned up the volume.

"This evening, a breaking story," the news anchor said, her voice grave. "According to Amarillo police, reports of cult activity have been steadily on the rise, and two potentially related crimes have the city on edge. Reporter Lindsay Cundiff has the full story."

Asher watched as the camera cut to a male reporter standing in the middle of a quiet suburban street. "Thank you, Monica. That's right. This middle class neighborhood is not as peaceful as it seems. Back in August, two teenage girls disappeared from their homes. As of this report, they still have not been found–but we have an exclusive interview with some of their closest friends."

"Creepy, right?" Destiny chimed in. "The whole potential cult story has actually made it as far as the Dallas media. I'm not usually conspiratorial, but a severe increase in cult-related reports is pretty striking."

Asher nodded. "I mean, it could be Satanic Panic type stuff, I guess, but yeah. I hope they find those girls, either way."

They focused back on the screen as the reporter sauntered up to one of the houses nearby and rang the bell. A woman invited her and her cameraman inside, and the shot changed to the same reporter sitting on the couch across from three teenage girls.

"You told the police that you think your missing friends have become involved in a cult. But the Amarillo police tell us there's no evidence that the reports of cult activity have any credibility. Do you stand by what you reported?"

"Yes," a slender brunette said as her friends bobbed their heads up and down emphatically. "Stacy and Ava talked about there being this little community out in the desert somewhere before they went missing. They told me that a couple people invited them to come and join one of their parties, though none of us ever got the details. I told them both it sounded weird, and to stay out of it."

Just as the reporter began to ask a follow-up question, the door to Destiny's room swung open, and Karlin returned alone, looking chastened.

Asher could only imagine how furious the doctor must have been now that the immediate danger had passed. Senera giving DX8 to people like Destiny was dangerous, no matter what the FDA had said.

And even that official seal of approval was questionable.

Perhaps Bajwa or someone higher up at Senera had

bribed regulators. If Asher could find evidence, that alone could be enough to get DX8 out of patients' hands, at least for a while.

Destiny clicked the mute button on the remote, silencing the TV as Karlin walked up to the head of her bed.

"I am so sorry," Karlin said quickly, her face pinched. "I feel terrible about what happened. How are you feeling?"

"Honestly, pretty much normal," Destiny said, a smile rising on her full lips. "I mean, I have a bit of a lingering headache, but right now, I'm mostly just upset about yet another failed treatment option for my schizophrenia."

Karlin said nothing, though Asher could tell by the way she gripped the railing of the hospital bed that she was trying to stop her hands from shaking. He desperately wanted to reach over and comfort her, but he couldn't risk breaking cover in front of Destiny anymore than he already had.

Destiny continued. "I'd read stuff online about people going into a psychotic state after taking psychedelics. It freaked me out, but I ended up convincing myself that a synthetic drug made to help people with their mental health would be safe. I knew better, and I should have trusted my conscience."

"I am deeply, deeply sorry for what happened," Karlin said again. She swallowed hard, and her eyes were starting to redden. No one would have blamed her for tearing up, least of all Asher, but she didn't. Instead, she cleared her throat and spoke again.

This time, her voice was colder, almost clinical. The empathy she had shown moments before seemed to have faded away in an instant.

It didn't take a psychologist to know that she was

putting on a mask, trying to distance herself from the pain she was feeling. Asher knew the tactic well. He was used to using it himself.

"I am glad that you're feeling better, at least physically," Karlin said. "Dr. Bajwa is faxing some papers over for you to sign. We are going to be investigating this incident further to ensure that nothing like this ever happens again."

Asher tried to shoot Karlin a questioning glance, but she ignored him, her eyes remaining trained on her patient. He remembered the non-disclosure agreement that he'd had to sign himself for the retreat. He'd had his almost-sister-in-law and Forge Brothers Security paralegal, Bristol, look it over. The document had been pretty weak, and he hadn't been concerned about it getting in the way of exposing Senera's illegal activities. He could only hope that Bajwa wasn't planning on bullying the vulnerable woman into signing something more airtight.

"Okay," Destiny replied, smiling weakly despite Karlin's abrupt demeanor. "But I'm starting to feel really tired. Can I deal with the paperwork stuff in a few hours?"

"Of course," Karlin said, getting up to leave. "Before we go, is there anyone we can call to come and stay with you?"

Destiny shook her head. "Not really. Dallas is pretty far, and I'm okay. I promise. Thanks, though."

They walked out of the hospital in silence, lost in their own thoughts.

Asher couldn't help but to wonder if Destiny, like Karlin, was used to getting through life more or less on her own–and he was incredibly thankful that he had no idea what that was like.

KARLIN

Silence hung between Karlin and Axel as they climbed into Bajwa's Jeep.

She was glad that he seemed to share her pensive mood.

After visiting Destiny, her thoughts were even more of a jumbled mess than they'd been before. She'd managed to hold it together for her patient's sake, but just barely. She'd have to continue to steel herself. She doubted that the rest of the day was going to get any easier.

May as well get back to it.

When she moved to turn the key and start the Jeep, however, Axel laid his hand on hers, sending a burst of electricity dancing through her.

Despite Axel's usually jovial demeanor, there was something about him that made him seem not only competent, but safe.

Not that she'd ever fully let her guard down.

The man would be going home in a week and a half, and all she'd have was herself, just like before. Especially if they got the evidence they needed to take Senera down. She wanted that victory, but she knew it would be bittersweet.

"You need to get some sleep before we drive back," he said firmly. "The DX8 will have worn off by now and the others will all be asleep, anyway. Let Bajwa handle them. Ned will be coming in today, too, right?"

When she'd called Bajwa from the hospital earlier, he had still been awake and already thinking out loud about the legal ramifications of what had just happened. And Ned would be coming in, though he wouldn't have the first clue about how to help the patients process what had just taken place. No. Whether she liked it or not, they still needed her.

"I don't even feel tired," she said finally. "And if I did manage to fall asleep, I wouldn't be able to wake up again until tomorrow."

"You've been through something traumatic, Karlin," Axel said. "You're not going to be able to just hop back in immediately and be on your game. Be reasonable."

"Fine," she snapped, a little more harshly than she'd meant to. "I'll get a little bit of rest, but I'm keeping my eyes open."

A smile broke out on Axel's face.

"What?" she prompted, trying and failing to conceal her annoyance. Despite the terrible night they'd endured, he could still flip a switch and look as happy as a golden retriever with a ball at a moment's notice. It was maddening.

"Well, I have some sightseeing to do. Since you want to keep your eyes open anyway, the timing is perfect."

"Sightseeing? Axel, we do not have time for *sightseeing*. I need to check on the other patients. I need to call the hospital and check on Destiny. I almost certainly need to do eight thousand hours of paperwork–"

With another one of his teasing grins, Axel leaned over in his seat until his body was halfway over hers.

For a terrifying, electrifying second, she thought he was going to kiss her.

She froze in place, mouth still hanging open, unsure whether to try and kiss him back or to punch him in the nose.

But no attempt at a kiss came. While she was distracted, he yanked the keys out of the ignition.

"Hey! Give me those!" she said, lunging for the keys as

he collapsed back down into the passenger seat. She tried to grab hold of Bajwa's plastic keychain, but Axel was too quick for her and was now holding the keys over his head.

"Ha. I win," he announced, easily deflecting her next attempt at swiping the keys.

"Cheater," she muttered, sitting back down and crossing her arms over her chest. "You're taller than me."

"Having the physique of a string bean with sexy forearms has its benefits."

"You've just made me picture Popeye. Congratulations," she said.

"Popeye definitely didn't skip leg day," he pointed out. "I do. Actually, I skip *every* day. The gym sucks. Whenever my brother Ben manages to rope me into working out with him, I end up needing to eat like three extra peanut butter sandwiches a day just to stop myself from losing weight. I run a little when provoked, but that's about it."

She made a face. "As fascinating as your fitness regime is, we seriously don't have time for this."

"You're right," he said, shaking his head. "We don't. Not if we're going to make it to the Palo Duro Canyon before sunrise. Now, get out of the way so I can drive. Please."

"What a gentleman," she muttered as she got out of the Jeep and moved over to the passenger side. "Fine. You drive. But you can't tell anyone that I let you. I think this Jeep belongs to Senera, and they'd be even more mad than Bajwa if something happened to it. And there's one more condition."

"What's that?"

She would have sworn she could see Axel's ears actually perking up, as though eager for the slightest opportunity to make her happy.

It was cute.

Annoyingly cute.

"You stop for breakfast on the way," she said. "Including coffee that doesn't come out of a vending machine."

"I was hoping you'd demand a kiss as the sun rises," he said, starting the Jeep and shifting it into gear, "but coffee and food sounds almost as good. Done."

CHAPTER
TWENTY-TWO

ASHER

Asher had never had such a delicious breakfast.

Then again, it had been so long since he'd last eaten that even one of Gabe's alleged 'salads' of lettuce, vinaigrette, and barely-seasoned grilled chicken would have probably tasted incredible. The McDonald's Egg McMuffin he had just scarfed down was basically heaven.

The sky was beginning to lighten as he finished up the final dregs of his coffee and watched as Karlin did the same.

She'd gone quiet again on the drive over to the canyon. Every time he managed to get her laughing and opening up, she always shut down again soon after. On some level, he knew that he should probably be annoyed, but instead, he couldn't help but to see it as a challenge.

And he loved a challenge.

Especially one that allowed him to indulge in outrageous flirting with a smart, gorgeous woman like Karlin.

For the moment, though, he decided to be a little more serious. They'd have to go back to the retreat site soon, and this might end up being the only time they had alone for a while. He couldn't spend the entire time hoping for a kiss.

Not out loud, anyway.

He cleared his throat, gathering up their breakfast trash and tossing it into the largest paper bag.

"So. We haven't really had much of a chance to talk about the real stuff, have we?"

Karlin glanced up at him, her face going decidedly pink. He smirked. Maybe she thought he was going to profess his undying love or something.

He wasn't, of course.

At least, he didn't think so. Probably.

"It feels like everyone and everything has been conspiring to keep us apart," he explained. "It's hard to investigate very well when I can't actually talk to my point of contact."

"I'm sorry," Karlin said, looking way more chastened than he'd wanted her to feel. "It's been so difficult. I should have found us walkie-talkies or something, though I think that might be risky when I'm in my staff cabin–"

"No, no, no, don't be sorry," he said quickly. "It's no one's fault. And you've done a good job, considering the circumstances. I mean, you didn't accidentally dose me with DX8. Total win."

Karlin didn't return his smile.

"The doctor at the hospital threatened to report me," she said. "That was after she chewed me out for putting my patient at risk. She wasn't wrong, but it still hurt."

Asher reached over and rested his hand on her shoulder. "This is the kind of thing that you need to let Bajwa handle," he said firmly. "Don't let it distract you."

She nodded, and he let his arm fall away. He didn't want to push her too much now. Not when she was clearly wrestling her own demons.

"I guess I'm still worried about my own reputation," she admitted. "I don't want to be shunned by the medical research community. I love what I do. I want to keep doing it, even after all of this is over."

"Have you always been passionate about mental health research?"

She smiled softly. "I've always been a nerd. I loved math and science in school. I thought I'd do something else with that interest, though. Something nice and solitary, and preferably something that earned a lot more money than I'd had growing up. But when my parents left, I realized that I had gifts that could help people. Witnessing John's struggle only solidified that plan for me."

"I admire that," Asher said. "It's not always easy to use the gifts that God has given you. Especially when there are easier paths you could follow instead."

"Right," she said after a brief pause. "It's not an easy field to be in, that's for sure."

Karlin looked a little uncomfortable at the mention of God, and he decided to change the subject.

"So, did you see the thing about the cults that Destiny was watching?" he asked.

She raised an eyebrow. "Oh, I've definitely heard about it. It's been in the news for months."

"You don't sound convinced."

"I'm worried about the missing girls," she clarified, "but the idea that they ran off to some crazy cult compound out in the desert somewhere? No. Not convinced."

Asher shrugged. "I've seen stranger things in my business."

"If there was anything to it, the authorities would have found something by now," Karlin said firmly.

"For someone with such a skeptical streak, why do you so readily believe in what the authorities say?"

She paused for a moment, considering this.

"As an authority myself, I can tell you that 'the authorities' screw up all the time," Asher joked.

"Oh, so you're an authority now?" she asked, returning his playful tone. "The Forge Brothers Security website made it very clear that you guys aren't actually law enforcement officers, at least legally speaking. So I'm pretty sure you're not the boss of me."

"Hmm. My brother Gabe thinks he's basically the president, emperor, and king of the world," Asher mused. "Maybe I should read that page to him. Knock him down a notch or two."

Karlin laughed. "Your brothers sound like fun, honestly. Including Gabe. I wish I could meet them."

"I'm sure they'd love you," he said, blushing a little at even the indirect mention of the L-word. "And even better, all the flirty ones except Jacob are taken, and he's across the world somewhere."

"All the flirty ones aside from you, you mean," she said, rolling her eyes.

"Obviously. Speaking of flirting, the sun's about to rise."

"Speaking of raisins, that's a non-sequitur," she replied without missing a beat.

Goodness, she was pretty.

Even when she was teasing him.

"Come on. You're going to miss it," he said, hopping out of the Jeep and striding around to the passenger side. He yanked open her door.

"Let's go."

KARLIN

Karlin wrapped her arms around herself as Axel opened the door and sent a burst of freezing wind whipping into the Jeep.

"Are you insane?" she snapped. "It's like forty degrees out! And I didn't exactly think to grab my jacket while we were rushing Destiny to an ambulance."

To her annoyance, Axel only smiled wider.

"Stop being a wimp," he said, sliding out of his hoodie and holding it out to her.

For a moment, she considered slamming the door and turning the heat up to max, but decided against it. "If I die of frostbite, I'm blaming you."

"Don't be silly. It would have to be like eight degrees colder for you to get frostbite."

"How reassuring."

She allowed him to help her out of the Jeep and into the hoodie. She decided it was too cold to waste precious energy arguing as he led her over toward the railing of the lookout.

Despite her discomfort, she found herself stunned by the beauty of the scene that lay before her.

Axel was right–it was insane that she'd never been here, considering she lived so close.

The Palo Duro Canyon stretched out in front of her as

far as she could see, and on the far end, she could see the sun slowly creeping up over the canyon's red rim.

They watched in silence as the colors below began to shift from cool blues and purples to burning oranges, yellows, and reds. Innumerable shrubs and late flowering plants blanketed the canyon's bottom, and needle-covered juniper trees clung to its steep cliffs.

Karlin wanted to comment, but the view had left her awestruck, stealing away any hope of finding the right words.

After a few more minutes, the sun had risen fully above the tallest stretch of cliff, and Axel broke the silence at last.

"It's like…it's like love, you know?" he said.

"What?"

The very mention of that word was enough to make her breath catch in her throat.

"I feel like we humans are always trying to quantify everything," he explained. "We try so hard to explain everything, to break it down to the smallest parts in hopes of examining our way to the truth."

Karlin stole a glance at him for a brief moment, but his eyes were still trained on the scene below. "I'm a scientist, so yeah. Trying to know things is what I do. It's how I live my life."

"There's nothing wrong with knowing things," Axel said. "But there are some things that the natural sciences can't touch. Like the beauty of a sunrise. Or love."

Long moments passed as she considered his words, turning them over and over in her mind.

"There was a time in my life when I would have considered that idea to be false. Maybe even stupid," she admitted.

"But?"

She chewed on her bottom lip, trying to form the right words.

These questions were not entirely new to her. She'd pondered them before, many times, but somehow, she always felt like a traitor, as though acknowledging the inherent mystery of the universe meant she was ready to throw her lifelong love of scientific truth away.

But she couldn't deny that her opinions had changed over the years, even if she hadn't reached a full conclusion yet as to what she believed.

"I used to think about these questions in purely material terms," she said, gesturing toward the sunrise, as though the glorious beauty could speak up and help her explain. "I thought of love as taking place in the brain. Just hormones, chemicals, neurons, and the rest. I thought beauty was the same."

Axel nodded. "There's truth to that, obviously. I just don't think that's where it ends. I think that beauty and love exist not only outside of us, but outside of what we can measure. At the end of the day, I think that theistic faith makes sense of things that science can't really touch."

"I've– I've had the same thought," she admitted. "I'm so used to looking for rational explanations for everything, but sometimes, I think we need to take our own experiences of the world into account. And my experience of the world tells me that there might be more to life than subatomic particles."

Her words hung in the air for what felt like a very long time.

It was the closest she'd ever come to admitting out loud that God could possibly be real. Actually, it was probably the closest she'd come to admitting as much even within the privacy of her own thoughts.

"Well," Axel said at last, finally looking over at her with a smile as he broke the silence between them. "I'm glad you don't think I'm stupid."

She laughed. Once again, she found herself realizing just how safe she felt around him. He knew how to press every button she had, but on the other hand, he also knew when to simply listen. It was a rare gift, and one she found herself extremely thankful for.

"You're shaking, you know," he said.

At that moment, she realized he was right. She'd pulled the hood of his sweatshirt up over her ponytail and the sleeves as far over her fingers as they would go, but she was still extremely cold.

"You must be freezing, too," she retorted. Having given her his hoodie, he was now wearing only a long-sleeved t-shirt.

"Nah. Nice and warm. I'm a man," he said. "We wear shorts in January."

"Whatever you say," she said, shaking her head as she tried to pull the hoodie more tightly around herself.

"Seriously, I'll prove it," he said. His teasing smile had reached the corners of his eyes. "Come here."

Before she had the chance to get away from him or even to argue, he'd pulled her in close, wrapping his arms around her.

He was warm all right, warm enough for his body heat to mingle with what remained of her own, but she hardly noticed. Her heart was beating so loudly that she feared he would hear it.

He'd hugged her at the hospital, but this was different.

She forced herself to breathe in and out slowly, trying

to let herself relax, but her mind was racing at a hundred miles an hour as she considered what this meant.

Axel made no jokes and offered no flirty comments.

There was a seriousness to the way he touched her now, holding on to her like she was a precious treasure for him to protect.

But then again, maybe she was reading too much into it. Perhaps he really was just trying to be a gentleman and keep her warm. He'd be flying home to San Antonio soon enough, and she'd probably never see him again.

She should be pulling away, not letting herself rest in his arms.

And yet, despite everything she knew and the kind of person she thought she was, she wanted to dream.

She wanted to believe so badly that this could be something real. That there might be objective beauty in sunrises, and true love, and a God who made both.

Just then, she felt her phone vibrating.

Who would be calling her this early in the morning? It had to be Bajwa.

For the first time ever, she found herself annoyed to have phone service.

She could have sworn that Axel actually let out an audible sigh as she extracted herself from his arms and pulled the phone from her back pocket.

But as soon as she read the name on the caller ID, she froze.

It wasn't Bajwa.

It was John.

"Hello? What's going on, are you okay?" she said as she picked up, not waiting for her brother to greet her.

There was a brief pause on the other end of the line.

"Hey, Karl. Don't freak out, but I'm in the hospital."

CHAPTER
TWENTY-THREE

ASHER

A sher got to his feet and pulled Karlin up after him, gesturing in the direction of the Jeep. Karlin followed mutely, gripping the phone with white knuckles as her brother talked. As they settled back into the warmth of the vehicle, Karlin finally spoke, her voice more angry than Asher had ever heard it.

"An overdose, John? Really?" she spat. "How can we be doing this all over again?"

He tried to catch her eye.

She ignored him, but he could see the tears gathering on her cheeks. He hated seeing her cry, and it had been happening way too often.

"I know," she said after a pause. "But I'm still going to come. I want to make sure you're—"

Karlin's fingers tightened more firmly around her iPhone. "Fine. I know I have a lot going on here, too, but as soon as I deal with all of it, I'm heading to Lubbock, and that's final. Okay. I love you, too. I'll call again soon."

She hung up the phone, a fresh volley of tears falling from her eyes as she curled up against the window of the passenger seat.

He let her get herself together for a moment, not wanting to make things worse, but finally, the longing to try and comfort her became too strong to resist.

"What happened?" Asher asked, taking her hand within his own. She allowed this much, but he didn't think it would be wise to try and get any closer, despite the moment they'd just shared. Trying to get Karlin to open up to him was like sneaking up on a doe. One too-quick movement, and she'd bolt for the hills.

"John had the brilliant idea to go to a party," she said, chuckling without a hint of humor. "But not just any party, of course. A party filled with drugs and alcohol, thanks to some alleged war friends that I've never heard of. He said that no one else gets him like other vets do."

Asher said nothing, though he could tell by the look on her face that she didn't buy her brother's excuse any more than he did.

"I wanted to tell him it was total crap," she continued, "and that other veterans who do drugs aren't helping him. But he knows that. Of course he knows that! It's the addiction talking, not reason. And it's just–it's maddening. It feels like all of this time sober was pointless in the end. And it's not the first time he's fallen off. It's just so unbelievably frustrating. I believe his pain is real. I wouldn't be in this field if I didn't. But I just…"

Karlin trailed off, putting her face in her hands and letting out a long groan.

"Pain can be an explanation, but it can't be an excuse," Asher said. "It's okay for you to be angry. He's put you through a lot."

"He's been through so much worse," Karlin said. Her voice was softer now, like all of the anger had been ripped clean out of it, leaving only a husk of sadness behind. "But yeah. His pain has hurt me, too. I'm not invincible. I've–I've had to learn that lesson, and it was a painful one."

Her eyes landed on his for a few seconds longer than necessary.

Somewhere within their depths, he could sense words she was leaving unsaid, but he wouldn't press her. He knew she'd unburden herself from her darkness only when she was ready, and nothing he said would make that happen a moment sooner. If anything, he'd only succeed in making her more afraid to be vulnerable with him.

"I hope you know that, whatever it's worth, I think you're an amazing little sister," he said, squeezing her hand. "He is so blessed to have you. He knows that, I think."

She offered him a weak smile. "I don't know about amazing. But I'm trying. If nothing else, I do think he knows I'll always be there. We all need someone to love us unconditionally. Our parents didn't, so that means it's my job to be that for my brother. I just wish his addictions didn't rob him of his ability to really do the same for me."

The passion in her words stirred Asher's heart, but they also made him a little bit sad. How could someone so brilliant be so blind?

"Karlin, even if you had no one at all, not one single person, you wouldn't be alone," he said quickly, hoping desperately that the words would come out right. "I know He might be hard to see or hear sometimes, but God is always there. God loves you unconditionally."

She was quiet for a long moment, watching the sunrise

through the window as it continued to light up the canyon in pinks and purples of a thousand hues.

"The funny thing is, I think John really does believe what you believe. Even though he keeps messing up, he has this faith that God is going to bring him through his pain in the end. Even if he has to say sorry five hundred times, he never stops trusting that forgiveness is possible. I'm actually jealous of him. How messed up is that?"

Several questions floated through Asher's mind, but he didn't say anything.

Instead, he offered a silent prayer to God to bring Karlin closer to Him. It was beyond clear that this beautiful, brilliant woman needed her Father as deeply as any struggling soul he had ever met.

"It's crazy to be jealous of him," she said, breaking the silence. "He really went through hell. He watched as his teammate was killed in front of him. Actually, it was worse than watching it. He got blood on his clothes. He got blood on his face. I just...I don't think we can imagine what it's like to go through something like that and find the will to move past it, let alone believe in this good God who loves us."

Asher tightened his jaw.

He had just been handed an opportunity to share his own story.

It was the perfect timing. She made it clear by the empathy she had for her brother that she would at least try to understand.

But he couldn't do it.

She wasn't the only one who was good at running away.

"You're right," he said at last. "I've never experienced

anything quite like that. Despite his flaws, John's faith is inspiring. I'll pray for him."

He looked out the window, not wanting to look at Karlin, even as he continued to cling to her hand like a lifeline.

He didn't lie. He had never experienced exactly what John had experienced.

But he did know what it was like to have a teammate of his own die.

And worse?

He hadn't been a witness.

He'd been the cause.

CHAPTER
TWENTY-FOUR

THE WOMAN

BEFORE

Mother did not keep the woman waiting.

It seemed that the closer the two of them grew, the more quickly the serpent could find her.

What had once taken hours of focus and great gulps of foul-tasting liquid now required only sips and moments.

The woman wondered if one day, she would be able to contact Mother without the need of drugs at all, but she was not yet prepared to ask.

For all of the kindness that Mother exuded, there was still something terrible and mighty about her. It always felt like she could break apart the world in an instant, sending the woman falling into the depths.

Perhaps she could.

"My dear child," Mother began, her voice honey sweet.

"Tell me more about her. Tell me about the woman that you have chosen for us."

"Do you not know everything before I tell you?"

Some questions were too difficult to resist asking.

"Some things are shrouded from me," Mother said, letting out a soft hiss with her forked pink tongue. "That is why you are precious. You must be my hands and my feet within this world."

"Amira has visited our compound many times already," the woman answered. "She's lonely. Her husband is busy with his career. He's starting a new company and has little time for his family."

"Very well," Mother said.

"But there is a complication," the woman ventured.

"Tell me."

"Amira cannot move in like the others have done. She has a daughter at home, and she is not willing to leave her behind."

Mother was quiet for a long moment. The woman imagined the floor beneath her feet cracking in two, followed by the dirt, the crust of the earth, the whole world.

"Do not worry, my dear one," she said at last. "None of that matters. Soon, we will all return to my planet. We will all be home, in the glorious dimension of light. Fear not."

CHAPTER
TWENTY-FIVE

KARLIN

By the time her alarm began to sound, Karlin was already awake.

She allowed her eyes to remain closed for several pleasant seconds before climbing out of bed and silencing the noise. For the first time in what felt like forever, she'd gotten more than enough sleep, and a burst of fresh energy seemed to fill her limbs.

After she and Axel had returned to the retreat site yesterday, they'd been relieved to see that the rest of the guests were doing as well as could be expected.

Bajwa, however, was in a sour mood.

The Senera higher-ups had advised him to postpone their next DX8 dose by a full day, supposedly to allow everyone to rest after the ordeal with Destiny. Of course, this meant twenty-four hours of lost time and data.

For her part, Karlin had taken a long nap and caught up with office work, though she could admit to herself that she'd spent more time than she should have thinking of Axel and what he was doing to pass the day without her.

Every time she'd have to read some boring report, her thoughts would wander back to Bajwa's Jeep, the sun shining softly at the window, and Axel's warm chest pressed against her cheek.

There were worse ways to get lost while catching up on emails, and the day had passed relatively quickly.

By now, though, in the bright light of a new morning, she was eager to finally get some answers.

Most of their first week at the retreat had flown by, and in another week, Axel would be gone and she'd be on her own. Aside from the small fact that she needed his help to figure out how to stop Senera, she could no longer deny that she would miss the pleasant distraction of his flirting.

Even if she couldn't bring herself to believe it would ever be anything more.

She forced thoughts of him from her mind as she left her cabin and headed toward the lab to get a head start before breakfast.

As she made her way down the familiar dirt trail, however, she heard something.

She froze where she was, glancing out into the desert and seeing nothing but a few cacti and a patch of dead grass. But she did hear the noise again, slightly more quietly this time.

"Creepy, aren't they?" a voice from over her shoulder announced.

She whirled around, her heart leaping into her throat, but it was only Lily and Cora standing in the path behind her.

"It's just coyotes, honey," Lily continued, shaking her

head in the direction of the now silent desert. "But boy, do they ever sound human."

Cora smiled. "Totally creepy, but I've kind of started to like hearing them. They're beautiful creatures."

"Right," Karlin said, forcing a little laugh as the two women fell into step beside her. She decided she may as well skip the lab and head straight over to the dining hall. Her work could wait a little while longer, and at the moment, she suddenly felt very glad not to be alone out here in the quiet of the early morning.

"So," she said after a moment, "have either of you heard anything about the cult rumors that are going around in Amarillo?"

"Ha!" Lily said, tossing her silvery braid over one shoulder. "My brother works with the sheriff. They've searched high and low for this so-called cult. If there was anything to it, they'd know it by now."

Karlin thought the same thing, and yet, something about the woman's words gave her pause, but at the moment, she couldn't remember what it was.

"There's nothing to it but wild desert stories, that's all," Lily continued. "It's boring up here. What else are people gonna do but talk? They've been at it since before I was born."

"I'm not so sure about that," Cora cut in. "Those girls really did go missing."

"Oh, sure. But that doesn't mean they got snatched up by some cult. More likely it was a gang. Or maybe a pimp. Something more ordinary, anyway."

"But maybe there's a *reason* these stories keep popping up," Cora argued. "I read about the history of this place. There used to be these people here called the Antelope

Creek phase Indians, but they disappeared. To this day, no one knows what happened to them."

Lily gave Karlin a knowing look out of the corner of her eye. "I did entire classes on the local history of this area in college, and you're half right, I guess. No one knows exactly why those Indians died out–"

"I know I'm right!"

"Now, hold on," Lily said firmly, stopping for a moment where she stood and gesturing toward the expanse of the desert that surrounded them. "Look at this place. It's a harsh climate, and it has been for a very long time. There are all sorts of logical reasons that those people might have disappeared."

"Sure," Cora said brightly. "A portal to another dimension. Or maybe alien contact."

Karlin resisted the urge to laugh out loud.

Portals? Aliens? It was completely insane. Once again, she found herself wondering about the rigors of Bajwa's patient selection process.

Lily did laugh, though not unkindly. "It might be fun to speculate about the sci-fi stuff, but I can almost guarantee that it's something mundane that brought the Antelope Creek phase to their end. Resource scarcity, a warring tribe, a mass illness–there are all kinds of rational possibilities."

"So why don't they know what happened?"

"Because it was over five hundred years ago and most of the evidence is gone. No conspiracy required."

Cora considered this, finally shrugging her shoulders. "You're no fun, Lily."

Lily grinned at her. "I am old, Cora. I don't know what you're expecting."

Karlin let the two women pull ahead of her, following

them in silence as they continued to talk and joke with one another.

She couldn't help but to look over her shoulder one last time, her eyes searching the horizon as the light continued to grow brighter. She could hear only the breeze now, interrupted by the occasional chirping of a meadowlark.

She could almost believe the sounds had never been there at all.

Almost.

ASHER

Asher awoke with a jolt, sitting up straight in bed.

It took a couple of seconds for his brain to catch up with his body and to realize that the terrible air raid siren he'd been hearing in his dream was, in fact, a ringing phone.

His bleary eyes settled on the dresser on the other side of the cabin. He was so used to reaching into his pocket for his iPhone that he'd actually forgotten he'd been given access to a corded phone for the duration of the retreat.

"Hello?" he answered as politely as he could, in case it was Ned, Bajwa, or, best of all, Karlin.

Not that she'd ever trust a phone owned by Senera, if she was paranoid enough to believe that her cell phone could be bugged.

"Yo, bro!" the deep voice on the other end of the line boomed.

It was his brother, Ben, and he suddenly wished he'd picked up with one of his usual, more colorful, greetings.

Alas, his opportunity had slipped away.

"Hey, what's up? Finally someone remembers I'm still alive," he said, releasing a yawn.

"I remembered," Ben retorted. "I've been busy. I've been digging into this Dr. Daman Bajwa character."

Now, that was something. Asher twisted the gray cord between his fingers, waiting.

"His history is a lot more complicated than it seems on his Senera website bio, that's for sure. He's spoken publicly about his family history in business back in India. His father was some fancy-pants businessman, super rich, all the rest. But as it turns out, the story didn't end there. Apparently, dear old dad lost the entire family fortune and his good name due to the dot-com crash, and in particular, his own reckless spending. Daman Bajwa's father's last name is actually Kapoor. But Daman Jr. wanted a fresh start in America, with no baggage for anyone to Google.

"First, though, he had to get to the United States. To bring in the money to get himself through an international grad school program, he got involved with some seriously shady business dealings back in the old country."

"Shady how?"

"He was never convicted of anything personally, but he helped manage a call center that was exposed as a front for insurance fraud. Oh, and did I mention they specialized in targeting the elderly in North America?"

"That's insane."

"Yep. And of course, after all of that, he legally changed his last name to Bajwa."

Asher's mind was racing. "No way. I wonder if Karlin—my client, I mean—knows anything about this."

"I highly doubt it," Ben said proudly. "Took me a ton of digging to get this info. I doubt even the big bosses at Senera Pharmaceuticals would have been willing to take on the risk of employing him if they knew."

"Well, it explains some things. Mainly, why Bajwa is so

desperate to be the pioneer behind DX8. It's the chance at redemption he's probably been looking for his entire life. His family, too. Thanks for the help."

"No need to thank me. You know I live for this stuff," Ben said.

"Can't relate."

Though the two men were twins, Ben was pretty much Asher's opposite. Where Asher liked to get into the thick of things and investigate on the ground, Ben usually preferred to hole up in his office, running software and searching databases. His skills served Forge Brothers Security well.

"So," Asher continued, "how's the wedding chaos going?"

"I'm trying to stay away from it as much as possible," Ben said gruffly. "Though I was forced to learn, against my will, that Bristol got her way and they're doing black bridesmaid's dresses."

"How does Grace feel about it all?"

Ben paused, letting out a long sigh before answering. "She's driving me bonkers. She's trying to act like she's totally not hinting about me proposing, but as you know, she has about as much tact as, well, you."

"You're right, I don't have any tact," Asher agreed. "So, I'll just say it. Ask that girl to marry you already and stop being a wimp."

Ben groaned. "Even Dolly wants me to hurry up and marry her."

Asher laughed. The older woman ran the daytime security crew at FBS, and Grace's chaotic office management style often drove her crazy. "Why?"

"She thinks that maybe Grace will quit and become a housewife."

"You know, she might," Asher mused. "I can see that. Knowing Grace, she'll be all in. Martha Stewart in hot pink heels and some kind of designer apron that costs a week's pay."

Ben sighed dramatically, but Asher could imagine him smiling on the other end of the line. His brother loved Grace deeply, even if it had taken him forever to realize that she was perfect for him.

"Hey, did you ever get in touch with Jacob?" Ben asked.

"I did right before I left," Asher said, "but not since then. Things got busy here. Why, is everything okay?"

"So far. He called Dad to let him know that he finally made it to his dream destination of rural Libya. He might be out of touch for the next while."

Asher made a face. "Gotta love our little bro. Some dream of a peaceful resort, others dream of a sand-filled tent and no running water."

"He's helping so many people," Ben said solemnly. "I could do more of that."

Asher sighed. He had a point.

"Yeah, me too," he agreed.

Silence fell between them for a moment. All of the brothers made fun of one another constantly, including Jacob, but the truth was, he was an easy man to admire.

The rough past he'd lived as a teenager and young adult made even Asher look like an absolute angel. But eventually, Jesus had fully taken hold of Jacob's heart, and he'd chosen a radical life of protecting their brothers and sisters in Christ in dangerous areas overseas, even though his mission often put his own safety in danger.

He should have made the time to call his brother sooner, he knew, but he had kept putting it off. Jacob had a way of bringing out the deeper things in people, and he knew he wasn't immune to his probing questions.

If anyone was going to get him to talk about what had really happened in Afghanistan, it was Jacob.

And some part of him wished he had taken the opportunity by now.

"Well, let me know if you learn anything else about Bajwa or Senera," Asher said at last. "Thanks, Ben."

"No problem."

The brothers said their goodbyes, and Asher made his way toward the dining hall, picking up his pace a little when he realized just how high the morning sun was getting. Eggs were basically the only protein to speak of, and if he didn't hurry, they'd all be eaten.

By the time he grabbed his plate, however, he'd forgotten all about his breakfast preferences and began piling it high with whatever food item happened to be closest. Karlin was standing off near the edge of the buffet table by herself, sipping a mug of tea. Everyone else was sitting at the long table, absorbed in the buzz of breakfast conversation.

Asher's heart swelled as he strode over to her, trying his best to look totally casual and totally not-suspicious. All he could think about was the morning they'd shared at the canyon, and how much she'd finally been willing to let him in. Even if the morning had been soured somewhat by the news about her brother's relapse.

Still, he'd only gotten to see her for approximately five seconds yesterday, and the unresolved tension between them was driving him crazy.

"Good morning," he announced, resting his tray on the edge of the table beside her.

"Shh," she said in response, narrowing her eyes. "We'll talk today. I have a plan for our next meeting."

"You know, I really was just saying good morning," he said, picking up a strawberry and popping it into his mouth. "I don't think that's suspicious."

"It's not," she said under her breath, "but the way you beeline toward me the second you enter the room totally is."

He considered arguing with her for a moment, but decided that straight-up honesty would be way more fun.

He waited a second for everyone else in the room to be focused on their breakfast before leaning over and whispering in her ear. "In my defense, I'm kind of struggling to keep my distance, now that I know what it's like to hold you in my arms."

She pulled away quickly, tea wobbling back and forth in her mug, threatening to spill over the edge. Her cheeks were visibly pink, which only made Asher smile.

"You seriously need to shut up," she hissed at him.

"You're pretty. Like, really pretty today, more than usual. Probably that much-deserved beauty sleep."

"Seriously? Just. Shut. Up!"

"Now who's being suspicious?" he asked innocently, turning his back on her and picking up his tray.

He headed off toward the others, trying to wipe the goofy grin off of his face. Man, driving her crazy was way too much fun.

"Hey, Axel," Cora said as he sat down beside Paul. The others greeted him and he tried to make small talk, but he found himself distracted by Bajwa, who was speaking in hushed tones to Karlin and Ned a little further down the table.

Ben's discovery of the man's real background had officially put Bajwa even more firmly on his radar.

It seemed obvious to Asher that he was no mere victim, caught up in Senera's demands.

He had every reason to want to push DX8 through to market, no matter the cost.

"Anyone feeling nervous?" Lily said, pulling Asher from his musings. "I'm actually feeling pretty optimistic about tonight."

"Me too," Cora agreed. "My first trip wasn't great–I felt pretty rough after Destiny freaked out, and I couldn't get back on track. But I think it's going to be a lot easier without that chaos in the background. Poor Destiny. However scary it was for us, it was fifty times worse for her."

Asher wanted to tell them they were crazy for taking DX8 again at all after what happened, but he refrained. "You guys are right. Psychedelics rely so much on what our brains are already doing. We need some peaceful vibes tonight. More rain sounds, less pounding drums. Maybe Bajwa can rig up some incense or something."

"Totally," Cora said, her brown waves bouncing against her shoulders as she nodded her head. "And maybe some better blankets. I was freezing my butt off in that hut."

Paul grunted. "I guess I'm the only nervous one. But I talked to Ms. McKenna, and she assured me that Destiny's reaction was rare and that she's already out of the hospital. I figure I'm already here. Gotta ride it out til it's over."

Asher nodded mutely, stealing yet another glance over at the retreat staff section of the table as he sent up a silent prayer for guidance and for strength.

Paul was right. They did have to ride this thing out

until it was over, which would happen only when Asher and Karlin had the evidence they needed to bring Senera to justice, ensuring no one else could be hurt by DX8 ever again.

And until then, they would continue to walk the careful line between truth and deception.

Human lives–and perhaps even human souls–depended on it.

KARLIN

Karlin stirred her teaspoon around and around in her mug, trying and failing to pay attention to whatever Bajwa was talking about.

Instead, she kept glancing over at her patients sitting further up the table. They were all deep in conversation and wearing serious faces. Even Axel looked uncharacteristically solemn, but she would talk to him later.

For now, it was Paul who worried her most.

He'd managed to catch her alone for a moment when she'd arrived at the dining hall, confessing his worry over taking DX8 tonight. Not for the first time, she wondered why he was so desperate to take this drug, but she felt foolish having to ask him directly.

All she'd wanted to do was to tell him to leave, right now, and never come back, but of course, she couldn't do that.

In a strange way, they were all trapped here, all waiting for the ties that bound them to break.

We're in Your hands, God. Please, let us all go home safe when this is over.

Karlin shoved her last forkful of egg white omelette into her mouth. The thought–the prayer–had arisen unbidden, and she wasn't ready to think about what that meant.

Just then, Bajwa set his napkin on his plate and moved to get to his feet. She reached out and touched his shoulder, intercepting him before he could get everyone else's attention.

It was time to put her plan for today into motion. It was risky, but she had a good opportunity and couldn't afford to waste it.

"Excuse me, Dr. Bajwa?" she asked in a whisper. She shouldn't have bothered. Ned was even more tuned out than she was. "If you can spare me, I'd really rather not join our planned Palo Duro Canyon hike today. I'm feeling a bit under the weather, probably due to stress and exhaustion, and Axel mentioned the same thing to me this morning. He didn't ask, but I think it would probably be wise to excuse him as well."

She held her breath, watching as the gears in his mind began to turn. If he suspected that anything strange was going on between them, now would probably be the time that his face would reveal it.

Instead, he merely looked annoyed.

"You're still tired? Surely you got way less sleep than this in grad school?" he asked, chuckling a little, though it didn't sound like he was kidding.

She decided to roll with it.

"I mean, Axel looks like he's used to rocking out with his band in his mom's garage all night," she joked. "Looks can be deceiving. What happened with Destiny was a lot. I'm also wondering if maybe we both picked up some bug at the hospital. Wouldn't surprise me."

Bajwa considered this.

"I know Axel wants to really be operating at one

hundred percent for his first DX8 journey tonight," she added. "Especially since we will have to give him a higher dose than last time."

"True," Bajwa conceded. "We've never had a patient totally fail to react to a normal dose before."

"Hey, at least it's interesting research data, right?" she said, offering a smile that Bajwa did not return. The man didn't look suspicious, but for whatever reason, he did seem a little anxious. He kept glancing around the room and shifting in his seat while she spoke.

"Fine, you both will stay here today," he said at last. "In that case, I'd really appreciate it if you can help Ned with the food inventory before you get some rest."

"Will do," she said, trying to hold back her grin. Finally, something was actually going right with this investigation.

Bajwa stood up at last, and she half-listened as he told the others about the hike that they would be taking for most of the day.

As soon as the group started to head for the door, she beelined straight for Axel.

"Thanks, Ms. McKenna," he said loudly, presumably for the benefit of anyone listening. "I haven't felt great. I just want to crash until tonight."

"Go to your cabin and stay put," she said under her breath. "I'll come get you soon."

"Will do, ma'am." He made a salute motion with his hand and headed outside with the others.

So far, so good.

"Ready to start on inventory, or do you need a minute?" Ned asked from somewhere behind her shoulder, almost making her jump.

She turned quickly. "Oh, no, I can start whenever

181

you're good to go," she said, plastering on a smile. Ned didn't exactly look thrilled to have her help, but oh well. She was glad for the distraction. This afternoon would present the best chance she and Axel would have to search the main Senera Pharmaceuticals compound, as most of the staff went home early on Fridays. With any luck, Ned would do the same.

And if they were careful, neither Bajwa nor anyone else would suspect a thing.

CHAPTER
TWENTY-SIX

THE WOMAN

BEFORE

The woman was cold, and no amount of warm blankets seemed to help.

She curled up against the edge of the hut, shivering. It had been nearly an hour since she'd swallowed the last of the drug.

She could no longer hold back her tears.

Mother was going to be so disappointed.

The woman knew that it was not her fault, and she did not think Mother would blame her, but that was little consolation.

After everything that Mother had done for their chosen one, she had betrayed them.

Like a selfish, foolish, thoughtless child, she had thrown away the greatest of gifts.

The gift of blood.

Amira had taken her own life.

And with it, she had swallowed up the hope of a whole community.

The woman continued to weep, rocking back and forth, alone. No other human could comfort her now, though she knew she would have to go to those who followed her, to dry their tears, to help them believe.

But for the woman, the empire of light had never felt quite so far away.

Neither had Mother.

The woman had grown used to her presence, the warm slithering feeling in her chest, even when she had not drunk the liquid.

Now, Mother was gone, and she felt impossibly hollow inside.

She swallowed a sob, reaching up with the edge of her blanket to wipe away the tears that dotted her cheek.

She had to be strong.

Because whether Mother came or not, whether she comforted her or not, it would change nothing.

The woman would keep looking until they found the one.

The true chosen one, the one who would bring them home.

She would search the very ends of the earth if she had to.

CHAPTER
TWENTY-SEVEN

ASHER

The knock at Asher's cabin door was the most beautiful sound he'd ever heard.

He'd been bored when he had to watch Tourmaline teach everyone yoga. He'd been bored when he had to watch everyone sitting around high on DX8.

But this morning might have been even worse.

He'd finished the final pages of Hunt for the Skinwalker, and there were no schizophrenic DX8 breakdowns to distract him in his cabin. He'd settled for calling his brothers and his father in turn, though somehow, all of them were apparently too busy to shoot the breeze for very long in the middle of a weekday morning.

He was also dying to see Karlin.

Especially after the way he'd made her blush so hard this morning.

Grinning at the memory, he jumped off his bed and opened the door, only to find Ned standing where Karlin should have been.

"Oh, hi," Asher stammered. "Uh, wanna come in?"

Ned shook his head, looking as awkward as Asher's stammering words sounded. "I'm actually heading home for the day, but I found this cross necklace in the dining hall. I thought maybe it was yours."

Asher instinctively raised a hand to his chest. Sure enough, the cross necklace he usually wore was gone.

He reached out and retrieved it from Ned's outstretched hand, trying to meet the man's eyes. "Uh yeah. It's mine. Thank you. I appreciate you bringing it."

"Of course, Mr. Bishop," Ned said, offering something that wasn't quite a smile. "I'll be taking off now. Good luck tonight."

With that, the man turned and was gone, and Asher found himself thoroughly creeped out. The man's vibes were seriously weird. Was Ned checking up on him? Then again, if he was, it wasn't like he would have been able to yank Asher's cross off his neck to use it as an excuse.

In any case, the morning of torture-boredom suddenly felt a little more worth it.

Had Karlin not ordered him to stay in here, he probably would have been snooping around, and Ned probably would have caught him doing it.

To his relief, after only about another fifteen minutes staring at a tiny imperfection in the ceiling paint, there was another knock.

This time, Karlin was the one standing on his front step, the sun at her back making her look like a redheaded angel, complete with a halo.

"Ready?" she asked by way of greeting.

"To pick up where we left off? Way back in the Jeep?" he joked.

She was blushing again, and it was all he could do not

to pull her into his cabin and start kissing her right then and there, which would be an insanely stupid idea.

Instead, he forced himself to step out into the warm afternoon, pulling the cabin door shut behind him.

He decided not to tell Karlin that he now had his handgun secured in a concealed ankle holster, just in case. He doubted they would need it, and there was no need to freak her out.

"How is John, by the way?" he asked.

She narrowed her eyes at him before answering. "Nothing to report. He left a message on my voicemail that he was fine and that he'd try to call me later today or tomorrow. Anyway, we need to get moving if we want enough time to search the Senera offices."

A smile had snuck its way onto her face, and he could barely contain his own excitement. "Sick! Good work, Karlin," he said, pumping his fist at the sky. "Finally some good, old-fashioned, reading-piles-of-irrelevant-documents investigating!"

"Oh, there's more," she teased, raising her hand to reveal a small ring with several silver keys and a plastic ID card attached to it. "Bajwa actually left everything aside from his Jeep keys behind. Apparently, he didn't want to risk losing them in the canyon."

Asher widened his mouth in mock horror. "You *stole* his keys? I can't believe my eyes!"

"Technically, I'm borrowing them. For very legitimate purposes," she argued. "Or maybe you're just a really bad influence."

He reached out his hand and brushed a few strands of hair out of her face, catching her gaze with his own.

"Definitely. I'm definitely a bad influence."

KARLIN

Karlin watched the passing desert out of the pickup truck's window, glad that Axel had volunteered to drive the maintenance vehicle they'd borrowed. Her hands were shaking way too much.

It wasn't very far between the retreat site and the main Senera compound, but the road twisted back and forth, went up and down steep, sandy hills, and was covered with an unreasonable amount of potholes.

The view was pretty, though she definitely preferred the softer light of sunset.

Or sunrise.

Not that she was going to start thinking about sunrises right now.

"So, what did I miss?" Axel said after a while, glancing over at her as he expertly navigated around a trapped tumbleweed.

"Well, I learned some stuff about Cora," she offered. "When I was talking to her and Lily this morning, she kept going on about some old Indian tribe that apparently went missing. She seems to think they might have been abducted by aliens or sent through another dimension."

Axel laughed. "I mean, that's totally weird, but I don't think it means she's secretly a spy on Senera's payroll."

She rolled her eyes. "Obviously not. But I do think it means she was never really here for mental health purposes. She's a conspiracy nut looking for an intense high. It's probably not important, but that's about all of the new information I've dug up."

"No, this is good," Axel said. "We now have at least two patients that never should have made it into Senera's patient pool, and that's information we can use against them. Investigative work rarely involves a smoking gun. Usually, it's just the slow process of building a case."

"You know, you're kind of a nerd. At least when you talk about your work."

Axel looked genuinely horrified. "No! No. Gabe is the nerd. *You're* the nerd. I'm the one who can parkour between two rooftops, guns blazing, and take down the bad guy without even making a big deal about it."

"There's no way."

"Well, maybe not literally, but you know what I mean."

She laughed. Despite his utterly ridiculous example, she did know what he meant.

"Okay, Jason Bourne," she teased. "Point taken."

"Oh!" he exclaimed suddenly, smacking his palms against the steering wheel. "I did learn something useful from the biggest nerd in my entire family."

Her playful smile quickly turned into a frown as he shared the truth about Bajwa's background.

He'd hidden his secrets well, and she couldn't help but feel a sting of betrayal.

He wasn't a good boss, and he wasn't an ethical researcher. He was obnoxious half the time, and he spent the other half of the time dragging her into his question-able decisions.

But she'd also seen the way he'd inspired her–and many other people they worked with–in the past. He'd encouraged her to learn and to discover. He had seemed genuinely fascinated by psychedelic research, and it hurt to know how much of his passion was probably based in nothing more honorable than his own pride.

"He's such a scumbag," she spat, allowing her anger to block out her hurt. "We need to take him down."

"Hold up, sheriff," Axel said, lifting both hands from

the steering wheel in surrender just as they shuddered over a pothole. "Just because he's a liar and probably a professional scammer doesn't mean we need to lose our focus," Axel said. "Senera itself has the most to gain here, and we need to tie in as many people as possible."

"Building the case, right?"

"Kinda," Axel said, a playful grin teasing his lips. "I was thinking more like that scene in The Dark Knight where Two-Face and Commissioner Gordon talk about tying all the Gotham crime lords to a single crime."

"What are you even talking about?"

"Hello? Batman? One of the most popular and cool movies of all time?"

Karlin shook her head. "I told you. Nerd. *Total* nerd."

Axel looked like he was about to argue, but they had just crested a hill and could now see the Senera compound stretching out below.

"Okay, let's do this," she said, her voice clipped.

No more teasing. It was time to focus.

A few minutes later, they'd parked in one of the staff spaces and climbed out of the truck. There were a few other vehicles peppering the lot, but this was as quiet as it was ever going to get.

"See that door?"

Axel followed her gaze and nodded.

"If you stay along this wall here, you'll be out of view of the cameras. Go to the door and wait for me. I'm going to go in the normal way and come let you in."

She moved to walk to the front entrance, but he grabbed her arm, easily stopping her where she stood. She was about to shake herself free of his grip, but the look in his eyes quieted her in an instant.

He took one step closer, then two, and all of a sudden he was very, very close.

She could smell the light mint scent of his breath, and now she realized that his cologne carried a faint note of leather.

Still holding on to her, as though she might bolt, he reached up with his free hand and stroked her cheek.

"I really did love watching the sunrise with you," he said, his voice barely above a whisper. It could have been a silly thing to say, but there was no hint of a joke in it. He was so painfully sincere, so honest about wanting to be with her. Why was it so difficult for her to believe in the obvious evidence, right in front of her eyes?

She wanted to say something in return, but no words would form. She was too busy thinking of what it would be like to kiss him, to feel his lips pressing into hers. She was surprised she could still think at all with so little distance between them.

Without any further comment, he let her go and pointed at the door. "I'll see you in there."

"Uh, okay," she stammered. He gave her another delicious smile before turning away and striding over to the wall, just as she'd directed.

She stood there for several seconds too long before remembering that they seriously did need to hurry it up. There was no way to know for sure exactly how long Bajwa and the others would take to return, and she didn't want to take any chances.

She headed for the main entrance, but just as she was about to unlock the door, she was sure that she noticed movement out of the corner of her eye.

She whirled around, glancing behind her and along the

edge of the parking lot, but found nothing aside from well-manicured flowers and a few bushes.

She turned the key, drawing a few breaths to settle her nerves. It was probably a mouse, or a bird, or even just a gust of wind. Axel's flirting had clearly put her on edge, but there was no more time for distractions. She had to focus on getting this done.

Hope rose in her chest as she walked quickly down the halls of Senera, listening to nothing but the hum of idle office equipment.

This could all be over soon if they found the evidence they needed.

This could all be over today.

CHAPTER
TWENTY-EIGHT

THE WOMAN

The woman waited, but this time, she did not wonder after Mother.

They had been together for years now. They were closer than sisters. Closer than blood.

She no longer had to take the drug in order to see the serpent. Mother was with her always, beneath her skin, curled up warmly around her heart.

She sometimes wondered if their souls had actually joined and had become one perfect, inseparable thing.

She did not know what she believed about souls, though. Not anymore. Certainly, they were not what she'd been taught they were.

They could be changed. They could be shifted.

And, she hoped, they could be brought to a new world. A better world, where they could finally leave their sufferings and difficulties behind.

She waited.

She was not impatient, but she was eager. Joy seemed

to tingle within her fingertips and toes, like she could scarcely hold herself to the earth anymore.

After all this time, after all these years, she was sure she'd found the one.

"Hello, my darling," Mother said without words, sending fresh tingles down the woman's spine. "You have news."

The woman could scarcely form the words. She was far too happy.

"Yes, Mother. I think...I think we have found her at last. The one who is open to the truth. The one who will get us home."

Mother said nothing for several long moments, but the air surrounding the woman was not silent, either. It seemed to hum and shiver, as though the fabric of the universe itself was pondering, considering.

At last, she spoke, and all else went quiet.

"I do have reservations, my dear one," Mother said gently. "It has been a long time, but we have made mistakes before. Once she sees our rituals, she may become afraid. She may leave us."

The woman drew a slow breath in, steeling her will. She did not like to contradict Mother, not ever, but she wasn't as scared as she used to be. Mother needed her, that much was clear. However great her power was, the beautiful serpent was not infinite. The woman, too, had choices to make for the good of their community.

"I do not think that will happen, Mother," she said softly. "This one is not like Amira was. She is a true believer, and more than that, she is brave. She will do whatever is necessary to find the truth."

"You speak well," Mother said.

The three words were enough to make the woman's heart soar.

But there was still one thing she did not dare to tell the serpent, one fear of her own that she still carried.

The chosen one may have been found, but that didn't mean the end would come easily.

Karlin McKenna was too close, too watchful, always trying to figure everything out.

They had to go to the empire of light soon, or she would figure out how to stop them.

And the woman would not let that happen. Not after everything they'd done.

No one would kill their hope.

Not this time.

CHAPTER
TWENTY-NINE

ASHER

"Here, you do it," Karlin ordered. Her fingers shook as she tossed Bajwa's office keys to Asher.

"Yes, ma'am," he said mildly, unlocking the door and ushering her inside the inner office confidently, like they belonged there.

Her nervous energy was kind of adorable, but unfortunately, he didn't have the time to tease her about it. They'd searched the Senera compound for two hours already and had found nothing but some somewhat troubling financial reports and a few lab documents with potentially manipulated data.

He'd told Karlin that this was all about building a case, and that was true. But the reality was that it would be a whole lot easier if they found something super solid instead of a bunch of standard-fare misdeeds.

Not that the afternoon had been a total loss so far.

He'd gotten to see the big lab where Karlin spent most of her days, and the brief tour had given him even more appreciation for her intellect than he already had.

Had they been back in high school right now, there'd be zero chance a girl like her would have ever given him the time of day. The fact that she seemed to be catching feelings for him despite their differences made him all warm and giddy inside.

Clearly Reilly, Cameron, and Ben had been on to something. Meeting a nice girl was a whole lot easier if you could impress her with your private security expertise. He should have really gone with that angle long before now.

"Let's dig," Karlin announced, reaching over to yank open one of Bajwa's desk drawers. "If there is such a thing as a smoking gun in this case, I think it'll be here."

Asher nodded and started riffling through a stack of papers, trying his best to shift the pile back into the correct order as he went. "I think you might be right. But like I said, Bajwa's past doesn't necessarily mean he's our big bad. We need to stay open to other possibilities."

"You mean all the ones we haven't found anywhere in this building so far?"

He tightened his jaw. "Yep. Keep looking."

They lapsed into a comfortable silence as they continued to search through Bajwa's belongings and paperwork. They couldn't get into his computer, but fortunately, the man seemed stuck in the eighties. Stacks of printed reports, old emails, and tidy folders full of various invoices filled several filing cabinets and covered every surface.

"Does your office look like this?" Asher asked as he skimmed yet another insanely boring document.

Karlin snorted. "I'm more of a minimalist. I truly don't understand how he can work in here."

"You'd die if you saw my brother Cam's office, trust me," he joked. "At least Bajwa seems to have something resembling a system. Also, note the lack of scattered garbage."

Karlin made a face. "I'd like his system better if I had any idea what it consisted–"

She raised a sheet of paper to her face, her eyes roving over the words.

"What?"

He dropped his own stack and sauntered up to read over her shoulder.

"No way," he said, realizing what she held. "May I?"

She handed over the document, her blue eyes lighting up as she smiled. "Emails from what seems to be a very close friend of Bajwa, with a very official FDA, government-issued email address."

"Hinting at very illegal strings being pulled with his fellow regulators," Asher finished. "Okay. Maybe not a smoking gun–I can imagine how Senera lawyers are gonna spin this–but it's good. Really good."

"Find more. I'll fire up the copier," Karlin ordered, striding through the door and back to the anteroom where Bajwa's secretary, Mayim, usually sat. Her office was immaculate down to the last detail, but hopefully, she wouldn't be paying too much attention to the copier's paper supply or its print history.

A half-hour passed as they worked. Asher dug through the papers, gathering everything with the same FDA email address and a few others that were potentially suspicious. They'd be sending all of it back to FBS, and he was confident his brothers and the rest of their team would be able to cut through the noise.

Karlin copied each document, stuffed the copy into a folio, and carefully returned the originals to Bajwa's office, where Asher tried to put them back more or less where he'd found them.

"Okay, I think those are the last ones," Asher called through the door to Karlin. She said nothing, but he could hear the whine of the copier as she worked.

Her nerves had apparently melted away completely as she focused on what she had to do. He could imagine her over in her laboratory, getting equally lost in some experiment, hours passing as she tipped chemicals into beakers and measured data in tiny lines of neat handwriting.

He loved her passion for what she did, and he hated that Senera's actions threatened to take it all away from her. And he would do anything he could to make sure they failed.

"Be there in a sec," Karlin called out at last.

He tapped his fingers against the smooth metal of the nearest filing cabinet. They had only checked the top three drawers. May as well check the bottom one while he waited.

He pulled it open and scanned the tabs. Fortunately, these were more traditionally organized, and the labels were typed rather than handwritten. They were names, male and female. Probably nothing, maybe just–

Halfway through the drawer, there was a name he knew.

"Woah. Woah. No way."

He yanked the file free just as Karlin strode back into the room and headed over to him, standing mere inches away as she tried to see what he was holding. Not even the scent of her shampoo could distract him at the moment, though, not after what he'd found.

"Look at this," he said excitedly, waving the file in the air. "I never got all of the details, but I know this name. I know this case."

"If you'd stop waving it around like a lunatic, I could see—"

Karlin's words fell away as she read the name on the tab.

She clasped a hand to her mouth.

"Hey. Hey, Karlin, are you okay?" Asher asked, but it was like she didn't even hear him.

She yanked the file from his hand and dropped it onto the desk, as though the papers might scald them if they touched it any longer.

Her face had gone white, and her eyes were filling quickly with tears.

KARLIN

Karlin stared at the file in horror.

The name on the label made it impossible to look away.

"Amira Gorsky," she said at last, swallowing the lump in her throat as she willed herself not to cry again. She'd spilled far too many tears in front of Axel already. And this time, she had no right to cry.

She wasn't the victim.

She was one of the perpetrators, and villains didn't get to cry.

Axel's brow wrinkled in confusion, but he didn't reach

for the file. He was clearly waiting for her to explain what about it had shaken her so much.

She'd been so stupid.

How could she have thought that he wouldn't find out she was on that trial? That she was partly responsible for an innocent woman's death? She'd signed off on it. Sure, she'd been scared, and there were a whole bunch of reasons for that, right down to the bad childhood sob story. But she'd still put her name to paper, and someone who would otherwise be alive was now dead.

"Are you going to report me? To the police?" she asked, unsure of why she'd asked, or how she expected Axel to understand. Her logical mind didn't seem to be working in order.

Panic was pressing into her from all directions, drowning her, choking her.

This had all been a huge mistake. She'd asked Forge Brothers Security for help, but if Axel did what he was legally supposed to do, she'd succeeded in nothing more than signing her own arrest warrant.

She could go to jail.

Senera wouldn't protect her, they'd made that beyond clear.

No, it was worse than that.

They only had this file in the first place as a form of insurance, she was certain of it.

She'd bet her life that it contained evidence against her, probably carefully curated to shield them as much as possible.

The more she thought about it, the more it made sense.

The whole thing had been designed from the start to place her as the scapegoat if it ever became necessary.

For all she knew, they were doing the same thing right now.

Maybe her name was somewhere on the papers that permitted Destiny and Cora to join the current cohort. Maybe the secrecy and lies ran even deeper than she'd thought.

She could go to jail.

She *should* go to jail.

That part, she could handle. It was the rest of it that she couldn't bear. John would suffer. Her patients would continue to be put at risk.

And Axel would hate her.

That might have been the worst possibility of all.

"What? Report you?" he asked, looking more confused than before. "You need to calm down and explain to me what on earth you're even talking about."

He reached out to her and pulled her into his chest.

She wanted to pull away. She didn't deserve to feel his warmth, not after everything she'd done. He had to be crazy. She'd all but told him that she'd committed a terrible crime, and his first reaction had been to cradle her in his arms.

It was enough to set the tears flowing all over again, as desperately as she wanted to stop them.

"Sweetheart, please. You're scaring me."

She could feel his breath whispering against her ear as he spoke, his words gentle and full of so much trust, trust she was about to destroy. But she had to do it. Even if it made him hate her.

She had carried too many secrets for too long. The burden had become unbearable.

"Amira Gorsky's death was my fault," she said at last, pressing her eyes shut, though she could see nothing but the deep green of his shirt. "I'm the reason she's dead. I took her husband's wife away. I took her daughter's mother away."

Her body was wracked with fresh sobs.

"Shh, breathe," Axel said, still stroking at her hair, still holding her, as though her confession hadn't just irreparably destroyed every reason he cared about her.

"I was fresh out of school, and when I got a junior researcher job with Senera, I thought I'd hit the jackpot. Brilliant scientists to mentor me, top of the line equipment, cutting-edge research–it was intoxicating."

Axel didn't say anything or ask for clarification. She paused to take a breath, wishing there were a way she could share the story without sounding like she was making excuses for the inexcusable. Then again, maybe that was exactly what she was doing.

"I noticed a few things that were ethically questionable about the way the company operated, but I'd seen enough even in grad school that I wasn't naive. I knew that boundaries were pushed all the time, even in something as serious as medical research. So I just kept going.

"When I worked my way onto a team for an actual DX8 trial–it wasn't called DX8 then–I was ecstatic. This was the real thing. This was everything I wanted to do. Keep in mind, Bajwa didn't work here back then, so the day to day environment was a lot less stressful. If I'm being honest, it was usually a lot of fun.

"They had me sign off directly on the patients that we accepted into the trial, including Amira. I had her medical history. I sat in on her interviews. I knew she had a history of major depression. I signed off on her anyway.

"During the trial, she had a severe panic attack, pretty similar to what you saw happen to Destiny. But we didn't take her to the hospital. We managed to calm her down, and since it was the last dose of the trial, we didn't bother formally releasing her, either. I honestly thought she seemed fine."

She drew a deep breath, struggling to keep her voice even.

If there was a God, she hoped He could forgive her for what she was about to say. Even if Axel never would.

"Until the minute the last patient flew home, I felt like I was going to pass out from nerves, but nothing else happened. I thought I was in the clear. I thought that we'd gotten away with skirting the ethical boundaries. But we didn't."

Her voice broke.

"Not long after the trial, Amira committed suicide," she finished in a whisper.

Axel pulled back just enough to look down at her face. The kindness in his eyes was too much to bear. She allowed herself to sob freely, once again pressing her face into his chest until his shirt was damp.

She didn't want to look at him, didn't want to breathe, didn't want to do anything. Maybe he could feel empathy toward her for the moment, but when he had the time to really think about what she was saying, he'd want nothing to do with her.

She'd be lucky if he didn't call the police, let alone stick around to help her with this investigation.

"It's terrible what happened," he said, lifting a hand and stroking her hair. "But I know you would never hurt anyone on purpose. You were under a ton of pressure."

"Why should that matter? I still made choices. I should have said no the very first time that I was asked to fudge a test result or break labor laws or any of the other zillion things they told me to do. I was pathetic. I cared more about keeping a job that I liked than about Amira Gorsky's life. I should have been stronger."

To her surprise, her voice had come out angry, but the only person she was mad at was herself. She'd tried to suppress the self-loathing, tried to bury it, but it always came back.

Always.

And when she forgot about what she'd done for even a day, the universe always reminded her. Maybe everything she'd been through with John was some kind of Divine punishment.

"Your desire to take accountability is admirable," Axel said. "It's easy to say that we should have been stronger in doing what's right. But you can't expect a younger you to know what she didn't know, or have strength that she didn't have. Other people made choices, too. People with a lot more power. Don't get so caught up in punishing yourself that you forget that."

She didn't want to blame anyone else.

She didn't want to open the door to making excuses for herself.

But on the other hand, she had to admit that he had a point.

There was no way that she could change the past. Some logical part of her brain could still realize that hating herself certainly wouldn't bring Amira Gorsky back from the dead.

There was only one way she could move now, and that was forward.

"Look at you today," he added. "You're risking everything to bring Senera to justice. You're in your crazy boss's office, with some weird guy from across the state that you managed to hire without spending a dime. You're smart, resourceful, and determined. You see an injustice, and nothing will stop you from making it right. I see so much strength in you. I hope you know that."

She didn't say anything for a long time.

Despite her cynicism, despite her fear, she could feel the weight that was crushing her getting a little bit lighter with every word that Axel said.

Because maybe, somehow, by some miracle, she was wrong about him.

Maybe he really did practice the forgiveness that she'd heard so many Christians in her life preach about. Maybe he could still wake up tomorrow and look at her the same way he had since they'd met.

She had to know. She had to hear him say it.

"Axel?"

"Mmm-hmm?" he mumbled, pressing his face into her hair and kissing the top of her head.

She took a deep breath, gathering all of her courage.

"Can you forgive me for what I did?"

"I already have," he said, without missing a beat.

"Thank you—"

"But it's not my forgiveness that you're looking for," he added. "In the Psalms, it says that God casts our sins away as far as the east is from the west. He's the only one who can free you from the darkness you've been carrying. He's waiting for you. He loves you, and He wants to forgive you abundantly."

"I'll have to think about that."

"I would hope so," he joked, giving her another kiss on the head and pulling her closer.

She let herself lay back against his chest.

Despite the new uncertainties and hopes at war within

her, she couldn't help but to soak in just a little of this present joy.

This, right here, with his arms around her–this felt like something close to heaven on earth.

But the moment didn't last.

They both leapt to their feet as they heard the sound of keys turning in the external office door.

CHAPTER
THIRTY

ASHER

The Amira Gorsky file still lay open on the desk.

Karlin was staring at it, stuck in place as the sound of jingling keys continued.

Asher swore. They should have photocopied it right away, but now it was too late. He scooped up the documents and opened the filing cabinet, shoving it into what he prayed was the proper place he'd found it in.

"Come on," he said, gesturing toward the en suite bathroom. "Even if that's the cleaning lady, we can't be caught here."

All at once, Karlin sprung into action, but to his surprise, she didn't follow him. First, she yanked open the filing cabinet drawer and took the file.

"I'll explain later," she said, rushing over to the bathroom. "Just trust me."

He didn't have a choice. He could hear footsteps coming from somewhere near Bajwa's secretary's desk.

Unlike in the main office, there was one window near

the bathroom ceiling that actually opened. He knelt down near the wall, placing his hands into a cradle position. "You first. Hurry."

Karlin shut the bathroom door quietly behind her and placed a foot into his hands. "Don't you dare drop me," she ordered. "I hate heights."

"We're on the first floor!"

"Still!"

He chuckled as she put her weight against his hands. It was easy to forget that not everyone was like him and his brothers. Jumping from this kind of window was child's play in his world.

She wobbled as he boosted her, but offered no further complaint. With some effort, she managed to shove the window open, just in time for him to hear someone entering Bajwa's inner office behind them.

Karlin looked out the window, and then back down at him, her eyes wide. He knew from experience that it looked a lot higher than it was, but it didn't matter. There was no option B.

He held her gaze and smiled up at her.

"Have faith."

Finally, she jumped. And taking hold of the windowsill, he pulled himself up and through, just seconds behind her.

KARLIN

"If someone goes into that bathroom, they might notice the open window and take a look outside, but I didn't see any cameras except for the ones in the parking lot," Axel explained as he pulled Karlin around the corner of the building. "I think we might have actually pulled this off."

His eyes were actually shining.

He looked like he was having the time of his life.

Karlin, meanwhile, felt like she was going to throw up. Or, at the very least, find the nearest ravine and toss the file folder she was holding into it.

She nodded mutely, pulling her arms around herself as a rush of wind sent a chill running through her. The sun was lower in the sky now, and it would only get colder with each passing minute.

"You okay?" Axel asked, pausing and resting his back against the brick wall.

"I'm fine," she said, drawing in a heaving breath, only just then realizing how exhausted she was. "You?"

"Oh, I'm great," Axel beamed. "I was just thinking about how, for once, I'm so thankful to be the scrawny one of the family."

"You know, I was kidding when I said you looked like a string bean," she admitted.

"I know, I know—by the standards of the general population, I'm totally buff," he said, his voice serious. "But my twin brother is the size of this wall. And the rest of them are somewhere in the middle of the string bean and wall continuum."

It felt good to laugh, even a little. "As much as I'd love to keep discussing this, we do need to get out of here."

"Lead the way," Axel announced, pushing himself off the wall and following her toward the dusty pickup. "But I'm really curious why you risked taking that file. I was thinking we have enough now to string together a warrant, especially if you're willing to talk about the pressures you faced when you started the job."

Karlin didn't answer for several seconds as they shuffled across the parking lot. One of her colleagues, a younger scientist she didn't know by name who had just started working in the lab a few weeks ago, crossed their path and smiled. "Hey, Ms. McKenna," he said, raising a hand in a salute. "I've got overnight lab duty tonight. Paying my dues."

"You got this, newbie!" she offered, unsure what else to say. She sounded cringe, but whatever. At least the man would have no idea that Axel was out of place here.

Finally, they reached the vehicle. This time, Karlin took the wheel, and as they began the drive back to the retreat site, they both kept a look out for Bajwa and the others returning from their hike. If they saw anybody, Axel would have to drop to the floor, and that was about as far as their contingency plans went.

"So, the file?" Axel prompted as soon as they'd reached a relatively less treacherous part of the road.

"Senera lied to the courts after Amira died," she said. "They claimed that a lightning strike took out their servers and caused a huge data crash, which happened to erase much of their trial data."

Axel snorted. "The courts bought that?"

Karlin nodded. "I always suspected they were lying, though. I was sure they had some evidence against me somewhere. An insurance policy, in case they ever ended up in a tight situation. I'd also suspected that Bajwa knew about it, based on some little comments he's made in the past. I've just been proven right."

"It's just nasty enough for me to believe that Senera would do it," Axel said, his jaw tightening. "Take a new hire, fresh out of college, put her on the hook for a risky trial...The good news is that I think a decent judge would be able to see through it. Remember, they wouldn't have wanted to fake the server crash if they thought it would be an easy slam dunk to pin it all on you."

Karlin shook her head. "I mean, sure, the best thing for them was just to keep me around and keep me quiet. But once we start threatening them legally, it's ultimately my word against theirs. And we don't even know everything that's in that file yet. For all we know, they embellished the details to make me sound even worse. So, yeah, that's why I took it. Whether they have another copy or not, I'm not sitting around waiting for the trap to close. I'm getting ahead of it."

She realized that she was gripping the wheel tight enough to turn her knuckles white.

Axel leaned a little closer, resting a hand on her shoulder, but even his touch wasn't enough to soothe her anxiety. She felt like every nerve in her body was humming, poised for action, though she had no clue what to actually do next.

"Karlin, you realize that you can turn around," he said. "You can just turn around, right now. We don't need to go back."

"No," she said, shaking her head. "Not an option."

"Even just based on what you've told me, we have enough to get the local authorities involved," Axel argued. "Look, we have this police liaison back in San Antonio, Allie? She's great. She'll know someone here, or Gabe will, or we'll find one of our contacts who does. They'll know how to handle the next steps. You're not facing this alone."

Karlin said nothing, considering his proposal as she navigated around several sharp turns. So far, there'd been no sign of any other vehicles, and though it was getting colder, sunset was still a few hours away. She was confident that her plan had worked and that they would beat the others back to the site before anyone realized they had ever left.

"We can't leave tonight," she said firmly. "I mean, you can if you want, but I'm not abandoning my patients. I'm going to observe their DX8 doses and make sure everyone is okay."

"If you think I'm leaving you, you're insane," Axel announced. "But tomorrow, however we make our escape, we need to leave. This is getting too big for the two of us to handle on our own."

Karlin nodded, risking a quick glance in his direction.

"Thank you for standing by me," she said.

"You're stuck with me now," Axel said firmly, giving her shoulder a gentle squeeze that sent a ripple of heat down her spine. "I'm not going anywhere unless you want me to."

She swallowed hard, not trusting herself to respond to the implications that his words held. Part of her was terrified to believe that he meant them. A bigger part was terrified that he didn't.

But she couldn't think about her heart right now.

Tomorrow, things were going to be set into motion that she couldn't undo.

Her life was going to change, for better or for worse.

God, please help me, she prayed silently, trying her best to focus on keeping the truck safely on the road. *Help guide me through whatever comes next.*

CHAPTER
THIRTY-ONE

THE WOMAN

Mother was waiting for her this time.

As soon as the woman awoke, she was there, somehow, in the dark.

She was in her bed now, but it didn't matter where she was, any more than it mattered if she took the drugs or not.

Mother found her whenever and wherever she was needed. The woman was important, precious. It was hard to believe Mother could need anything at all, but somehow, in some miraculous way, Mother needed the woman.

Now, she had been awoken from sleep, long after the moon had risen over the earth.

She tried not to yawn, but she couldn't help it. She had struggled to fall asleep the night before, her mind filled with a mingling of worry and excitement.

"I have disturbed you, dear one," Mother said. There was no apology in her tone of voice.

The woman searched the room, but Mother had not

revealed herself as a serpent tonight. Often, she preferred just to exist at a more primal level, something disembodied, above and greater than anything in all the earth. It always filled the woman with awe, even if she did like to see Mother's dark eyes and glittering scales.

"I spoke to our chosen one today," the woman said, shaking off the last remnants of her exhaustion. Sleep could wait.

Or maybe it wouldn't need to.

Perhaps humans did not need to sleep at all once they arrived in the empire of light.

"What did she say?" Mother prompted. The woman could sense something in her tone, almost an impatience. It was always fascinating to note even the slightest hint of imperfection in the godlike being. Not that the woman would ever dare to point it out.

"I spoke to her about our rituals. I was careful. I wanted to tiptoe around the subject until I knew that she wouldn't balk."

"So wise, dear," Mother said. "Always so wise."

The woman blushed at the compliment, though she didn't know how much Mother saw of her in the dark, or if she could see at all now, lacking the eyes of her serpent form.

"Her response was better than I could have hoped for, Mother," the woman said, struggling to keep her voice calm. "She actually told me about how she had learned of these magics in the past, and the way that every culture knew its power, until the Christians came with their centuries-long campaigns of hate and murder. She is ready to partake. Eager, even."

"It seems you were right," Mother said. "She does not sound like Amira. She will not allow the foolishness of shame to stop her from doing what must be done. Good. Very good."

Without another word, Mother was gone.

The woman was not sure exactly how she knew this, but she did.

She was alone in the dark again, listening to the sound of her own breathing.

She wanted to be happy. Mother was pleased with her, and their chosen one had come.

But she couldn't shake her worry.

She couldn't shake her fear that they would be found out, and that all of their enlightenment would be shrouded in shadows once again.

She swallowed hard, forcing her eyes shut, pushing away the fear.

No. She was strong. She would make it.

And if she couldn't do it for Mother, she would do it for the Professor.

He had started her on this journey, and she had come so far.

She would make him proud.

CHAPTER
THIRTY-TWO

ASHER

Asher unclipped his seatbelt the second that Karlin brought the truck to a stop behind the staff cabins.

He'd felt jittery for the rest of the drive back to the retreat site, like he couldn't sit still. They were so close to the end now. All he had to do was get through one more DX8 session, and they'd be able to go to the authorities. Finally, Senera Pharmaceuticals would face the consequences of their crimes.

"No vehicles," Karlin announced triumphantly as she took her own seatbelt off and climbed out of Bajwa's Jeep. "We made it, but it's probably close. You should get to your cabin. I'm going to run over to the small lab. If we're leaving this place tomorrow, I have a few personal items that I don't want to leave behind. I also have to put Bajwa's keys back."

Asher hesitated, glancing around the quiet desert.

Even though the sun hadn't set yet, the empty retreat

site gave him the creeps. He could hear nothing at all. Even the birds and insects seemed to be holding their breath, like they knew something had shifted. He almost wished for those weird coyotes to howl in the distance. He'd prefer it to the oppressive silence.

"Are you sure you'll be okay on your own?" he asked.

Karlin nodded firmly. "It would be suspicious if we were caught hanging out together right now. I'm telling you, everyone is going to be back any minute now. Safety in numbers, right?"

Asher couldn't find a good reason to argue.

Sure, they'd almost been caught back at Senera, but he was fairly confident that it had only been by a janitor or another employee entering Bajwa's office at random.

No one had come after them in the parking lot, and they hadn't seen a single vehicle behind them, either. They could check the few cameras they had at some point in the future, but he'd deal with that when–or if–the time came.

"Okay," he agreed. "I'll come out as soon as everyone arrives."

He had hoped for some kind of proper goodbye, maybe even a hug, but Karlin was back in pure focus mode. With a quick nod in his direction, she locked the truck, turned on her heel, and headed toward the building that held her on-site laboratory.

He watched for a moment, making sure she'd made it safely inside the door, and then headed for his own cabin. Now that he was truly alone, he felt even more freaked out, though he couldn't exactly explain why. He wasn't really the type of guy to jump at shadows. But there was something about the quietness of the place that–

He rounded the corner of one of the empty cabins,

nearly colliding with Lily and sending his train of thought shuddering to a stop.

"Hey," he said, letting out a puff of breath as he waited for his heart rate to slow back to normal. "You guys are back already? You scared me to death. Man, I must have slept longer than I thought. What time is it?"

Lily smiled up at him. "Oh, no, you're right on time, hon. I ended up staying behind at the last minute. I have a pretty bad left hip, and I felt bad slowing the others down."

Asher muttered something noncommittal, wondering why Lily was so far from her own cabin and so close to his own, and why she hadn't announced her intentions to stay behind sooner when she knew her hip was weak. It was odd, but it was hardly odd enough to call her out on it.

The most likely explanation was that he was being a tad paranoid.

He had to keep his eyes on the ball.

"Now, I thought I'd try and get the sunset," Lily was saying. "There's that nice hilly spot past the dining hall. Thought I could make it up that slope, at least."

The sun would be setting soon, and if he wasn't so creeped out by the silence, he had to admit it would be a pretty evening to watch it.

"I'll walk with you to the parking area," he offered. "I want to wait for everyone else, anyway. I'm excited for tonight. Hopefully I'll get the right dose of DX8 this time."

This was only half a lie. He really would be getting the right dose. It just so happened to be a placebo that he had been supposed to take the first time that would cause some physical symptoms and make his acting job a whole lot easier.

And he was excited. He just happened to be excited

that tonight was the final hoop to jump through before he could get Karlin away from here and help her to take Senera down once and for all.

Lily accepted his escort, and the two of them headed toward the central area of the retreat site. She was chatting happily, and he engaged in the conversation as best he could, though his thoughts were elsewhere.

He considered tomorrow's possibilities, turning the options around over and over in his mind, never quite managing to settle on anything. He was pretty sure about how the investigation related stuff would go. That was routine enough, especially once he dragged the rest of FBS into action.

But Karlin was still a mystery.

He knew she had feelings for him, and he was well beyond denying that he had hopelessly fallen for her. But he also knew she was scared, stubborn, and independent to a fault.

Would she want to stay close to him? Or was she just going to push him away the second that they were no longer forced into close proximity?

"No time for a sunset, apparently," Lily said with a sigh, pointing toward the access road that led into the retreat site. "Looks like everyone's back."

Asher saw two headlights traveling toward them.

Either Senera security was after them after all, or Bajwa and the rest of the trial participants had indeed returned.

He pushed his worries about Karlin aside, steeling himself for whatever came next.

Just one more night. All he had to do was get through one more night.

KARLIN

Karlin glanced over her shoulder as she stood at her desk, gathering up a few of her most well-used notebooks and stuffing them into a tote bag she'd left hanging on the door handle.

She usually loved the silence of the lab, especially the small one here at the retreat site, where Bajwa almost never ventured. It was her sanctuary.

But today, the air in the place felt different. She didn't feel at peace. Instead, a steady sense of anxiety seemed to grip her.

She looked around the space again, trying to think of anything else that she felt she absolutely had to take with her. Up on the wall above her desk was a large collection of carefully curated art, motivational quotes, and clippings from research articles she'd participated in. She saw a few things she wouldn't have minded pulling down and shoving in her bag, but she didn't reach up to grab them.

The wall represented years of memories, and despite the terrible things she'd been part of, she couldn't deny that the majority of those memories were still good ones. She still didn't know exactly how she felt about the moral implications of psychedelic drugs, but the very thought of her research area now made her feel off-balance.

Would tomorrow bring an entirely new life? Would she realize that she had spent so many years on something that was not only corrupted, but dangerous to its core?

She didn't know if she could bear it. And worse, she didn't know if Axel could bear it either.

Could God?

Axel would say He could. He'd say she'd be forgiven, no matter what she'd done, but it was hard for her to believe it now as she stood looking at the dozens of academic papers, a record of the lives her work had influenced.

She was no Marie Curie–the world would never know her name–but she knew that didn't really matter. In her own way, she'd been a big part of the psychedelic revolution in mental health research, and years from now, her name was still going to come up on a PubMed search.

The thought didn't make her proud. More than anything, she felt ashamed.

She turned away from the desk, giving the rest of the room a final once-over.

She knew she was probably leaving evidence behind tying her personally to some of Senera's more mundane unethical activities, but what did it matter at this point?

All she really cared about now was taking care of John, and making things right. For Amira, for Destiny, and for everyone else that DX8 had hurt.

She could only pray that the authorities would be able to investigate the lab before Bajwa or anyone else started destroying evidence. Like the majority of Senera's main compound outside of immediately accessible public areas, this building had no cameras.

She felt a shiver running along her back as she grabbed the labelled DX8 doses they would use tonight. She couldn't seem to shake the creepy feeling that somehow, somewhere, she was being observed.

She was relieved when she stepped out of the building and locked the door behind her.

It was already getting dark, but the fresh air and open space felt positively inviting. She was sure everyone had to have returned by now, and soon, it would be time for the patients to take DX8. And those doses would be their last.

Whatever was going to come tomorrow, she had no choice but to face it.

Lord, please protect my patients for one more night. Please protect Axel. Please, just keep us safe until we can bring an end to this madness. Amen.

The prayer seemed to rise within her naturally, like talking to God was something she'd been doing all her life. But there was still one request she was too afraid to ask for, even in the silence of her heart.

She desperately wanted Axel to be a part of her life when this was over. She wanted him to kiss her every night, to hold her in his arms, and to be there to tell her that everything was going to be okay.

She was so tired of carrying her burdens alone.

CHAPTER
THIRTY-THREE

THE WOMAN

The woman was no longer anxious.

Her heart pounded now with pure excitement that overshadowed every other feeling.

The ritual had gone well. Better than she could ever have expected. Any last shred of doubt she had about the identity of their chosen one had been cast aside.

"You have done well," Mother said, a sudden voice in her ear that echoed the thoughts in her mind. "I always knew you would."

The woman sat up a little straighter, pride swelling within her chest. Her years of service to Mother and to their community had not always been easy, but now, she could hardly remember the difficult times.

Mother showed herself now, her green scales glistening, somehow, even in the dark.

"The Professor would be proud, too," Mother added in a hissing whisper. "He always told me you were special.

He would stand in awe at the woman you have become today."

The woman's heart felt like it would burst with joy.

"Thank you," she said, unable to say anything else for fear she would begin to cry. There was no time for that. They were near the end now, but it wasn't over yet. Until it was, she had to keep her guard up against the dark forces that threatened their mission.

"I imagine you need more of the drug," Mother said, once again seeming to read the woman's mind. "The DX8. I believe we have nearly used up the remainder of our stores, and I don't think we have enough to finish our task."

The woman nodded.

"I apologize. It's been difficult to get more."

"Because of the others?"

"Yes. Especially Karlin McKenna. She always seems to be watching everything."

Mother let out a hiss again. This one was not a whisper. The woman could almost see the anger that escaped the beautiful serpent's forked tongue.

"It will not matter soon. Do what you must," she commanded.

"I will."

They were silent for a few moments.

"Mother?"

"Yes, my dear one?"

"Is it really time now?"

The woman knew that she sounded overeager–childish, even–but Mother's voice had softened into kindness.

"There is one last ritual, and then, yes. We will be home."

A sound like screaming wind filled the woman's ears,

and she felt the ground beginning to rumble beneath where she sat.

Mother was in front of her now, growing larger and larger, so big that the room could no longer contain her.

The woman could not see the room anymore. Somewhere, a great distance away, she could see a blanket of ink-black sky dotted with stars, but her eyes were trained firmly on Mother.

She had grown to a gargantuan size. Each one of her scales was now as big as the woman's hand. Mother's face was so high up now that she couldn't see her mouth, her flicking tongue, or her fangs, but she was sure they had to be enormous.

"Listen well, dear child," Mother continued, her voice booming, seeming to fill eternity with its volume. "There is no power without sacrifice, and there is no sacrifice without the spilling of blood. We have our chosen one. She will give up her life for the salvation of all, and she will do so willingly. We will not fail."

Her final words rang in the woman's ears.

She could hear the sound of blood pulsing through them. They ached from the noise, and her body trembled with terror. How awesome, how powerful Mother was!

The woman would not fail her. No matter what it would take, she would go home to the empire of light. She would share in Mother's power, in her greatness.

She, too, would be unstoppable.

All she had to do was get away from this wretched, dying earth.

She closed her eyes and smiled, speaking in a loud, clear voice.

"I love you, Mother. I live, and die, and kill for you."

And when she opened her eyes, she was in her simple room again, alone in the dark.

CHAPTER
THIRTY-FOUR

ASHER

A sher took his place in the now familiar hut, trying to focus on not staring at Karlin while she tinkered with DX8 doses.

Yet again, Bajwa was giving one of his sermons about how revolutionary and amazing DX8 was. And as usual, Lily and Cora looked as though they were about to leap up from their mats and bow down to his brilliance, while Paul looked like he was considering thwacking him with a hot cattle brand.

"What happened with Destiny will not happen tonight," Bajwa was saying. "You are going to experience a wonderful, joyful journey. You are going to do the work on yourselves that you came here to do. You are going to experience healing."

He sounded so confident that Asher had no trouble believing that he really did believe all of this to be true. In the mind of Dr. Bajwa, DX8 was a miracle, and nothing was going to shake that faith.

Asher's experience of this retreat had created an oppo-site unshakeable conviction.

Knowing what happened to Amira and to Destiny was enough to drive away any lingering curiosity of what it would be like to experience the high for himself.

DX8 and all other psychedelic drugs were undeniably dangerous, and the public's recent embrace of them should have already been ringing warning bells in the minds of regulators, politicians, and the media.

And he was confident that those red flags would be noticed, especially if Karlin actually went to the authorities tomorrow as they had agreed.

This was about more than just Senera.

It was about bringing light into a place where darkness reigned.

He stole a glance in her direction.

Tonight, she was dressed more formally than she had for the rest of the retreat. She'd even brought a lab coat to the hut, though it was discarded on top of Bajwa's CD player at the moment.

Ever since the others had arrived back at the retreat site and she'd rejoined the group, her smiles had been cold, and any conversation she made had sounded forced. Asher knew her well enough now to see the gears turning. She was in deep focus mode now, single-mindedly set on only one objective until this nightmare ended.

He shared her determination, but his acting would have to be a lot more convincing.

"Mr. Bishop, are you feeling fully prepared?" Bajwa asked him, as if on cue.

He was prepared, all right. Right down to the concealed handgun he wore. Tonight, he wasn't taking any chances.

"You bet, Doc," he said, giving a thumbs-up and a carefree smile. "We got this. Let's do it for Destiny!"

With this, he let out a cheer, and everyone joined in. Even Paul offered a weak whoop, though his face was etched with confusion, as though he was expecting a hidden camera to pop out at any moment and tell him that all of this was a joke.

Which, Asher supposed, it kind of was. But it was a joke he'd have to be in on for the next several hours. May as well do it justice.

"Your dose is perfect this time," Karlin said, lifting up a glass cup and gesturing in Asher's direction. "You're going to actually feel what it's like to experience DX8, I promise."

Bajwa clapped his hands together, his dark brown eyes gleaming. "Excellent. We wouldn't want you missing out on this once in a lifetime chance to grow and to explore our universe."

He looked so excited that Asher could actually pity him. He could only wonder how the man would react when he learned that one of his best scientists was risking everything in order to put an end to his research entirely.

"I think we're ready to get started," Karlin said, getting up from her spot near the plastic cooler of DX8 and beginning to hand out doses to the others. When she reached Asher's mat and passed him his own, her fingers lingered on his a few seconds longer than necessary. But before he could offer her so much as a surreptitious wink, she'd already moved on to Cora.

A new fear struck at him as he waited for the others to receive their doses.

He'd been so worried about whether Karlin would have the courage to go through with leaving the retreat tomorrow that he hadn't considered what would happen if she did. Would they continue to grow closer together without the forced bonds of the retreat, or would Karlin push him away as soon as she no longer needed him?

He wanted to believe that they had a real connection, that her feelings for him were just as real as his feelings for her, but he knew that nothing was guaranteed. Worse, he also knew that even when things were going well, he had an epic knack for messing everything up.

He gripped the glass cup more tightly.

He couldn't let himself worry about how Karlin felt about him. The life and death reality of dealing with Senera had to be his only priority, at least for now.

Glancing around the room, he let his eyes linger for a moment on each of his fellow retreat patients.

He'd failed the people who'd relied on him back in Afghanistan, and those men had been soldiers. Lily, Paul, and Cora were not. Neither was Destiny.

Neither was Amira.

He couldn't turn back time and help her now, but he could certainly make sure that justice was truly served on her behalf, even as she awaited it in death.

Finally, his eyes alighted on Karlin, who was moving her lab coat and saying something he couldn't hear to Bajwa.

She looked so fierce and determined, like some invincible goddess, but he knew that wasn't true. Deep down, she was vulnerable in ways that few other people could fathom. Whatever choice she made about continuing to want him when this was over didn't matter. She'd still trusted him, still shared things with him that she had carried by herself for years.

He would be strong for her. He would protect her.

Even if it was the last thing he ever did.

KARLIN

The sound of drumbeats filled Karlin's ears as her patients downed their doses of DX8.

She realized she was holding her breath, but so far, nothing seemed to be amiss.

Everyone was sitting quietly, listening to Bajwa as he gave a few final instructions, including letting everyone know that he and Karlin would be monitoring their vital signs and taking notes.

She was glad that they'd managed to give Axel the proper placebo this time. His acting was convincing, but he couldn't exactly fake a higher blood pressure or an increased heart rate. She didn't think that claiming an underdose would work a second time.

They wouldn't start drawing blood or measuring vitals for another hour or so, so she sat down and tried to relax. Even Bajwa seemed to have lost some of his usual energy, choosing to lean against the wall instead of wandering around the room.

Despite her boss's assurances to their patients, she knew that the incident with Destiny had to have rattled him. Not that it would come close to being enough evidence for him that DX8 was dangerous.

After fifteen minutes or so had passed, she got to her feet and did a quick circuit to check on each guest. Everyone had their eyes closed, and both Paul and Cora were rocking back and forth slightly. When she approached Axel, she noticed that he was doing the same. He didn't even open his eyes to try and sneak a smile in her direction. It was as though he hadn't noticed she was there at all.

Well, whatever. So long as it convinced Bajwa and everyone else that he was high as a kite, she wasn't going to–

A surprising sound from outside broke through the pounding of the drums.

A dog was barking loudly, and a few seconds later, the sound of sirens joined the chorus. Bajwa hit pause on the CD player and looked over at her with confusion.

"What on earth is going on?"

Karlin opened her mouth, and then shut it again as the sound of voices and footsteps grew louder.

A second barking dog joined the other one. She could distinguish it by the low rumbling of its bark, and for one absurd moment, she found herself thinking of John and the service dog he desperately needed.

"Karlin, what is going on?" Bajwa demanded, pacing back and forth in place. She stood completely still, her heart rattling against her ribcage as she tried desperately to think of a possible answer to his question.

At that moment, four police officers, a black Labrador, and an enormous German Shepherd burst through the door and entered the hut.

"I have no idea," she said honestly, trying desperately to catch Axel's eye as the chaos rose to an immediate fever pitch.

"Everyone stay where you are, and stay calm!" one officer–a compact man with dark skin who seemed to be in charge–commanded.

"We're looking for Dr. Daman Bajwa," the man contin-ued, his fellow officers fanning out behind him, weapons

233

drawn. One, a tan-skinned man who looked to be easily six and a half feet tall, kept guard at the door.

Karlin looked at her patients, all of whom were now making noise, rocking quickly back and forth, or covering their ears. Axel was doing the same, and while she knew he had to stay undercover, she desperately wanted him to acknowledge the insanity of the situation.

Had he called this in even though they'd agreed to wait until tomorrow?

She couldn't think of any other explanation as to why the retreat had suddenly become overrun with armed law enforcement. She tried to catch his eye, hoping for a reassuring glance, but he was ignoring her completely. Undercover or not, he was seriously ticking her off.

"I'm Dr. Bajwa, but this is–this is preposterous!" Bajwa said, stepping forward with his hands raised. His face had gone red, and his eyes looked like they were going to bulge out of his skull. "For what possible reason am I in trouble with the law? I'm an American citizen! I have all of my documentation, and I can explain any discrepancies!"

Karlin resisted the urge to let out a snort.

There were discrepancies, all right, if Benjamin Forge's research was to be believed. But she highly doubted that was why Amarillo PD had shown up now.

The officer in charge nodded to the other two standing nearby. Within seconds, they had produced handcuffs and closed in on Bajwa. "You are under arrest in connection with the suspicious death of Amira Elizabeth Gorsky. You have the right to remain silent–"

Bajwa interrupted the man immediately. "This is an outrage! I hope you are prepared to be sued for all you've got! I did not even work at Senera Pharmaceuticals at the time of Amira Gorsky's death!"

To Karlin's horror, he managed to yank one hand free of the police officer trying to cuff him, and pointed it in her direction.

"I wasn't there, but she was. I've seen the file! She was the one who signed off on a severely depressed woman's participation in a Phase I medical trial. Arrest *her*!"

Karlin's heart felt like it was going to burst right up into her throat, but she said nothing, figuring that holding her ground was the best option.

She had taken the aforementioned file with her and hidden it in her cabin. There was no way that Bajwa knew it was gone, and it was far from guaranteed that there were other copies of it floating around, especially if her theory was correct and it contained additional false information designed to bring her down. Senera–and therefore Bajwa–wouldn't have wanted anyone to see it unless they found themselves in a truly tight situation.

"You can explain everything down at the station," one of the other officers grunted, finally managing to secure the silver cuffs around Bajwa's wrists. "I'll make sure you get a chance to contact a lawyer."

She knew the truth about what she'd done was going to come out, but if there was any way she could choose, it was going to be on her terms.

Once again, she found herself looking to Axel for comfort, only to find him sitting with his back pressed to Cora's, his eyes pressed shut. Cora was shouting something incomprehensible at the hut's wall. A few feet away, Lily was rubbing a weeping Paul's back. What a disaster.

Bajwa, too, noticed the deteriorating situation, and decided to change tack.

"I can't leave now," he begged. "This is an active medical trial. I have four participants currently under the influence of a powerful psychedelic. They could hurt themselves. Please."

The dark-skinned officer nodded to the huge man by the door, who called the two K9s away from the cooler of empty DX8 vials that they were currently investigating.

"We already spoke to another scientist at Senera," the officer in charge explained, turning back to a defeated-looking Bajwa. "Unless you have immediate proof of your serious accusations about Miss McKenna, I have been assured that she is perfectly capable of monitoring the group on her own for the rest of the night. Am I correct?"

Karlin couldn't decide if she had gotten extremely lucky or extremely unlucky.

Senera's offices would be even more empty by now. If the cops had only spoken to the young scientist she and Axel had run into, he would have had no idea that Bajwa wasn't even part of the company at the time of Amira's death.

"Yes, sir," Karlin said quickly, deciding to roll with the situation for now. "Once you guys clear out, I should be able to calm everyone down."

The officer nodded, and with the help of the other men, began shoving Bajwa in the direction of the door.

"I'm cooperating! I'm cooperating! Get your hands off of me, you beasts! Don't you know who I am?" Bajwa shouted, nearly stumbling as they finally maneuvered him out of the door and into the night.

For several long seconds, Karlin stood where she was, staring after them as Bajwa continued to ramble.

Though she knew that she'd had no other choice but to let them go, every instinct was screaming at her to follow them and to tell the truth.

The whole truth, and nothing but the truth.

She rubbed at her temples. Now that she thought about it, that one was definitely for the courtroom, not talking to the cops.

Not that it mattered now.

The truth was a luxury she couldn't afford.

CHAPTER
THIRTY-FIVE

KARLIN

To Karlin's relief, the other patients did calm down, though she struggled to get her own heart to stop racing.

She spent the next little while checking vitals, monitoring each patient individually, and trying to talk to those who could do so, which at the moment seemed to be only Paul, and presumably Axel, though he was acting like he couldn't even hear her.

As the minutes ticked past, she found herself actually missing Bajwa. At this moment, despite everything, she wished that she could share his rock-solid faith in DX8– even if just to get through the night and figure out what on earth was going on.

Once again, her anger at Senera flared. Trip killers should have been synthesized specifically for use with DX8. If the company had funded this basic precaution, she would have been able to get everyone sober within an hour or so. Now, she was trapped here until morning, left with no choice but to hope that no medical complications or even bad trip experiences would arise.

No, that wasn't strictly true.

She could also pray that God would protect her patients, and she took a moment to do so as she waited for the blood pressure cuff to inflate on Paul's upper arm.

The more that the idea of faith had intruded into her life, the more her life's work felt like a sham. Even if DX8 was safe, or could somehow be tested ethically–neither of which she could agree with any more–could she ever be okay with working with psychedelics again?

Could she ever be okay with helping other people to leave their rational minds behind?

She shook her head, attempting to clear her thoughts as she slipped the cuff off of Paul's bicep. His blood pressure was a little high, but not enough to be truly worrisome, considering what he'd just witnessed.

Her existential moral crisis would have to wait. Even though everyone was medically fine at the moment, she knew that the current situation was untenable. Senera may have thought she was capable of handling the rest of this trip by herself, but she knew the FDA would not agree.

She had to call in another scientist for backup. If there was any chance at all that she would be able to work in the medical research field again, she had to be able to say that in an emergency, she'd done the right thing and sought help.

She needed to find a sat phone. Had she been thinking ahead, she would have asked Bajwa to leave his behind, but unfortunately, it was too late for that, unless he'd left it in the Jeep.

It was worth checking–Bajwa didn't always remember

to lock his vehicle–but if there was no phone there, she'd be leaving her patients alone for nothing.

On the other hand, it would take her only a few minutes if she hurried, and maybe she wouldn't need to go at all.

She looked over at Axel.

His eyes were closed, and he and Cora were now sitting calmly together. Lily had scooted her mat over to be closer to them. Paul was no longer crying, in fact, he looked more peaceful than she'd ever seen him.

She considered telling the whole group that she'd be back in five minutes, and that Axel was in charge–with Bajwa gone and with her promise to leave the next day, it no longer really mattered that he remained undercover as a fellow patient–but decided at once that it would be too risky.

Everyone was still high on DX8, and them finding out during a trip that Axel wasn't actually one of them could trigger dangerous levels of paranoia. Another panic attack was the last thing she needed.

She settled on leaning over and whispering in his ear that she was stepping out and would be back in five minutes. He was hardly a scientist, but at least he was sober. If chaos was going to break out in the next five minutes, there wouldn't be much she'd be able to do on her own, anyway.

She lingered several seconds longer than she had to, admiring the slight scruff on Axel's face and ignoring the mad urge to press her lips against his.

Surely, he hadn't been the one to call the police on Bajwa. She trusted him when he'd said he'd stick with her until tomorrow.

But if he didn't, who did?

Before she could consider the matter any further, Lily shot up from her mat, mumbling something about feeling like she was going to throw up.

Jumping into action, Karlin rushed over and took the woman's hand, guiding her out of the hut. The cool air outside was refreshing, but unfortunately, it didn't seem to have much of a soothing effect on Lily's stomach.

Karlin led her a few meters from the hut to where a convenient stand of thick bushes would provide a little bit of privacy.

"I'll be right here, okay?" Karlin said gently.

She waited for several long minutes, but no repulsive sounds came.

Instead, she found herself actually enjoying the chance to escape into the calm night for a moment, even if it delayed her plan to go call for backup.

It felt good just to be alone in the dark and quiet.

Finally, after indulging in the silence for a couple more minutes, Karlin turned around to ask Lily if she felt any better.

But before she could say anything, her words were stolen away in a gasp.

Everything felt like it was beginning to move in slow motion as the peace she'd felt mere seconds ago slipped away in a single heartbeat.

A gun was now pointed directly at her head.

ASHER

Bajwa. Police. Dogs. Noise.

Asher was trying to think, but his brain didn't seem to be working properly. It was like it could only process a single word at a time. Everything felt slow and thick, like he was trying to muscle his way through a tidal wave of quicksand.

Bajwa had been arrested. That much he could gather, but he didn't understand why. The sounds of the barking dogs and the loud voices of the police officers had hurt his head.

The drums are gone, so why is it so loud?

Asking this question suddenly seemed very important. The police and the dogs and Bajwa were gone. It didn't make sense. He knew somehow that the hut was relatively silent, so why did his head feel like it was pulsing with noise from the inside out?

He wanted to talk to Karlin.

That's what he really wanted to do. He had to get up, go over to her, and tell her that he must have taken the wrong DX8 dose.

She seemed impossibly far away.

He would have settled for calling her name, but he couldn't do that, either. He thought he managed to open his mouth a little, but maybe that was only his imagination. It was useless, anyway. No words came.

So instead, he just sat.

He tried to pray, but could barely think of the name of Jesus without feeling confused and exhausted. He could feel that his heart was beating fast. He could hear it in his ears. But other than that, he thought he felt okay. He was breathing.

He just had to focus on breathing.

Time passed.

He wasn't sure how long it had been. He felt adrift, like there was nothing left pinning him down.

He opened his eyes at one point, not realizing that he had closed them, and he saw something.

Lily was standing up and following Karlin into the night.

The fact made him afraid–he *knew* he was afraid–but he didn't feel it.

It was like God was shouting at him from Heaven itself, but he was too far away to hear anything but a vague whooshing in his ears.

No, surely, that was just his blood making that noise.

Right. That made more sense. It was loud.

So loud.

It reminded him of Afghanistan. It reminded him of the way his ears felt after the bomb that killed Nico went off.

The thought still scared him, even through the haze.

No. He had to focus on what was happening right here, right now. He didn't have time to go back to the past, to things he couldn't take back or do over again.

Lily. Karlin. Lily.

There was something he should have mentioned to her earlier. It hadn't seemed important, but now, it was. It was like the drugs had unlocked something in his brain and it had become totally clear, but he couldn't get to it.

He tried to force air in and out of his lungs.

Maybe he was just deluding himself. Everything was quiet. The others looked okay, and Karlin would be back in a minute. He had his gun if he needed it. He'd protect them all, and everything would be okay.

He closed his eyes again as gleaming stars and dancing lights played at the edge of his vision.

He just had to keep breathing. He just had to hold on.

CHAPTER
THIRTY-SIX

ASHER

A sher's tongue felt like it had been permanently glued to the roof of his mouth.

He forced himself to open his eyes, ignoring the pounding of his headache, and pulled himself up into a sitting position on the hard floor. He could see his sleeping mat several feet away, and his screaming back told him he had to have been sleeping for a while. Probably at least a few hours.

As he glanced around the hut, he tried to remember recent events, but it was difficult.

He could, however, figure out that he must have been high on DX8 by mistake.

He remembered lots of colors and twisting shapes. He remembered feeling like he'd lost his place in space and time, like he was floating in an infinite blackness.

He remembered his ears pulsing with blood. He remembered the mixture of silence and buzzing that followed the sound of an explosion...

But there had been no explosion here. No. Even DX8 hadn't made him delusional enough to believe that. All it could do was force him to remember Afghanistan, to make him relive things that he wanted so badly to forget.

Even now that he had sobered up somewhat, his brain still felt riddled with holes. What else had he seen?

He was curious, but a bigger part of him was thankful that he didn't know. Perhaps God was protecting him from those memories.

But as for the real world, a few details began to emerge from the haze of his exhausted mind.

Police had shown up here, and they'd arrested Bajwa. He remembered that. They had big dogs that barked, and then the drumbeat sound had been turned off.

He could see Paul and Cora sleeping on their respective mats nearby, looking normal. That was good, at least.

He craned his neck to look for Karlin, to ask her how on earth she'd accidentally given him the wrong dose, and then he remembered.

She had gone outside, and he'd seen Lily following after her.

And even though hours had passed, neither of the women had returned.

Asher sprung to his feet, gripping the wall of the hut for a moment to steady himself before taking off at an unbalanced run. His legs were filled with rubber, but he had to push through it, along with the general feeling that his head was stuffed with cotton balls.

The desert was dark and empty, but there was a thickness in the air, like a storm might be rolling in soon.

He wanted to run, but he had to think. He needed direction. By now, Karlin and Lily could be anywhere.

Despite the remaining fogginess in his brain, he was

sober enough now to remember what he wished he'd told Karlin. She didn't know that he'd caught Lily lurking around his cabin when they got back from the Senera offices the day before.

At the time, he'd wanted to accept the woman's excuse for being there. He liked Lily, and he'd been so focused on stopping Senera that digging into the other patients' pasts felt like it was mostly a waste of time.

But now, nefarious possibilities began to unravel in his mind.

Lily had probably been at his cabin for the most obvious reason–she suspected that he wasn't who he claimed to be and was digging for clues. She could have swapped his DX8 dose, too, probably at the lab before-hand. How she'd gotten in, he didn't know, but security there wasn't exactly tight.

Giving him the real drug would have allowed her to both confirm he was lying and take him out of commission in one blow, allowing her to get to Karlin.

It all fit. It was certainly a more plausible explanation for the DX8 switch than Karlin simply making a careless mistake. He knew her well enough to know that she virtually never made them.

That, and how out of it he still felt. He should have been a lot more clear-headed by now than he was, which made him think he'd been given a much bigger dose than anyone else.

But nothing he could think of settled the most obvious question: why?

Was Lily involved with Senera somehow? Was she working with Bajwa?

If she was, why had he been arrested? Was it all part of some ruse?

He pressed his fingers to his temples, as though he could push through the haze somehow. All of this attempted deduction was not helping his headache, either.

He had to get ahold of dependable, brilliant, and always sober Ben so that he could do a deep dive into Lily Moonchild.

Finding a phone was now his next objective.

But before he could consider where to look, he heard the sound of angry voices coming from inside the hut.

KARLIN

Every inch of Karlin's body ached.

She forced one foot in front of the other as she and Lily hiked through the desert in the dark, stumbling over rocks and pricking herself on unseen plants.

The air felt dangerously heavy, and the wind was beginning to pick up, sending a bitter cold breeze rushing over the sand.

Despite the exertion, she struggled to keep herself warm, and the business-like skirt and thin cardigan she wore did little to protect her from the cold gusts of wind that swept up every few minutes. Her simple flat shoes were only moderately warmer than a pair of sandals, and she would do almost anything to go back and choose a pair of sensible sneakers with thick socks.

She couldn't stop shivering, and yet, she longed for a glass of freezing cold water.

She knew that she had more important things to think about.

Everyone was in danger now, most of all herself, but it was incredible how the needs of the body could draw her thoughts even as she faced a real risk of death.

She tripped over a root and fell to her knees, gasping in pain as she felt a cut opening up on the top of her right foot.

She felt Lily jabbing the gun into the back of her head.

"Keep moving," the woman said, her voice void of emotion. "I need you out of my way."

Karlin yanked her body upright, knowing that it would be dangerous to argue.

Ever since Lily had ambushed her outside of the retreat hut, she'd hardly spoken, but everything she did say filled Karlin with cold terror. It was like the cheerful older woman had disappeared, replaced by a monster in an instant.

But there had to have been signs. Signs she–and apparently, Axel–had missed.

Not that she was casting blame. Whatever the reason for her deception was, the act Lily put on had been extremely convincing.

"We have a ritual to do, and we're already late. It was supposed to be performed at midnight," Lily continued. It was the most substantial sentence she'd uttered in hours.

Karlin decided she'd risk a question, though she didn't dare to ask specifically what the woman meant by needing her out of the way.

"What do you mean?" she choked out.

Her mouth was so dry that the words nearly got stuck in her throat.

Lily stopped walking for a moment, and Karlin stole a glance behind her. The woman actually looked almost sad.

"You almost found out, back then," she said at last. "Amira liked you, trusted you. She was going to tell you everything, but she never got the chance. I couldn't risk history repeating itself. You were getting too close."

Karlin's stomach clenched as she stared at Lily, realization dawning.

It was all she could do not to throw up.

Everything was finally beginning to make sense.

ASHER

Asher followed the raised voices back into the hut, just in time to see Paul begging Cora to leave with him. "We need to get back to the main site," he was saying, his voice pleading. "We need to call for help."

"No way," Cora argued. "Listen to the wind. There's a storm starting, and it's pitch black out there. I don't even know if there's still a Jeep to drive, and the trail will be rough if it starts raining. We need to wait for Karlin to get back."

"She might not come back," Paul snapped, sounding angrier than Asher had ever heard him. "Dr. Bajwa is in jail, Ms. McKenna has disappeared, and so has Lily. Maybe she had a bad reaction and Karlin had to take her to the hospital like they did with Destiny. This whole retreat is cursed."

Asher considered this.

If he hadn't spent most of the night high out of his mind, he probably would have considered that possibility first. He hadn't even looked to see if Bajwa's Jeep was still outside.

Surely, it was a more likely possibility than the explanations he'd been tossing around.

He was about to suggest that they go see if the Jeep was there and if the keys were in it when Cora spoke.

"That's not gonna happen," she said, shaking her head, as though Paul's idea was ridiculous. "Lily has way more experience with DX8 than Destiny did. There's no way she..."

The woman cut herself off mid-sentence, shutting her mouth like a trap.

Asher paused for a moment, confused.

What did she mean?

He was all but certain Lily had said she'd never tried anything more severely mind altering than weed.

Man, his head hurt. It felt as though each time he tried to form a thought, he was killing off a few more brain cells and causing a little more pain.

He needed to drink some water, he needed to talk to Ben or one of his other brothers, and he needed to get his theory straight.

Most of all, he had to find Karlin.

"Fine, do what you want," Paul said at last, wiping invisible dust from the front of his jeans. "I'm finding a phone to call for help. If I can't manage that, I guess I'll wind up back here or find some other shelter."

"Be careful," Asher warned. "If there's no phone in the Jeep, the next one will be at the main compound. It takes a while to get there on foot in the daylight, let alone at night with a storm brewing."

Paul considered this. "It would be a lot safer if you came with me."

Asher shook his head. "Honestly, man, I feel way too sick. I'm just gonna hunker down here with Cora for a while."

It was true.

His head was still pounding, his mouth was dry, and he knew that if he was going to find Karlin in this weather he was probably going to need to take a few minutes to get himself together. Everything still felt muddled, and he was afraid that in his impaired thinking, he could make things even worse.

Paul headed for the door, giving them a final wave as he strode out into the brewing storm.

For several moments, neither he nor Cora spoke.

The hut felt lonelier than ever.

Asher longed for the normalcy of his life in San Antonio. Failing that, he would have settled for a few hours of sleep back in his guest cabin down at the main area of the retreat site. Anything but here, unable to think straight, his body and mind rebelling against him even as he knew he had to start taking action.

"Hey, thanks for staying with me," Cora said after a little while, moving her mat a little closer to his. "It would be seriously creepy by myself."

"Yeah, seriously," Asher agreed, not wanting to tell her that as soon as his head stopped spinning, he was heading back out into the rain. Hopefully, Paul would be successful in calling for help, and she wouldn't be alone for very long, but he couldn't stick around when Karlin was in much more danger.

"It's better this way," Cora continued, reaching for something in the pocket of her baggy jeans.

"Sorry?"

He had no time to think, no time to react.

In a single motion, Cora lashed out like a snake, and a sudden flash of pain jolted through him.

He glanced down just in time to realize that the end of a syringe was now stuck firmly into his thigh.

CHAPTER
THIRTY-SEVEN

KARLIN

Karlin forced her legs to continue carrying her forward as she tried to make sense of everything.

She knew the truth about Lily's identity, but should she play her hand and confront her, or should she wait?

The rain was beginning to fall now, quickly dampening the sand and dirt beneath her shoes. It took most of her concentration just to keep walking without slipping.

Lily had gone quiet again, more interested in jabbing her with the gun and snapping at her to keep moving than in explaining herself further.

At last, after several more minutes walking in silence, debating what to say, Karlin finally realized where she was.

Up just ahead was the downward slope that led toward the old cabin where she had met with Axel.

"Careful on the rocks," Lily said, breaking the long silence. It was everything Karlin could do not to laugh as she navigated down the steep, wet slope. The rain was picking up by the minute, and the trail was becoming downright treacherous, but if Lily was so concerned about her safety, why did she have a gun pointed firmly at her back?

Any hope that the woman might be somehow on her side was dashed as they reached the door of the old building.

"Get inside," Lily said flatly as she opened the door.

Karlin shook her head, but the woman only jabbed her harder with the gun until she stepped over the threshold.

"You can't leave me here," Karlin protested. The dark interior looked suddenly frightening. Sure, it would be mostly dry, and warmer than outside, but as far as she knew, no one but herself and Axel–and apparently Lily–knew the cabin was here. Who knew how long it would be until someone came to look for her, even assuming Axel was still safe?

Even assuming he was still alive.

She swallowed hard, not wanting to even entertain that thought for a second. Whatever was going on, she was sure he'd be okay. He had to be.

"I told you, I need you out of my way," Lily said, raising the gun again as she reached for the handle of the door.

She looked so different now from the sweet hippie grandmother she'd once appeared to be. Her long gray hair hung loose, and thanks to the rain and rising wind, it now looked as wild as her eyes.

Karlin knew those eyes.

And had she been looking closely, she would have recognized them a long time ago.

"Dana, please don't do this," she pleaded. "You can

just let me go. I just want to get away from here, I promise."

She'd been expecting some kind of surprise to show on the woman's face, but instead, she could see only contempt.

"Are you planning to start calling Axel by his real name, too?"

Before Karlin could think of a response, Lily had shoved her backwards. She stumbled on the leg of a chair, crashing to the ground just in time for the door of the cabin to slam shut.

She got to her feet immediately and rushed back through the darkness, but it was too late. No matter how much she shook the door and yanked on its handle, she couldn't open it. She shouted after Lily until her voice felt hoarse, knowing all the while that it was pointless.

She was alone.

Leaning back against the door, she pressed her eyes firmly shut, trying to adjust to the dark as much as she possibly could and forcing herself to breathe deeply.

She was scared, but she knew this cabin.

She knew there were candles and matches here somewhere. In a cabinet near the far side of the room, if she remembered right.

After a few moments of fumbling, she took hold of the box of matches, drew one out, and struck it. The light was blinding as she hurriedly lit a jar candle she found sitting on the table, filling the cabin with a scent that she assumed had once resembled vanilla.

She could see for certain now that the few windows were too small to provide an escape route.

Outside, the sound of wind battering the cabin walls had joined the pounding of the rain. If she was going to break a window and try to call for help, she was going to have to wait until morning at the very earliest. There was zero chance she'd be heard now.

There was a little firewood beside the stove, some canned food in the cabinets, and a case of water bottles still stuffed in the corner of the room like they'd been last time.

This was the good news.

She wasn't going to die of thirst or starve. If Lily had wanted to kill her, she would have done it with the gun–unless she'd just assumed it would be empty in here. But she didn't want to think about that option.

Now that her immediate panic had passed, her mind was reeling.

Every answer she knew seemed to lead to several more questions.

She knew that Lily Moonchild was, in fact, a woman she'd met before–a woman named Dana Corbett, who had been part of the same retreat as Amira Gorsky.

She could imagine Dana in her mind now, and she could almost forgive herself for not recognizing her.

Though it had only been a decade, she looked a lot younger than Lily did now.

She had been at least fifty pounds lighter, and she'd worn her hair in a pixie-like brown crop.

The most distinguishing feature that Karlin remembered, however, was Dana's dress style. She'd usually worn tailored dress pants, crisp white shirts, and simple gold jewelry. Karlin could remember being impressed by the way she managed to look elegant in the middle of the desert. She reminded her of a slightly more androgynous version of Destiny.

Everything about the way Dana had presented herself

back then was a complete one-eighty from how she looked now as Lily.

But there was one clue that Karlin could not forgive herself for overlooking.

Dana had frequently thrown up after taking the earlier iteration of DX8.

She had never seen anyone else experience the same side effect, and it should have rang warning bells immediately, but it hadn't.

Clearly, Axel hadn't suspected anything about the woman, either–by the sound of it, his twin brother Ben would have been able to dig up the dirt on Lily if he'd decided to look.

No, the woman had them both fooled, and now they were paying the price.

Karlin rubbed her hands up and down her arms to warm them, considering whether or not she could focus long enough to start a fire.

The weather seemed to be getting even worse outside, and try as she might, she couldn't shake her fear that something terrible might have happened to Axel, not to mention Cora or Paul.

Not that she had any idea as to what Lily's motives were, or what was even going on. Clearly, the woman knew Axel was undercover, and if she knew that, she probably knew that he and Karlin were trying to take down Senera.

But why did Lily care?

Try as she might, she couldn't imagine any scenario where Lily was working with Senera, and especially not with control-freak Bajwa.

Then again, the woman had managed to come across as

harmless. For all Karlin knew, she was actually the evil genius mastermind, and Bajwa was her lackey.

Nothing would surprise her any more.

She pressed her fingertips to her temples, feeling the twinges of a headache coming on. She was missing something.

There was some connection that she wasn't making, but no matter how many times she turned over the information she had in her mind, she couldn't seem to find an answer.

ASHER

Asher stared down at the needle.

He expected the world to go black immediately, like it always did in the movies.

Instead, he found himself staring open mouthed up at Cora, who had crossed her arms firmly over her chest.

"You can take that out now," she said. "Just be careful. It'll probably bleed a little."

"What did you do?" he asked, taking hold of the syringe and pulling it carefully out of his thigh. Despite the droplets of blood it left behind on his jeans, he couldn't feel anything now that the momentary pain had passed.

Which probably wasn't a good sign.

Cora ignored him.

"What did you do, Cora?" he demanded again, forcing the last of his energy into raising his voice at her.

"It's just a sedative that Lily stole from the lab. You'll be fine soon."

"Are you going to hurt Karlin?" he asked.

He hated the fear he could hear in his own voice. Even the gun he carried did little to reassure him.

For the second time in less than twelve hours, he'd been drugged against his will. If he didn't have the clarity of his own mind, even a powerful weapon wouldn't be enough to save him.

He could threaten Cora now, but if he did, she might stop talking.

And getting her to talk was his best chance at figuring out what on earth was going on.

"I would if I had to," Cora said, her voice sad, "but I don't think she's going to give me a reason. Neither are you. Just go to sleep. This is all going to be over in a couple of hours."

He could feel the effects of the sedative intensifying now.

His vision seemed to be ringed with a halo of darkness, and every limb felt unbearably heavy. All he wanted in the world was to lie down and take a nap.

"What will be over? I just want to understand."

Cora paused, standing over him.

"We need to finish our ritual," she said. "Once it's done, I'll be able to go home. My entire family will be able to go home at last."

CHAPTER
THIRTY-EIGHT

ASHER

Asher leaned back against the wall of the hut, desperate to figure out what on earth was going on.

Cora had drugged him, and was apparently preparing for some kind of ritual.

Lily and Cora were connected somehow.

Lily was with Karlin.

And Karlin was in grave danger.

None of the pieces fit together, and yet, he was surprised by how quickly his mind was working now, turning the information over in his head, trying to put together the impossible puzzle.

He had pressed his body carefully between the wall and the floor, expecting to pass out at any second, but instead, something strange was happening.

As the seconds wore on, he thought that he might actually be starting to feel better.

The onslaught of tiredness that he'd felt a moment ago

was lessening, and he was beginning to feel the stinging pain left behind by the needle once more.

Hope stirred within his heart as a vague plan began to form.

God, please, grant me a sound mind. Let me stay awake. Help me to find Karlin.

"What ritual?" he asked, trying his best to sound like he was close to losing consciousness. He even managed to let a little bit of drool fall onto his chin.

To his surprise, Cora answered, leaning down to rest on her heels beside him. "The final one. This is a big day for my community. I wish you'd just gone with Paul, but I promise, you're going to be fine, anyway."

She didn't meet his eyes. She seemed lost, as though her mind was somewhere else even as she helped him to lay down on his mat.

He complied, not wanting her to know that her drug had seemingly failed, but dozens of questions threatened to spill out.

He didn't like the sound of a ritual, particularly one described as being 'final.'

Both he and Karlin had dismissed the cult rumors out of hand, but now it was clear that their lack of interest had been a huge mistake.

It seemed impossible to believe that this ritual wasn't connected to the missing teenage girls.

However the whole cult thing fit together, it was clear that Cora Trejo had gotten caught up in something terrible.

He wanted to know what it was, and to try and help her if he could, but for the moment, he had only one priority.

"Wait," he said, laying his head obediently against the

top of the mat. "Where is Ms. McKenna, exactly? Can you at least tell me that?"

This time, he didn't have to fake stumbling over his words. His terror had done that work for him.

He could barely bear the quiet seconds that passed as he waited for her to answer. The very thought that Karlin might not be okay was enough to send him reeling.

At last, Cora spoke.

"All you have to know is that she'll be fine, and so will you," she said, getting to her feet and adjusting the belt of her jeans. "We just need you guys out of our way. Tonight, we only need one victim."

His heart was pounding so loud that he was sure she would hear it.

The temptation to pull out his gun was strong, but he forced himself to remain where he was, breathing in and out as slowly and deliberately as he could. He watched as Cora's combat-boot clad feet walked toward the door of the hut.

He would take a chance and ask one more question, and then he was going to have to put the rest of his plan into action.

"You–are you–are you going to kill her?" he said, closing his eyes as he slurred each word out slowly, guessing at the sex of the ritual victim.

Cora stopped short and turned to look back at him, but she did not move to speak.

Her eyes looked hollow now, like some dark, malevolent force had taken over the woman's being.

"Cora? Cora, are you planning to hurt someone?" he pleaded, remembering at the last second to slur his words.

She didn't seem to suspect anything. She didn't seem to hear him at all.

Without another word, she turned again and walked out into the night.

As she opened the door, a gust of freezing wind swept into the hut, sending a shiver rushing along Asher's spine.

He hardly noticed it.

The emptiness in her eyes had already chilled him straight through to his bones.

KARLIN

Apparently, knowing how to start a fire and actually doing it were two very different things.

Karlin's legs were aching as she knelt in front of the old cabin's woodstove, watching as yet another pile of kindling ignited, only to burn out a few seconds later.

It probably didn't help that outside, she could hear a deluge of rain pounding on the roof and gusts of wind blowing over the top of the chimney somewhere above her.

The only consolation was that there was no thunder, at least, not yet. Thunder had terrified her ever since she was a little girl.

Her parents had never had much sympathy for her fears, but John had always tried to soothe her, explaining why there was nothing to be scared of. She'd never been fully convinced–even now, her rational understanding of the science of thunderstorms did little to comfort her–but she was thankful that he'd cared.

She shivered in her damp clothes, wishing she still had her lab coat that she'd tossed aside back at the hut.

Actually, that was a lie.

What she really wished for was Axel.

He'd know what to do.

And best of all, he'd hold her in his arms, warming her straight through until she never wanted him to let her go.

She had to believe that he was out there somewhere, looking for her. She refused to let herself consider any other possibility. And in the meantime, she had to focus on taking care of her basic needs.

"Here goes nothing," she said aloud, striking another match and lighting a few balled-up old newspapers she was using as tinder. They caught easily, filling the cabin with a pleasant warm glow.

But this was the easy part.

"Come on, come on," she coaxed the fire, blowing slightly as the flames licked against the kindling. To her relief, they caught, and this time, the flame only continued to grow instead of going out.

Karlin plunked herself gracelessly onto the floor, figuring she should wait for a few moments before trying to add any actual logs. She took a sip of water from a bottle she'd set nearby. Now that the fire was starting to actually produce heat, she might be able to open a can and eat something for breakfast in a few hours.

Satisfied with her physical well-being for the moment, she reached into her pocket to take out the photo of John that she always carried.

Even though they had different biological fathers, she'd always thought they'd looked alike. John was blonde and she was a redhead, but they both shared the same bright blue eyes. And being born only eleven months apart seemed to have given them the same closeness as actual twins.

She held the photo to her chest, wishing desperately that he was here, too.

Aside from Axel, he was the one person who she knew

truly cared about her. Unfortunately, it would be a while before he realized she was gone.

She pulled herself to her feet and eyed the old futon sitting against the back wall. Thoughts of bedbugs, spiders, and other nasties made her shudder at the thought of actually sleeping on it, but she knew that getting some rest might be the smartest course of action.

She wanted Axel to burst through the door and rescue her immediately, but she knew it was unlikely.

Even if he was still safe with Cora and Paul, the storm outside was fierce, and the cabin was surrounded by steep, rocky hills.

An even worse realization struck her at once.

Bajwa was in police custody, but he also thought Karlin was still with their patients, so she doubted he'd think to try and send in any backup. Even assuming the police allowed him to try.

Until Ned arrived at work on Monday, the patients would be on their own.

It was highly likely that Bajwa's Jeep keys were still in his pocket along with his sat phone, which meant the others would have to get back to the main retreat site on foot. At least she'd left the maintenance truck parked behind the staff cabins. They could take that back down to the main Senera offices, but the road would be a nightmare in this weather.

Of course, this was all assuming that crazy, gun-wielding Lily didn't get to them first. Then again, she, too, was on foot and would be hindered by the storm.

She took several deep breaths, walking over to the table and laying John's picture next to the old scented candle. It had gotten totally soaked in her pocket.

She had to stay positive, or she was going to drive herself crazy.

At least the effects of DX8 had to have mostly worn off for her patients by now, and the hut was definitely warmer than this cabin. Like her, they were in no immediate physical danger–at least, not any danger posed by natural causes.

She leaned against the back of her chair, trying to get comfortable in some way that wouldn't require her to lay on the old futon. Her head hurt, and her racing thoughts certainly weren't helping.

Something else was still bothering her about the entire night, aside from the obvious.

Who had called the cops on Bajwa?

She had assumed immediately that it had to have been Axel, or maybe someone from Forge Brothers Security, but now she wasn't so sure.

Could it have actually been Lily?

It seemed possible.

After all, she'd been on the retreat with Amira, and she knew what happened to her afterwards. Then again, Lily also knew that Bajwa hadn't been at Senera when the trial took place, so why hadn't she just called the cops on Karlin, instead?

Was she conspiring with Senera somehow, or was she on some other side of this thing all on her own, desperate to get rid of anyone, including Bajwa, who might put a stop to whatever ritual she was planning?

The stuff they'd heard about cults didn't seem so ridiculous anymore.

She got to her feet with a sigh. There was no way she was going to be able to rest, let alone sleep, with such a fascinating puzzle in front of her. Instead, she grabbed a couple of logs from the little woodpile and tossed them onto the burning kindling. Within a few minutes, the cabin began to warm.

With nothing else to do, she bowed her head and tried her best to stumble through a prayer that Axel, Paul, and Cora were safe, and then help would arrive soon.

She wasn't sure God was listening, but if he was?

Now would be a really, really great time for him to work a miracle.

ASHER

Asher stared up at the ceiling of the hut, forcing himself to count slowly to thirty.

It wasn't easy.

Everything in him was desperate to rush out there after her, guns blazing, but that wasn't the plan. If he threatened her, she might just refuse to speak, but she could also lead him away from Karlin on purpose. He didn't think it was worth the risk.

"Twenty-six Mississippi, twenty-seven Mississippi, twenty-eight Mississippi…"

He could almost imagine Karlin wrinkling her adorable nose at him and announcing that he counted like an eight year old. The thought made him smile in spite of his worry.

The second that he hit thirty Mississippis, he sprang up from his mat and slowly snuck out into the darkness.

Just as he'd hoped, Cora was still well within sight, peering into the window of Bajwa's Jeep and fiddling with the door handle. As he'd suspected, it was locked, and the woman moved past it quickly.

He followed at a safe distance, wrapping his arms

around his chest tightly as the harsh wind turned the otherwise harmless raindrops into freezing barbs against his face and neck. Cora, on the other hand, hardly seemed bothered by the cold at all, even though she was wearing a cropped hoodie that revealed a couple inches of midriff.

He shuddered, imagining how the cold water would feel touching his belly button.

Totally yuck.

What was wrong with this girl?

Well, with any luck, he would find out soon enough. Despite his discomfort, he was thankful for the horrendous weather. Between the constant battering of the wind and rain, he could keep up with his quarry. There was no way she would be able to hear his hurried footsteps.

At first, she had seemed to be headed toward the main area of the retreat site, but it wasn't long before she veered off onto another, narrower path.

The trail grew more winding and hazardous as they went, and soon, Asher had completely lost not only his bearings but any sense of how much time had passed.

All speculation as to where they were going fell away as they went. All of Asher's focus went to putting one foot in front of the other, trusting that somehow, Cora would lead him to Karlin. If she didn't, he had no idea of plan B. If he didn't keep walking, he could become dangerously cold very quickly.

Aside from that, he had to stay close, for the simple reason that it was dark and he had no clue where he was going. It would be way too easy to walk off an unseen ledge and fall to his death.

Even Cora, who had looked invincible when they started their hike, was beginning to look miserable. Her wavy hair hung in dark strings over her shoulders, her jeans were plastered to her legs, and her face looked almost blue.

Still, she pressed on, until at last they came to a small clearing ringed by bushes and tall cacti. She paused for a moment and he did the same. Without movement, he found himself shaking so hard that he could feel his teeth clicking together.

Fortunately, she started walking again quickly, seemingly spotting something in the thick flora that he couldn't see from his current position.

Though he had paused just long enough to let her get a little ways ahead, he realized immediately that he'd made a grave mistake.

Up ahead, just around a tall clump of spiny cacti, was a red ATV.

Asher swallowed a bad word.

As usual, despite his best efforts to analyze the risks, he'd chosen the wrong course of action.

He should have subdued her immediately and demanded answers, not let her get away in hopes of her leading him to Karlin.

He was bigger than her, and as far as he could tell, she was armed with nothing aside from the syringe she'd already used on him.

He pulled out his gun and quickened his pace, trying desperately to catch up, but just when he thought he might be able to make up the distance, his foot slipped on a patch of muddy rock.

Those few seconds as he fell were all she needed to get onto the ATV, turn the key in the ignition, and race off into the wilderness.

CHAPTER
THIRTY-NINE

ASHER

Asher pushed his body up against a nearby rock and rested there, defeated.

He had managed to land directly on a patch of gravelly dirt, which had torn through his jeans and, apparently, the skin covering his knee cap.

Awesome.

It was bloody, but at least it didn't hurt. Much.

He could hear the ATV roaring somewhere in the distance. Even if he'd had full daylight and knew exactly where she was headed, there was no way he'd be able to catch up with her on foot.

He glanced around the clearing, once again trying and failing to get his bearings.

The rain was still falling steadily, and now that he'd stopped moving, he was getting cold fast.

How was he going to find Karlin?

He supposed he could try and find his way back to the main retreat site and call for help, but he might end up even more lost, and in any case, it was possible that Paul had made it there by now, anyway. Not that that meant help was on its way. There was a solid chance that the buildings would be locked, seeing as no one was supposed to be spending the night there.

On the other hand, there was the maintenance truck, assuming Paul could find it.

In any case, Asher hoped the older man hadn't dared to try and make it all the way to the Senera offices in this weather, and especially not before sunrise.

He pulled his arms against himself as tightly as he could, a long shiver wracking his body. All he wanted in the world was to hold Karlin in his arms.

Okay, that and a roaring bonfire, a thermos full of coffee, and his favorite totally dorky fleece Christmas pajamas. But still.

Less than twelve hours ago, he'd been certain that he and Karlin were almost out of this mess, and then everything had completely and utterly fallen apart.

"God, I don't know what your plan is, but this part of it? This sucks. I'm rating it at a zero out of ten, in fact. Karlin is probably in terrible danger right now, and there's nothing I can do, and I seriously need you to make the path clear to me, because I'm lost. Please. I just need you to cut me a break," he said.

Once upon a time, his mother would have scolded him for 'murmuring against the Lord as the Israelites did.'

She was right, but he wasn't sure he had the ability to care at the moment.

And then, as if on cue, a giant bolt of lightning struck the ground, impossibly close.

Asher yelped and shoved his body closer to the rock,

nearly falling a second time before steadying himself. The smell of ozone clung to the insides of his nostrils.

"Well played," he muttered in the general direction of the heavens. "A little dramatic, but totally well deserve–"

Before he could finish his sentence, thunder tore through the sky.

Asher's heart began to thump faster.

No.

He seriously could not have this happen.

Not now.

It was just noise. Nothing else. It couldn't hurt him.

Sure, that lightning bolt? That could have barbecued him instantly. But the thunder was just a sound. Nothing to be afraid of.

There was another lightning strike, and this time, the thunder followed almost immediately after it. The rain was coming down in freezing sheets now as the storm rested directly on top of where he now sat, helpless, clutching at the rock.

His head was swimming so much that it was all he could do to keep himself upright. His heart was pounding at a rapid clip, which didn't help with the sudden rush of dizziness.

He shouldn't be having a panic attack. He didn't *want* to have a panic attack.

He knew that thunder couldn't hurt him.

The problem was that his body didn't know that.

His body remembered that loud sounds meant terror, pain, and death.

His body remembered Afghanistan, no matter how hard he tried to forget.

KARLIN

The ancient futon was even more uncomfortable than it looked at first glance.

After spending ten minutes struggling to open it up flat, Karlin had given up and lay down anyway, her arm hopelessly squashed no matter what position she tried. Already, her spider paranoia was enough to have her scratching at her neck every thirty seconds.

She shivered and stared up at the ceiling.

Even with the help of the fire she'd made–admittedly, it probably wasn't a very good one–it was still extremely chilly. Worse, the fabric of the futon felt almost damp.

How long had she been here?

She kicked herself for forgetting her smartwatch on its charger that morning. It was impossible to trust her perception of the passing time.

Outside, thunder and lightning had joined the deluge of rain. If dawn was close, she had no way to tell. The windows revealed only blackness, lit by an occasional burst of blinding white.

She flinched with every strike, awaiting the enormous clash of noise that always followed. Once more, she longed for Axel's presence, even if she had no doubt he'd tease her about her fears. She'd happily accept a little ribbing if it meant she'd get to rest in his arms until the storm passed.

But Axel might not be coming. Help, in general, might not be coming. At least not for a while.

She scratched at an invisible spider on her neck again.

She couldn't just stay here and wait around for someone to save her. She had water and some hopefully edible food, but the firewood would last maybe one more night, if that, and then she'd be in an even worse position than she was now.

When morning came, she needed to get out of this cabin.

She twisted on the futon, freeing one arm and pinning the other beneath her body.

Even the little rest she'd had was enough to light a renewed fire within her, but she'd force herself to lay down a little longer.

Another lightning strike lit up the windows.

For less than a second, she could see the familiar clearing and the rocky hills that surrounded it, which were now slick with mud. Even if she somehow managed to break out of the cabin itself, getting out of the valley might prove even more difficult.

But she had to try.

"There's always a solution. You just have to find it," she said aloud.

One of her favorite professors from grad school always used to say that. He'd even added it to his email signature.

At first, she'd found the message to be corny, but over time, she'd learned to appreciate it. For the rest of her time at school, and afterwards at Senera, it had gotten her through many seemingly impossible projects. This one was no different.

She was smart. She could rely on herself, just as she always had.

She closed her eyes as another crash of thunder shook the cabin.

It was the biggest one yet, loud enough to leave a ringing in her ears. She curled her arms around her sides, trying and failing to ignore the pervasive chill that had taken hold of her bones.

She wanted to believe there was always a way forward, but in truth, she had never felt so helpless.

Maybe she couldn't always rely on herself.

Maybe that had always been a lie.

Before Axel came along, her world had been painfully, desperately lonely.

John needed her, but he wasn't capable of giving her the support she needed in return. Her parents were off in Florida, enjoying their retirement without a care in the world. Her childhood friends in Michigan had probably all forgotten she existed by now.

And whenever a colleague or anyone else had made even the slightest attempt at trying to get close to her, she'd always kept them at arm's length.

Because at least when she was alone, the only person who could fail her was herself.

ASHER

Asher pressed his hand to the rock behind him, forcing himself to notice the little details.

It was cold against his palm. Most of the surface was smooth, but near his pinky, he could feel a bit of grittiness that tugged at his skin despite the damp.

He was able to take a deep breath, and then another.

Okay, what else?

He closed his eyes as another flash of lightning lit the sky. He had to ignore the thunder. He had to focus on the rock.

He moved his hand up higher, noticing the way the formation grew steeper as it reached upward. It was huge, taller than him. It was solid and unyielding. When the thunder struck, it didn't shake.

He was okay.

He breathed again.

He could feel his heart slowing down as the panic attack abated.

He'd always thought the whole thing with touching the ground or feeling your abdomen expand in and out was dump therapy talk, but maybe the Veteran's Freedom Society had a point on this one.

Maybe.

Not that it was enough to do anything but push the pain aside temporarily.

No amount of grounding exercises or deep breathing or talking it out would bring Nico Delgado back.

He was dead in the ground, bombed to pieces at twenty years old, and it was all Asher's fault.

Lightning crashed again.

He couldn't afford to get lost in the shadows of his past.

For now, coping and suppressing would have to be enough.

He kept breathing, even as his body tensed in anticipation.

The thunder came a few seconds later, but he barely noticed it.

There was something else that cut through his terror.

He smelled smoke.

He looked around in the darkness. His night vision was even worse now thanks to the lightning, and it unsettled him, further destroying any remaining sense of direction he had.

He blinked quickly, trying to get rid of the starbursts

275

behind his eyes, but he had no idea where the smoke was coming from.

There were few trees here, but there was plenty of brush and shrubbery. Even in the rain, he knew that those could still burn if they got hot enough.

And lightning would certainly do the trick.

He pulled himself to his feet, ignoring the lingering sting of his torn knee. With a final touch of the rock, he set his jaw and started to walk forward. He was glad for the chance to focus on an enemy he could quantify instead of the demons in his head.

He had to find shelter. Thunder wasn't going to hurt him, but a brush fire certainly could, especially if the rain decided to let up.

With the next strike of lightning, he pressed his eyes shut hard, shielding them with his arm. After the thunder came, he opened them again.

He could see a little better, but not enough.

The smell of smoke caught on a gust of wind, filling his nostrils. Despite the danger, he found the smell oddly comforting.

The next time lightning hit, he was ready.

He kept his eyes wide open, using the half-second of light to survey the scene.

And to his amazement, he could see the top of the old cabin that Karlin had showed him up ahead.

There was no brush fire.

Thick, black smoke was pouring out of the chimney.

It was all he could do not to run toward it.

Instead, he walked slowly, not wanting to risk another fall. He knew there were several steep drops of rock ahead, and he'd have to navigate them using only the sporadic bursts of lightning to see.

He didn't know who was in the cabin.

It could be Paul, but it could also be Lily.

Still, it was his best shot. He desperately needed to warm up, and hopefully find something to wrap his wound with before it got infected.

As he began his descent down the slippery rocks into the little valley below, his heart began racing fast again.

This time, it wasn't his fear.

It was hope.

Karlin probably wasn't inside, but she could be. It could be her sitting there, warm and beautiful in the firelight.

And the very possibility was enough to drive him the rest of the way, even as the thunder hammered all around him.

CHAPTER
FORTY

ASHER

Lightning split the sky, flooding the valley with light as Asher approached the cabin.

An old chair was shoved under the doorknob on the outside, which was a good sign that Lily wasn't the one inside.

His heart soared.

Paul couldn't have locked himself in there.

It had to be her.

He yanked the chair free, but before he could open the door, he leapt backward, narrowly avoiding a flaming piece of kindling that Karlin had just swung directly at his head.

"Yo! Cool it with the stick!" he shouted, raising his hands in surrender.

He'd been expecting a warm welcome. Maybe even a kiss.

Oh well.

He smiled as he looked her over, relieved just to know

that she was safe.

She was missing her lab coat, and her outfit didn't look very warm, but aside from that, she looked just as stunning as ever.

And, judging by the swing that had almost connected with his face, she still had some strength to spare.

"I'm so, so sorry," Karlin stammered. "It was supposed to be a torch."

She leaned out of the cabin, tossing the dishcloth-wrapped stick out into the rain. The flame flickered against the sand for a moment before burning out, filling the air with yet more smoke.

"I'm surprised you managed to light it with whatever terrible fire you have going in there," Asher joked. "You can smell the smoke a mile away."

"Ha. Whatever. You're lucky I didn't knock you out."

Karlin was trying not to smile, but he could see how happy she was to see him. He wondered how long she'd been trapped in here alone, but before they caught up, he seriously needed to get dry.

"Are you going to invite me in? And maybe help me find something I can use to bandage my knee?"

She stepped back at last, allowing him to slip through the door before closing it behind them.

The fire in the woodstove was far from raging, but at least Karlin had managed to keep the smoke traveling in the generally correct direction. After the chill of the rain, the old building felt almost cozy.

They spent a few minutes rooting around the cabinets until they found a dust-covered roll of paper towel and used it to wrap Asher's leg as well as they could.

"You scared me, Axel. I thought you were Lily," Karlin said, collapsing onto one of the chairs. He followed suit, all thoughts of further banter forced immediately from his mind.

"Why did Lily lock you in here?"

He listened for several minutes as she recounted the events of the night, and then he took his turn doing the same. But when the moment came to tell her that Cora had mentioned some kind of ritual killing was about to take place, he hesitated.

He hated the thought of scaring her even more. She'd already been through so much stress. Then again, she deserved to know the extent of what they were dealing with.

Before he could figure out how to share the grim news, however, Karlin interrupted him. "What did Cora inject you with?"

"I have no idea. She just said it was a sedative."

Karlin pressed a finger to her lip.

Immediately, Asher could imagine the wheels turning.

"I'm confused. You're a small guy. It shouldn't have been difficult for her to figure out a large enough dose to put you to sleep. The real danger should have been giving you too much and accidentally killing you. Hmm."

Asher opened his mouth to tell her just what he thought of her calling him 'small,' but a second later, her eyes lit up.

"Wait. Wait. You did get the placebo dose of DX8, didn't you?"

"Uh, no. Somehow, it was switched with the real thing. I assumed you knew, considering I was high off my butt even before Lily kidnapped you."

Karlin's eyes grew wide.

"I had no idea! If I hadn't thought you were sober, I never would have gone outside with Lily in the first place and left you all alone. I just assumed you were trying to stay undercover."

Asher shrugged. "To be fair to you, my acting is pretty great."

He expected some kind of retort, but she hadn't seemed to have heard him.

Instead, she was looking off into space, a smile spreading across her face. "Well, that explains why the sedative didn't work like Cora planned. It acted as a trip killer instead."

"You know, I did notice that I started feeling better after the–"

He didn't even have a chance to finish his sentence. The woman was off in her own world already, smiling to herself.

"Fascinating," Karlin was saying excitedly. "Most of the sedative drugs we had in the lab shouldn't have worked. We hadn't really tested them thoroughly, but there was a lot of data to cross-reference, and I've been tinkering with that for years. Most of them have been tested against ayahuasca extensively, and the dimethyltryptamine that interacts with the 5-HT2A receptor is primary within the DX8 synthesis–"

That was it.

He couldn't wait any more.

He was going to kiss that gorgeous, infuriating dork and make sure she knew without a doubt how he felt about her.

This wasn't the right time, but fireworks and flowers were in short supply right now.

Asher leaned toward Karlin and cradled her jaw gently.

Before she had a chance to argue–or finish talking

about whatever incomprehensible science stuff was currently rattling around in her brain–he pressed his lips to hers.

Kissing her felt like he was high on DX8 all over again, but it was so, so much better.

His heart was thumping as her soft lips touched his, and when she reached up to stroke the back of his neck, he thought he was going to pass out right there.

The moment ended way too fast for his liking.

He sank back down into his own chair, grinning stupidly. Karlin was already narrowing her eyes at him, her cheeks going red.

"What was that? Seriously, you need to warn me before you–do that," she stammered.

"You interrupted me first."

She considered this for less than a second.

"Fine. I guess. But not with–not with *that*."

He formed his fingers into two circles and held them over his eyes as if they were glasses. "No, you went with telling me all about the blah, blah, blah, 123BXY Periodic Table."

For a second she looked so annoyed that he thought she might actually slap him, which of course only made him smile even more.

Goodness, she was pretty.

Even when–especially when–he got a glimpse of how brilliant and passionate she was.

Just as he was considering silencing her fury with another amazing kiss, a fresh bolt of lightning struck somewhere outside the cabin.

This one was close.

He could smell it.

There was no time to breathe deeply, or to touch the floor of the cabin, or even to pray.

The thunder boomed ferociously, rattling the old windows in their frames and making the light of the candle in the middle of the table flicker.

He gripped the edge of the chair until his knuckles were white, trying to ignore the fear that was currently trying to steal away his happiness at finally getting to kiss the girl of his dreams.

"Hey, are you okay?" Karlin asked, reaching over to rest a hand gently on his shoulder. "You're shaking."

He tried to shake his head no, but unfortunately, the rest of his body decided to shake at the same time.

"Here, have some water," she said, reaching over and grabbing a plastic bottle sitting nearby. He took several long swallows, all the while listening for the inevitable sound of the next lightning strike. This time, he wasn't going to be surprised.

By the time it came a minute or two later, he was breathing calmly and the shaking had passed.

"Sorry about that," he muttered, looking down at the table.

She reached over and pressed a fingertip against his chin until he looked up into her concerned blue eyes. "I'm pretty well acquainted with PTSD and other traumas," she said. "You have nothing to hide from me. I promise."

He wanted to tell her he didn't have either, but of course, that would have been a lie, and he chose instead to keep his mouth shut as she continued.

"I used to have a lot of panic attacks," she said softly, glancing toward the window as another nearby jolt of lightning shot through the sky. "They used to be really bad. Sometimes they'd happen at work, and I'd lock myself in the supply closet."

"That's awful, Karlin," he said, glad that the conversation was shifting away from his own problems. He hated the idea of her seeing him as weak, even if it was true. "I'm so sorry. Do you...want to talk about what caused them?"

He cringed at the way the sentence came out.

He wanted to be supportive, but apparently, the whole sharing-your-feelings thing was harder than he thought. He was used to leaping into action. Having to simply sit still and listen was a very different beast.

She offered him a weak smile. "Private security operative, Oscar-worthy actor, professional class clown, and a therapist too? Be still my heart."

For a brief moment, he considered silencing her with another kiss, but before he could, she continued, clearly trying to change the subject.

"Anyway, it's going to be dawn soon, I think," she said. "We need to get out of here. We need to get help. I hate the idea that Paul could be out in this storm somewhere."

She looked troubled, and he could see that the rims of her eyes had gone red. Clearly, her teasing words hid something deeper. He just hoped he could get her to share what it was.

He nodded. "We will, but let's just get warm for a little while longer."

The thunder was still coming every few minutes, and though it would be dangerous to go out in it again, especially when it was still dark, that wasn't his main reason for wanting to wait.

He didn't trust himself not to have another panic attack.

And if he lost control again out there at the wrong time, he could put both himself and Karlin in danger.

She didn't argue.

Instead, she inched her chair closer to his, leaned onto his shoulder, and started to cry.

KARLIN

Great. Just great.

Karlin pressed her face into Axel's shoulder, preferring another snot situation to having to look him in the eyes right now.

"Shh, sweetheart," he was saying softly. "Just cry. Just let it out. You'll feel better."

"I'm so sorry," she choked out after several long seconds, struggling to get the sobs under control. At the moment, she would have strongly preferred the solitude of the Senera main lab's supply closet.

"How many times have I cried in front of you? Or in your arms? It's getting ridiculous at this point."

"Five," he said without missing a beat. "But I'm not counting."

That got her attention.

She pulled back a little and looked up at him. "You literally are counting, though. You gave me a number."

He didn't argue.

Instead, he leaned down and kissed her, slow and gentle.

Even after getting drugged twice, traipsing through the desert for hours, and getting soaked in the rain, he still smelled way too good.

She didn't want the kiss to end.

Everything about it–everything about him–was pure

comfort, security, and another word that she was scared to name, even to herself.

She'd never met anyone like him before, that much she could say with certainty.

When he was close, she felt like she could actually breathe, like the heaviness of her past suddenly didn't seem so unbearable. It felt like a miracle.

So why was she still so scared to tell him everything?

Why did she hold back, when her heart was begging her to open up?

He pulled away at last, giving a contented sigh as he pulled his arms more tightly around her. Even though his clothes were wet, he still felt warm.

"You know, you are the most argumentative woman I have ever met in my entire life," he announced. "And I work with some serious contenders. Our head of security, Dolly? Yeah, she used to scare me, but she's a pussycat compared to you."

She might have tried to give him a playful smack, but he had her gripped too tightly against his chest. "Whatever. To be fair, you *were* counting my tears. I'm sorry that I'm such a mess."

He chuckled. "The Bible talks about that, actually."

"What?"

"There's a verse about God counting our tears. I think it's in the Psalms somewhere."

"Well, in that case, I guess I can't be too upset with you for counting mine. I mean...thank you. I appreciate that you care. Even if I'm a mess."

Axel cleared his throat, saying nothing for a long moment.

She snuggled in more closely, trying to warm up. The woodstove could probably use another couple of logs, but she wasn't going to let him get up right now. His body heat would have to suffice for the two of them.

"God is always listening, Karlin," he said gently.

"I know. I'm starting to see that. Even if I still have doubts."

He nodded. "I'm glad, but that's not all I wanted to say."

She said nothing.

For once, she didn't want to interrupt, to argue, or even to tease him. After everything they'd been through together, she was questioning her lack of faith more than ever. She was far from having it all figured out, but maybe John was right about a whole lot more than she'd ever given him credit for.

"We can always talk to God, but the Bible also tells us to confess our sins to one another. I think that also applies to other burdens we carry. I think part of the reason that you struggle with faith isn't that you can't believe in a God who loves you, but that you don't want to be part of His people. You don't want to rely on the church. You want to do everything on your own, because if you let people care about you, you also risk letting them let you down or leave you."

Karlin stiffened.

That was a gut punch.

But she wasn't sure she could actually deny anything he'd said.

Axel let go of her, pulling back a little and fiddling with the candle in the middle of the table. As much as she loved his touch, she was thankful for a moment to breathe.

"God promises to never leave us or forsake us," Axel continued. "And part of trusting in that promise is trusting Him to work in the lives of those around us, to bring everything together for our good. Even when people are weak. Even when people fail. Even when people make mistakes that hurt us."

Karlin swallowed hard, remembering.

Her parents had let her down. As much as she wanted to pretend she had moved on, the feeling of abandonment and rejection always stung.

But if she was being honest, John had let her down worse than they ever had.

His mistakes hurt more because she expected more from him. He was her big brother. He was a Christian. He loved her.

And still, he had failed, and his failure had left her with deep scars that she wasn't sure would ever go away.

She had to tell Axel the full story of what had happened. If she didn't tell somebody the truth about that day, she was going to go insane.

But before she could say anything, he held up the photo of John that she'd left on the table earlier.

His face was white, and his hands were trembling.

CHAPTER
FORTY-ONE

ASHER

t was all Asher could do to stay where he was, grasping the picture in his fingertips.

He had never wanted to run away so badly in his life.

He didn't care about the thunder, or the chill of the rain, or anything else. Nothing could possibly be more terrifying than facing Karlin with what he had to say.

Nothing.

But a saner part of him knew that it was already too late for that.

Apparently, looking at a photograph could be enough to change his life in an instant.

This was a surprise to him, but God had always known. He had to trust in that.

He had to take his own advice to heart.

"Axel, what's going on?" Karlin said, reaching out and taking the photo from him. "You look like you just saw a ghost."

The words she chose felt like a physical blow.

A ghost was exactly what he'd seen. A ghost he'd been trying not to think about for the past fourteen years of his life.

"It's–it's complicated," he started, annoyed at his own cliched words as he tried and failed to think of any possible way he could soften the blow.

So many clues were falling into place now.

Little details he could have probably put together had he been looking for them, but of course, he hadn't been.

Not until now.

"What? Axel, chill. It's just a picture of my brother, not some guy I'm in love with. I like having him with me, that's all."

She was clearly trying to joke, but her voice was wavering. He had already scared her. The least he could do was to spit the truth out as quickly as possible.

"I wish it was," he said, shaking his head as tears began to prick at the corners of his eyes.

"What?"

"This is a photo of Rome, isn't it? Rome Collins...not McKenna."

Karlin's brow knit in confusion.

"Yeah, we have different dads," she said slowly. "His is even more messed-up than mine, if you can believe that. Ran off while our mom was pregnant. But how did you know his nickname? I haven't heard anyone call him that in years. Probably because he isn't so 'built' anymore."

Asher smiled through the tears that were now impossible to hold back.

Rome, the gym junkie, who didn't get built in a day.

"I knew him," he admitted, struggling to say the words.

He had to get this out.

There was no running from it. Even if she hated him for it, this beautiful, wonderful woman deserved to know the truth now that he did.

"I–I was with him in Afghanistan. He was part of my platoon."

His voice broke as the memories came flooding back, choking him, drowning him, threatening to pull him under right then and there.

It had been years since he'd cried about that day, but here he was, sobbing as Karlin tried to console him. The tender touch of her fingers against his shoulders felt like he was being burned.

"Please don't touch me," he snapped. "I don't deserve it."

"Axel–"

The sorrow within him was beginning to simmer into rage.

Rage at the war, rage at the Taliban, rage at the United States government, rage at everything and everyone that led him to an isolated outpost in the middle of that desert hell.

"I was the one who fell asleep on watch that night!" he nearly shouted at her. "I was supposed to be paying attention. I was supposed to be stopping people at the gate."

Karlin shrank back like she'd been slapped, but he continued on, unable to stop the angry words that were pouring from him freely now.

It wasn't everyone else he was angry at.

It was himself.

He had no one else to blame but himself and his own incredible capacity for messing up.

"I knew better. I'd been out on exercise, sleeping on the

ground for a couple of days beforehand. I was way too exhausted by the time we got back to base to take a shift on watch. but I was too proud to ask for help when my partner didn't show up. I thought the Red Bull my mom had sent would be enough to keep me awake, but it wasn't."

He kept waiting for Karlin to yell at him, or slap him, or do anything at all.

Anything would have been better than the way she was staring at him now, her eyes filled with hurt.

But still, she said nothing.

Her silence was too much to bear.

"It's my fault that IUD made it into camp," he snapped. "It's my fault that Nico Delgado was blown to pieces. It's my fault that Rome ended up with PTSD. It's my fault that I was never there for him, or for anyone else in our platoon, because I was too much of a coward to face them. It's all my fault."

Karlin got to her feet and walked over to the wood-stove, picked up a piece of firewood, and tossed it inside.

"I finished out the rest of my contract with a different unit, and left as soon as I could," he continued, desperate to fill the silence. She wasn't even looking at him now. If it wasn't for the small amount of space between them, he could believe she hadn't heard him at all.

"By that point, Gabe had already started Forge Brothers Security, so I had a job to come home to. I ran away and never looked back. I never checked up on any of my old platoon mates...I just wanted to forget my past. I never thought–Karlin, I had no idea that Rome was your brother until I saw that picture. I am so sorry. Please."

But no matter how much he tried to stammer out an

292

apology, she stayed where she was, staring into the flames without a word.

KARLIN

Karlin's body seemed to be moving of its own volition. She felt like someone else was putting on her wet shoes and opening the door of the cabin.

She was a thousand miles away, too angry and too hurt to think very much about what she was doing.

But she knew one thing.

If she didn't keep moving, she was going to break.

Axel was saying something, getting up and trying to bar her from leaving, but she ignored him and shoved her way past.

It was windy and raining, and there was still no hint of the coming sun, but she observed these details with indifference.

Her nerves were already burning with anxiety, waiting for something terrible to happen.

She didn't feel the cold, the damp, or anything else.

She was too caught up with remembering.

Remembering that day and the other cabin.

John's cabin.

Lightning flashed, and she made her way across the valley, her feet carrying her over crevices in the rock, her body on autopilot.

Axel was still talking, still pleading, but she was getting ahead of him now. She knew this area better than he did.

She smiled to herself as more thunder crashed.

The first time she'd discovered this cabin, several years after starting this job with Senera, she'd hated it.

It reminded her too much of that day.

But after a while, her feelings had changed.

She'd never spent any time in it or attempted to tidy it up, but in the back of her mind, she liked that it was there. If the time came to run, she liked knowing there was somewhere nearby that she could go.

She'd never told John that she understood now why he'd chosen a cabin of his own, off the grid, away from everyone and everything. Away from the life that was just too painful for him to live. The perfect place for running, and just as broken and damaged as the person who sought refuge within its crumbling log walls.

She'd never told him she understood.

But she did.

"Karlin, please, wait," Axel was calling from somewhere behind her. She looked up at the steep rock path ahead and started to climb, not bothering to look back. Even in the dark, she knew this would lead to the main retreat site. She didn't know what she'd do when she got there, but some detached part of her logical mind figured it was the logical next step.

The rain was worse now, she realized.

As she clambered up the steep path, she could feel her feet slipping every minute or two, slowing her progress.

It was stupid to be out here. Her logical mind knew that, too. But to go back? To turn to him, after everything he'd just said? She couldn't do it. She wouldn't.

"I promise I won't try and stop you from leaving," Axel called up to her. "Just wait for the storm to pass first. Please."

She paused where she stood, her fingers aching as she gripped a nearby branch, trying to keep her balance as anger coursed through her. It felt so much better than the pain and hollowness she'd been feeling.

She turned to look down at Axel.

He was trying desperately to catch up with her, but every time lightning flashed and thunder struck, he paused, touching the rocks with his palms. One of his shoes had come halfway off, and she could see blood leaking through the paper towel they'd used to try and bandage his knee.

"Let the storm pass, huh?" she called out, her voice thick with bitterness. "That's how you deal with everything, isn't it? Let the storm pass. Let the good times roll. Make your jokes and goof off and live your life, all while John—"

She struggled to get the rest of the words out. The rain mingled with her tears as sobs clutched at her throat.

She was so sick of crying over one man already.

Two was a real kick in the face.

Axel was gaining on her easily now that she'd stopped, but she was too tired to keep moving. Going back to the cabin seemed too difficult, too. Everything did.

"Just stay there, okay?" he was saying, his voice gentle, like she was a frightened desert hare that was going to bolt at any moment.

If he was smart, he'd realize that, if anything, she was a copperhead.

"I'm coming."

She watched him through tears as he made his way up the final stretch of the path.

She was too exhausted to run away. She was too exhausted to fight, too, but all she wanted to do was to lash out, anyway.

The anger and pain was too heavy to keep inside of her

anymore. Her head hurt, and her heart felt like it might give up on beating if she didn't calm down. Every part of her was determined to let him take on the wrath she'd been burying for so many lonely years.

Axel was closer now, close enough to see the way he trembled a little with each clap of thunder, but they didn't seem to be slowing him down anymore.

Maybe he was good at running away. But she had to admit it—he was also pretty good at pushing forward.

By the time he reached her, she couldn't bring herself to yell at him.

She wanted to, but something inside of her had gone quiet and still.

Even her tears had dried. Somehow, the rain had slowed a little, though she doubted the reprieve would last.

She wasn't crying.

But Axel was.

When the lightning struck, she could see the redness in his eyes. He kept swiping at his tears with his soaking wet sleeve.

"Karlin, I'm so sorry," he said again. He'd said it so many times already, but the words hadn't lost their meaning. He sounded just as sincere as he had the first time, not that she'd wanted to listen. "I don't think there's any way I can ever apologize enough, and I don't expect your forgiveness, but please just…hear me."

His voice broke on the final words, and her heart broke right along with it.

She slid to the ground, resting against a muddy rock, already so wet and uncomfortable that she didn't think it could get much worse.

Even the wind seemed to be listening now.

It was still blowing across the desert, but it wasn't as fierce as it had been a few moments ago. The lightning and thunder continued, but more slowly, as though they were taking turns to eavesdrop in between their bursts of fury.

And finally, Karlin knew beyond a shadow of a doubt that it was time to speak.

CHAPTER
FORTY-TWO

ASHER

Asher sat down next to Karlin, keeping a couple of feet between them.

He didn't want to say anything, didn't want to disrupt her thoughts.

Finally, she was talking to him.

Her fury toward him—as well-deserved as it was—seemed to have slipped away.

"John's trauma from the war didn't just affect him," she was saying, her voice soft. "It rippled out into everything around him. His job, his friends, everything else in his life was damaged, too. I was damaged. I *am* damaged."

Her words broke his heart.

All he wanted to do was hold her, maybe even remind her that God wanted to take all of that hurt and redeem it, but he knew that it wasn't the time. It was his turn to be silent now.

She was right.

He was good at waiting for the storms to pass, running

away from things that hurt, trying to make jokes instead taking real responsibility for his mistakes.

But he wasn't going to do it anymore.

God had forgiven him, but he had to forgive himself.

But before he could do that, he had to face every ugly piece of what he had done.

He had to hear whatever Karlin had to say, even though he was sure it would break his heart all over again.

"After Nico was killed, John stopped writing me letters. We used to write back and forth all the time. I'd send him care packages like our mom should have, and he'd tell me what he was thinking. A lot of those early letters had been happy, despite the hardships."

Asher could believe it. War was hell, but the brotherhood that was forged within it was second only to the bond he shared with his brothers through blood.

"I assume he mentioned you, actually, but it was probably by some dumb nickname I never picked up on," she continued.

He had to cut in. "They called me Mosquito back then. And I tell you this within the Cone of Silence, by the way."

For the first time in way too long, Karlin actually smiled, and it was even more beautiful than he remembered.

"Why? Because you're annoying?" she teased.

"Shockingly, no. It's part of a lyric from the song *Smells Like Teen Spirit*. I don't even like Nirvana, but I guess I *look* like a guy who would like Nirvana, so it stuck. Mosquito. But please go on."

Karlin cleared her throat and wrapped her arms more tightly around her chest.

He felt shivery and freezing himself and considered offering to go back down to the cabin to finish this conversation, but he couldn't risk interrupting her any more than he already had.

Whatever she was trying to tell him, he could tell it had been burdening her for a very long time.

He didn't want her to carry her pain alone anymore.

Not if he could help it. If she could handle the cold a little longer, he would happily do the same.

"Anyway, after the bombing, I was lucky if I got a quick note every six months," she continued. "I was worried about him so much. When he finally was able to come home–by then, I was in Amarillo, and he decided to start a construction job with another ex-military friend over in Lubbock–I was actually relieved. I thought things would get better."

"They didn't?"

She shook her head, sadness clouding her face once more.

"No. Everything fell apart. I'd go to visit him, and he'd be drinking. Then he was smoking weed, and probably doing other things, too. He got fired from his job, and he wouldn't really let me help financially at that point, so I'm not sure how he was surviving. Probably selling drugs along with using them."

She paused again, and Asher risked scooting toward her, close enough to rest a hand on her shoulder. He could feel her taking a long, slow breath.

"He was living in this shabby old cabin at the time, about forty minutes outside of town. It had solar panels and a well and all the rest of the prepper-waiting-for-the-apocalypse stuff. Clearly, he didn't want to be near people, but he did let me visit. I tried to get down to Lubbock as often as I could, even just to check on him. One day, I decided to stop by without telling him first. I'd randomly gotten a Friday off when they had to paint my lab."

Asher rubbed Karlin's back, dread pooling in his stomach. Several possibilities for where this story was going rose in his mind, and he didn't like any of them.

"When I pulled into his driveway, I remember knowing immediately that something was wrong. I couldn't explain why, or how, but I knew. John and I technically aren't twins, but we've always had that sixth sense about one another. So I guess I shouldn't have been surprised when I found him on the kitchen floor, surrounded by oxy tablets, but I was."

Asher's gut twisted. "Karlin, that's–"

"You know the funny thing?" she continued. "I actually didn't panic in that moment. I remember this rush of calm seemed to wash over me. I had cell phone service, thankfully, but the 9-1-1 operator warned me the ambulance would take a while. I put the phone down and started CPR.

"It was only after doing that for a while that I started to freak out a little. I knew that his chances of survival were low, and his chances of surviving without catastrophic brain damage were even lower. My arms were in so much pain. I kept going, long past the point where I thought I had nothing left to give. I kept digging deeper, reaching for one more minute of strength, and then one more second. I don't know where the strength to keep going came from, but it was there. I felt it. One second at a time."

Asher wanted to tell her that God was the obvious answer to that question, but he knew it probably wasn't the best time. Especially considering the fact that God wouldn't have needed to intervene at all if he hadn't screwed up, gotten Nico killed, and then left John and the rest of their team to face their own trauma without his support.

"How long did you perform CPR?" he asked instead.

"I found out later that it was twenty-six minutes. His chances weren't good from the start. We don't know how long he was out before I even got there. But…somehow, he made it. He recovered. The doctors all said it was a miracle."

Karlin's words were happy, but she couldn't hide the sadness in her eyes.

"Just because he survived doesn't mean it wasn't a traumatic experience for him. And for you," Asher ventured.

"So much of my life seems to hinge on that day," she admitted. "There's before, and then there's after. Before, I was worried about my big brother. But after? It was–it is– like I'm living on edge every moment of my life. Every time the phone rings, I expect the voice on the other end to say he overdosed again. That he's suffered brain damage. That he's dead."

"Like the other day."

"Exactly. It wasn't the first overdose since the Big One, either. Does it make me a bad person to say it makes me angry?" Karlin didn't wait for him to answer. "Maybe. But I can't help it. It does."

Asher shook his head. "Dealing with an addict has to be hard. I know you're doing all you can to help him make sure he has the resources he needs to stay healthy, and that hasn't exactly been good for you, considering you've been stuck working at Senera."

"That's true," she admitted. "But honestly, his faith is the most frustrating part of it all. I know that his belief in God is sincere, so why does he keep screwing up? Why does he make such dumb decisions? If God is real, I just wish He'd hurry up and help my brother."

Asher wanted to explain why she was wrong, to refute her objections, to act like he had all of the answers, but he didn't.

For now, he just sent up a silent prayer of thanks. Karlin didn't have to go through all of her troubles alone.

God had always been there with her, and now he'd be there, too.

KARLIN

Karlin's words hung in the air, the silence interrupted by the occasional strike of lightning. The wind had died down quite a bit, and the rain had slowed, but the reprieve didn't feel comforting. The whole valley felt like it had simply paused to take a breath.

"Can I hold you?" Axel asked beside her.

His voice was so gentle, so unlike his usual way of doing things. It melted her heart in an instant.

"You kind of already are," she pointed out.

He shook his head. "No. I need to really hold you. I...I need you to know."

She didn't ask what he meant. She was too afraid to.

All at once, he'd swept her up against his chest again. She tilted her chin upward just in time to meet his lips as he leaned down to kiss her. Feeling his lips against hers spread warmth straight through to her toes, and she could sense that his longing went deeper than either of them would dare to say aloud. But there was a gentleness mingled with the hunger. A promise that a kiss would remain only a kiss. A promise that...

She felt her breath catch in her chest as she let the kiss

come to an end, resting her head against his chest as he stroked her hair.

She realized she knew the words she wanted to share with him. They terrified her, but they were difficult to hold inside, all the same.

Ever since the day she'd first called him up on a Sunday afternoon, for better or for worse, she'd managed to show him all of her. All of her blame, bitterness, and ugliness. Perhaps most difficult of all, she'd shown him her weakness.

And none of it had phased him. All of it seemed to have only made him care about her even more.

It was hard to believe it could be true, but everything about his embrace made her want to believe.

"We need to go inside and warm up for a second, I think," Axel said. She shivered a little as he got to his feet, taking her hand and guiding her up from the rock. "Before the fire goes out. The sun should be up soon, too."

She followed him quietly, back down the steep rock and into the little cabin, still deep in the winding caverns of her thoughts. The fire had burned down somewhat, but it was still much warmer than being outside. Axel was right. Despite the moment they'd just shared, they were still in a precarious situation, and they had to be smart.

The two of them were lost in their own thoughts for several minutes as they curled up on the old couch, trying to soak in all of the heat they could from the smoldering flames.

Karlin's mind kept wandering back to Lily, replaying everything she'd said over and over again. How could she have missed so much, even when the truth had been right in front of her?

Maybe she just didn't want to believe it.

Maybe she'd been blind to Dana's identity because, deep down, she wanted to be.

She didn't want to face the tragedy of Amira's death, to keep reliving that guilt. It was so much easier when her ghosts stayed dead and gone.

"We can't get too comfortable," Axel muttered next to her, already sounding half asleep. "Paul needs us–"

But a sound from somewhere outside interrupted him mid-sentence.

Karlin sat up straight, instantly on alert. "What was that?"

With a finger pressed to his lips, Axel got up and headed over to the door, opening it just a crack. The sound came again, louder this time.

"Look," he said, gesturing for her to follow. She did so, and the two of them stepped out onto the rotting porch. She could see nothing but dark desert. For a long moment they listened to nothing but the rhythmic pattering of rain.

And then it came again.

Axel gave a nearly imperceptible nod.

There was no mistaking it this time. No convincing herself that it was coyotes or anything else.

The sound that had haunted her since she'd arrived at the retreat was louder now. And it was unmistakably and terrifyingly human.

CHAPTER
FORTY-THREE

ASHER

A sher had always thought that 'bone chilling' was a really weird way to describe something.

But now?

He couldn't think of anything else that explained the way the sounds made him feel. It was something deeper than just fear. There was a wrongness to the human voices, as though they had somehow mingled with something else.

Something dark. Something evil.

He wanted to call the sound chanting, but the voices occasionally shifted into yelling and cheering before changing back again. How had he ever convinced himself that this was anything natural?

Then again, it had never been so loud before now.

"I've heard this before," Karlin said as the yelling rose and crested once more. "I thought it was an animal or something. It always stopped just when I thought for sure it had to be human."

"Me too," Asher agreed. "In hindsight, the truth seems pretty obvious."

The side of Karlin's mouth pulled up in a half-smile. "The cult?"

"You can't seriously still think I'm being paranoid."

"Not at all," Karlin admitted. "I actually heard the sounds once when I was with Lily and Cora. Lily tried to convince me they were nothing, including assuring me that her brother worked with the sheriff. At the time, I thought I remembered her mentioning she was an only child, but I forgot to double-check on her story."

Asher sighed.

"There's a lot we missed," he said, "and I'm the one who should have known better. I'm sorry."

"Is there anything else we haven't accounted for?" Karlin asked.

"Kind of," Asher admitted. "I didn't want to freak you out, but you need to know. Cora told me that she had to get rid of me temporarily—"

"Lily said the same thing."

"Cora also told me why."

That got Karlin's attention. She didn't look thrilled with him for not telling her, which he supposed he fully deserved.

Especially considering the painful secrets she'd been willing to share about her own past. "I'm sorry, what? I thought it was for some creepy ritual."

He nodded and let out a long breath. "I mean, yeah, but she told me that you and I would be fine because only one person had to die tonight."

He expected her to look afraid, or maybe to yell at him for not sharing this information sooner, but to his surprise, she did neither.

307

Instead, she reached down and took off one of her shoes, shaking out a couple of tiny rocks before shoving it back onto her foot.

"No more fooling around. We have to find them. We have to stop this. Right now."

Asher reached up and placed his hand firmly on her arm. "No. *I* have to stop this. This is what I'm trained to do."

He tried not to think about the times he'd failed, making some foolish mistake, or worse, starting to panic and putting his team or a client at risk.

But he'd succeeded a whole lot of times, too. And this time, he was especially determined. Messing up simply was not an option.

Not when it came to keeping Karlin safe and putting an end to the nightmare they were currently trapped in.

"You can't do this by yourself," she argued. "You need backup."

"Ideally," he agreed, pulling out the handgun that remained holstered to his ankle. "But in this case, this is the backup I have available. It will be enough."

Karlin opened her mouth to argue, but before she could, a jagged bolt of lightning raced across the sky, followed by another clash of thunder. The wind was picking up, too, joining in the storm's renewed ferocity. They were protected by the roof of the cabin's porch, but just beyond it, the rain was now coming down in thick sheets.

"What if you have another panic attack?" she asked, her voice apologetic.

"I might," he admitted without hesitation. "But that doesn't mean I'm putting you in harm's way just so you can hold my hand and tell me the scary noises won't hurt me."

He stepped off of the porch steps and onto the ground.

And at that very moment, a rush of water began flowing over the tops of his shoes.

"Axel!" Karlin screamed, pointing toward the hill.

"On second thought," he said, reaching out to grab her hand, "you're coming too. Move!"

KARLIN

There was no chance for either of them to speak.

Karlin followed Axel at a run, the entirety of her focus dedicated to remaining upright as the mud at her feet grew thicker and thicker.

Up ahead, sticks, brush, and other debris were rushing down the hills that led into the valley, carried in a flood of brown liquid.

It was surreal how quickly the water had risen, racing over sand and rock, submerging everything in its path in filthy sludge. Bushes were yanked from weak roots, toppling over and mingling with the rest of the deluge as it continued to flow downhill.

"Come on!" Axel yelled, shoving her forward until she was in front of him. "Run!"

She could see what he was looking at immediately.

Up and to their right, maybe seventy feet ahead, she could see a steep ridge of rock that was still wet, but mercifully free of the slick mud that now covered the floor of the valley.

Allowing Axel to support her body from behind, she rushed toward it and began clambering up the stone, still managing to slip on the craggy surface thanks to the pouring rain. Her arms were aching as she gripped a sturdy-looking bush overhead, allowing it to take some of her weight as she pulled herself up and onto a flat plateau.

She helped Axel up behind her as best she could, only then pausing to rest, her chest heaving as she collapsed hard onto the stone ground.

"You okay?" Axel asked, but she barely heard him.

Her attention was focused behind where he stood.

The valley below was filled with churning mud. The cabin was already half buried, and the entire front porch had been torn away by the force of the water.

Karlin felt suddenly rooted in place, shaking in the cold as her adrenaline began to wear away. "If we hadn't–" she stammered, struggling to get the words out. "If we hadn't heard those noises outside and decided to move–"

"But we did move," Axel said firmly, reaching over and giving her hand a squeeze. "God saw us. He protected us, even using the evil of this cult to do it, because He's in control. And hopefully He's using us to save someone else's life tonight. I need to keep moving."

She couldn't argue with his reasoning. Not after what they had just survived.

"Fine. But I'm still coming with you," she said.

This time, he didn't bother to argue.

"I think the voices were coming from this direction," he said instead. "Hopefully, the desert wind isn't playing any tricks on us tonight."

ASHER

The lightning and thunder had stopped, and the lingering

rain slowed once more to a gentle patter as they wound their way through the wild, flood-torn desert.

Asher's knee still hurt, but it was manageable, and now that the wind had let up, the chill of his damp clothes felt a lot more bearable. Karlin was keeping up with him easily, and if she was uncomfortable or exhausted, her face didn't show it. Her blue eyes were filled with pure determination.

To the east, he could see that the sky was beginning to lighten just a little, though as far as he could tell, the coming sunrise was still shrouded in heavy cloud. Still, so long as they didn't encounter another flash flood, he could handle a little gloom.

In the distance, they could see a building that Karlin didn't recognize, and every so often, the chanting and shouting sounds started up again.

He felt confident that the ritual sacrifice had not yet been completed.

Somehow, some way, he could feel in his heart that the person Cora and Lily were planning to kill, whoever she was, was still alive.

He had to believe that was true. He couldn't bear the thought that he could be putting Karlin in more danger for nothing.

Part of him was lost in worry, wondering about what was to come, but a bigger part was just thankful that this endless night was almost over.

However this ended, it was going to end.

And so long as he kept Karlin safe, he would call it a victory.

That was his only prayer now as they walked together in silence, Karlin's hand gripped firmly in his own.

CHAPTER
FORTY-FOUR

KARLIN

"Whoa," Axel said, stopping short beside her. "Did this place used to be a prison or something?"

Karlin knew exactly what he meant. The sun had finally risen, and despite the lingering clouds, she could finally see in detail what the compound in front of them looked like.

It was made up of several small concrete buildings surrounding a larger one in the center. There were at least three guard towers that she could see, but there was no indication that anyone was inside of them. Were it not for the sounds that were now emanating from the central building, as well as the handful of ATVs that she could see parked nearby, she would have assumed that the place was abandoned.

It seriously gave her the creeps.

"Ooh, listen. They have drums now," Axel said, smiling as he started forward again. "That's good news."

"Why? I thought your band already had a drummer. You," she joked.

"You know full well that the band is part of my cover," he retorted. "My true passion is listening to music. Actually learning to play it seems way too hard, and trust me, no one wants to hear me sing."

"You just keep getting better, don't you? Man of my dreams–"

Without missing a beat, he closed the space between them and quieted her up with a kiss.

Despite the imposing structure before them and the eerie drumbeats coming from inside, the moment felt almost romantic. Axel had a way of making that happen. It was honestly pretty impressive.

"Anyway, as I was saying," he said, gesturing for her to keep walking. "It's good that they're drumming. I don't think they were drumming before."

She caught on to where he was going immediately. "It's a change in the pattern, which probably means they might be actually performing their scary murder ritual now."

"Exactly!" Axel crowed.

She gave him a look. "There's something seriously wrong with you. You know that, right?"

"I'm going to scout up ahead a bit. I want you at least a hundred feet behind me." He drew the gun from its holster and clicked off the safety. "Oh, and be quiet or I'll have to kiss you again."

"Ooh, so scary."

"See you in a second. Be careful."

In a certain way, despite the teasing smile he gave her that totally melted her into goo, he kind of did scare her a little. He was the picture of competence now, sneaking along the side of the building, his elbow bent as he raised his gun. She wouldn't want to be on his bad side, that was for sure.

She waited as he slowly made his way along the wall in front of them, his eyes alert as he scanned the area.

But just as she was about to start following behind him, she saw him come to a stop. Her heart pounded so loudly that she swore she could hear it in her ears, but when she looked around, she saw nothing.

The desert behind them was so empty it was almost peaceful. Birds had begun their morning songs, and the sky no longer seemed to be threatening anything worse than a few clouds.

There was nothing that should have made him stop. But there he was, pressed against the wall, his hands gripping the gun so tightly that she could see the white of his knuckles even at a distance.

Her stomach sank as realization dawned.

He was having another panic attack, and if he didn't come out of it soon, they would be in serious trouble.

ASHER

Asher pressed his face against the cool concrete wall.

He wanted to scream at the top of his lungs, but of course, he knew that he couldn't.

Years of frustration were bubbling over now, mingling with his terror.

"Seriously God? Seriously?" he said quietly, not wanting Karlin to hear his anger at the Lord, but at the same time, not really caring if she did.

It wasn't like there was any chance she was going to stay where he told her to, so now she was exposed like he was, which just gave him one more panicky thing to panic about.

Just perfect.

"I learned my lesson, okay?" he continued in a whisper, slamming his free hand against the wall. It made a dull, ineffectual thumping sound. He hadn't even managed to make himself feel pain. "I've never even been scared of drums before. I actually *like* listening to loud drums. Is this a sign? Because I hear you loud and clear. I'm sorry I'm out here in the field. I'm sorry I didn't listen last time."

He didn't want to think about the recent fiasco he'd accidentally caused on one of their last cases, a kidnapping that brought him and Ben to South Padre Island.

He should have told Gabe the truth, that he'd been struggling with panic attacks for years, but he hadn't. He hadn't wanted to be held back at the office while his brothers had all the fun.

It was clear to him now how prideful and stupid he'd been. And it was way too late to do anything about it. All he could do was hope that God's mercy would be granted. He didn't deserve it, but Karlin did.

And so did whoever it was that the cult was trying to murder within these walls.

CHAPTER
FORTY-FIVE

KARLIN

Karlin rushed along the wall, trying not to stumble on the rocks and other debris littered all over the ground. Finally, she reached Axel, who was standing in place, muttering something to himself. Pity swelled within her chest. As much as it saddened her to see him like this, it had to be so much worse for him to *let* her see him.

"Hey," she said, pressing a hand gently to his back. He stiffened, but didn't pull away. Then again, he didn't turn toward her, either.

"I guess this desert keeps reminding me of the other one," he said flatly. "I'm sorry this keeps happening. I'll be okay in a second. Just gotta keep breathing and remembering that I'm standing on solid ground."

She wrapped her arms around him from behind as best she could, feeling the shudder in his chest as air rushed in and out of his lungs.

"I hope you know that none of this changes anything

about how I feel about you," she said. "If anything, I'm thankful to see more of who you are."

Finally, he turned toward her, pulling her into his chest before she had a chance to try and look into his eyes. "More than just a pretty face?" he joked.

"More than just the class clown."

"I'll take it." They waited like that for several long seconds. She could feel his heartbeat beginning to slow and his breathing to even out. But that didn't mean her own fears would pass so easily. What if the same thing happened again five minutes from now?

"What happened in Afghanistan was a tragic mistake," she said after a while. "I don't blame you, and I don't blame you for struggling with the consequences of that trauma now. But I do think we're in over our heads. We should run and get help before we get ourselves killed."

For a moment, she thought that he might actually agree with her.

The thought of running away was so tempting, especially now that the sun was beginning to bathe the desert with light. She could feel the hints of a warm day ahead. They could get away from here, and with what they knew now, they could take down not just Senera, but Lily and Cora and their cult, as well.

Instead, Axel leaned back and looked down at her, cupping her jaw gently in his hands. "We can't do that, Karlin," he said firmly. "If there's any chance that the sacrificial victim is still alive, I need to save them. I need to do it for Nico. And for Rome."

"You might have another panic attack."

He nodded. "I might, which is why you should leave. Go for help. Let me handle this."

She was smart enough to know that, logically, he was

right. It was the best thing to do. But she also knew her heart well enough to realize that leaving him was absolutely not an option.

"I promise I'll wait to follow you until it's safe."

He shook his head. "Promise to pray for me."

"I will," she said.

God had clearly been with them when they'd escaped the cabin just in time for it to be struck with a flash flood. Maybe He'd been there all along.

Axel leaned down and kissed her again.

A few moments later, he was pushing on ahead, gun raised as he slipped silently along the wall.

ASHER

"Third time's the charm," Asher said to himself as he jiggled the knob of yet another locked door.

With a slight groan, he pressed on. There was another metal door up ahead, and this one had a few boxes leaning against the wall beside it. Maybe that was promising.

He could feel the sun beginning to warm his back now.

Even at this early hour, it was obvious that it was going to be a hot day for Amarillo in late October.

The same desert that had become a life-threatening nightmare mere hours ago would transform into something beautiful. Flowers would peek out in search of the light. Mineral veins would glitter in their barren red stones. Beauty would follow the darkness and gloom, and shine all the more brightly for it.

Maybe that was promising, too.

He stopped in front of the door and leaned down to peer into the tops of the cardboard boxes. They were filled with cans of Pepsi, which was totally not what he expected a bunch of cult members to drink, but whatever.

He paused to get Karlin's attention, pointing at the door. She gave him a thumbs-up from her position. Shockingly, she'd kept her promise, and was staying safely out of the way. Hopefully, she'd continue to keep it.

The door swung inward easily, and he kept his gun carefully ahead of him as he slipped out of the growing sunshine and into a shadowy, slightly musty-smelling room. He could hear the drumbeats again, mingled with the occasional yell and round of chanting, but it was quieter now. Somehow, that made it even creepier.

He moved through several rooms–the cult clearly used this area for cargo and storage, or maybe the prior inhabitants of the building had simply left it that way–and headed in the direction of the noises. He could hear Karlin behind him somewhere, but he didn't want to stop and direct her. If she got lost in the cargo area and stayed away from the action, all the better.

At last, he entered a long hallway. Up ahead, he could see that the room opened up into a larger space, and he could hear the sounds echoing off of the concrete walls.

Gripping his gun like a safety blanket, he moved forward slowly, realizing to his horror that he was actually using a couple techniques he'd been taught at the stealth course Gabe had forced all of the FBS operatives to go to. Not that he'd ever actually tell his bossy big brother he'd been right about anything.

As he reached the edge of the wall and the end of his cover, he felt his adrenaline beginning to surge. He was going to be hopelessly outnumbered, and he wouldn't be surprised if the cult was armed–he knew at least Lily had a gun– but he couldn't let such details deter him. Not if someone might be facing their imminent death, and not when Karlin was behind him somewhere, trusting him to keep her safe.

But none of his thoughts prepared him for what he saw when he poked his head around the corner and peered into the room.

There was no crowd.

The drumbeats surrounded him, the sound pouring gently out of huge speakers that had been set up at intervals around the perimeter of the room.

The spooky cult chanting had been about as authentic as Bajwa's get-in-the-mood-for-drugs mix CD.

But the room wasn't empty, either. Several people milled around the large space, which was surprisingly modern and well-maintained considering the rest of the building. It sort of reminded him of a nicer version of a high school gym.

He saw several scrawny guys, two of whom were wearing dreadlocks and presumably ironic Britney Spears t-shirts, along with several girls who couldn't have been out of their teens yet.

Well, that was one local mystery solved. So long as he managed to get the girls out of here safely.

But where were Lily and Cora?

He took two steps forward. He would be exposed if anyone looked in his direction, but so far, he hadn't seen any other weapons.

As his field of vision expanded, he noticed a huge photograph on the wall. It featured an older man with thick glasses, who was mostly bald and dressed in a short-sleeved button-up shirt. It was such an odd decoration that for several long seconds, he didn't realize what was located directly beneath it.

He gripped the gun more tightly, trying to stop his hands from shaking.

He had found the two women at last.

Cora was lying on what he could only describe as a wooden altar, and Lily was standing in front of her.

When she shifted her weight, Asher's terror deepened.

Though there was no sign of a gun, Lily was holding a large dagger in both hands, and its point was pressed firmly against the younger woman's throat.

CHAPTER
FORTY-SIX

ASHER

There was no time to think, but Asher didn't need to.

The momentary fear he'd felt ebbed away more quickly than it had come, leaving behind nothing but pure instinct and the years of training that had honed it.

He reacted in a mere heartbeat, rushing out from the shadows and into the center of the room, his gun a comforting weight in his hands.

Lily turned and spotted him. Her eyes were filled with genuine surprise, and he could see by the way she stood trembling now that she realized it was far too late for her to try and run.

He pointed the gun at her.

"Drop the weapon. Now!"

His voice was firm, and loud enough to echo through the space.

Behind him, he could hear the rest of the small crowd moving around and calling to each other in panicked voices. There was a chance one of them would pull a weapon and try to sneak up on him, but he couldn't afford to turn around.

Not until Lily dropped that knife.

He knew now what she was capable of.

"Lily, move now or I'll shoot!" he called out again, louder this time. He stared at her, refusing to let his gaze waver even an inch. He didn't want to hurt the woman, but he would if he had to.

He wouldn't hesitate.

But to his relief, this time, she obeyed immediately.

The dagger clattered loudly against the floor, the sound mingling with the insistent pounding of the drumbeats.

He glanced behind him, but no one was close. Already, the space was clearing out. The others were rushing off in all directions, retreating into the hallways that surrounded the central room. Hopefully, they would hop on their little ATVs and head for the hills. The authorities would have to round them up later, but at least the missing girls would be safe.

"Hands above your head," he said, no longer shouting. He didn't need to. Lily's face had sunk with defeat, and Cora was now sitting up on the altar, watching blankly as the others scurried away.

Suddenly, the sound of the drums went quiet.

Asher looked behind him, expecting trouble, but instead he found Karlin in a far corner of the room, clicking a button on a large black stereo.

Lily and Cora stared at him, and he stared back, keeping the gun pointed in their direction as he waited for Karlin to cross the room and join them.

For a few more moments, they listened to the retreating sounds of running feet, and then there was only silence.

KARLIN

Karlin forced herself to walk slowly toward Axel, Lily, and Cora.

Though she knew he had the gun–and therefore, control–the situation still felt terrifyingly volatile, like a tiny spark could set off a conflagration at any moment.

So many questions loomed in her mind, but before she could choose anything to say, Axel began with something practical.

"Where can we find a phone, Lily?"

In a heartbeat, the older woman's face transformed into a mask of fury.

"There isn't one," she said, leaning forward and spitting onto the ground near Axel's feet. He didn't move, but she could see the slightest twitch of his jaw muscle and the way his finger drifted a millimeter or two closer to the trigger.

In that moment, he reminded her so much of John.

Despite the vastly different lives the two men had lived, they shared so much thanks to their time at war. Both of them had a way of subtly scoping out a room the second they walked into it, always on high alert for danger. She doubted the battle-won instincts would ever leave them, no matter how much they tried to leave their memories of Afghanistan behind.

And at the moment, despite the pain she knew that Axel felt, she couldn't help but to be thankful for it.

"Don't lie to me," Axel said firmly. "There's a phone. Tell me where it is."

Lily kept her mouth pressed into a thin line, but Cora's eyes flicked between the older woman and Axel, clearly debating whether or not to speak.

She was perched on the edge of the altar, bobbing her legs back and forth like a little kid waiting for a needle at the doctor's office. The sight made Karlin's stomach turn all over again.

Cora and Lily may have both been adults, but it was clear just who was in charge here.

Fortunately, it seemed the younger woman had decided it was safe enough to talk. "There's a sat phone down that little corridor at the back, next to the big crates of water."

After a moment's hesitation, Axel nodded in Karlin's direction, and she set off for the phone, expecting all the while to find an ambush, but there was none.

She made the 911 call quickly, giving as little detail as she could while still ensuring a strong police presence. She was eager to return to Axel's side and, more importantly, she was certain the dispatchers had received more than one fake call claiming to have information about their friendly neighborhood cult.

When she stepped back into the room at last, everyone was in the same place they'd been a few moments before. She moved toward Axel, glad to know his gun was still resting firmly in his practiced hands.

"While we wait for the police," Karlin began, "I'd like an explanation of what on earth is going on here. I think you both owe us that much."

CHAPTER
FORTY-SEVEN

ASHER

Every muscle in Asher's body ached.

After being drugged twice, traipsing through the desert all night, and not getting any sleep, his body was finally beginning to protest in earnest.

Fortunately, he'd learned a long time ago how to push the pain away, whether it was physical or mental, and he could do so now. Especially knowing that help was on its way at last.

Cora was safe. The teenage girls were most likely safe.

And most importantly, Karlin was at his side, his loaded gun standing between her and Lily.

He could hardly believe how much the older woman's appearance seemed to have shifted. Her slightly messy, hippie-inspired look had been nothing but a facade, designed to conceal not only her true identity as Dana Corbett, but the warped depths of her clearly unstable mind.

"She's right, Lily," he said at last, nodding toward

Karlin. "You locked her in a cabin and Cora drugged me. It's over now. You may as well tell us how we got here."

The woman's lip curled up in a snarl. "I have nothing to say to you. You've ruined the ritual. You've taken our hope. You've destroyed everything!"

He'd gathered that much already.

Sorry, not sorry.

Careful to keep Karlin behind him, he stuck his gun into the waistband of his jeans and raised his empty hands.

"Can you at least tell me about this ritual?" he asked, letting his voice take on its usual, more lighthearted tone. Lily ignored his plea, but to his relief, Cora nodded.

"Well, you've probably heard about our community on the news," she started. "Though it's not quite as big as everyone on Facebook is saying. I've only just joined, but it's been around for a while now."

He wanted to let her keep talking, but he wasn't surprised that Karlin was unwilling to tamper her own curiosity any longer.

"How long? How did it start?" Karlin prodded.

"It was founded by a brilliant man. His name is Dr. Peter Rorhart, but we all call him the Professor."

"Do not speak of someone you've never met," Lily snapped. "I knew him intimately. He was a world expert on the history of the Texas panhandle, with a special knowledge of the Antelope Creek phase Indians. But the academy shunned his ideas."

Asher shot Karlin a glance. He remembered Cora had told Karlin something about some Indian tribe that had supposedly gone missing. Was this the same one?

"What do you mean?" he pressed, glad that Lily was

starting to talk after all. By the sounds of it, she knew a lot more about the cult than the younger woman did.

"The Professor was willing to follow the evidence where others would not," Lily said proudly. "This tribe disappeared almost six hundred years ago. The main-stream wisdom is that they left their settlements due to drought, resource exhaustion, or being driven out by the Apache, but that's not where the evidence leads."

Karlin raised an eyebrow. "If my memory serves me, you yourself said that their disappearance was down to mundane, earthly causes."

"I couldn't exactly tell you what I really thought, could I?" she sneered.

"So you and this Professor actually think these people were abducted by aliens?"

Asher couldn't blame Karlin for pushing. The whole thing sounded completely insane, and yet, after everything he'd witnessed tonight, there was little he would doubt.

Lily scoffed. "Hardly. They were *saved* from imminent extinction by benevolent, interdimensional beings. They contacted them through their traditional plants–"

"Psychedelics?" Asher clarified.

Lily nodded.

"–and eventually, the tribe was brought to a new planet, where they could live in peace."

"Now your community is seeking the same contact? Seeking to leave this world for a better one?" Asher asked.

It was Cora who answered this time, and Lily made no effort to stop her. "Primarily, our goal is to serve Mother, but yes, in the end, we know that our final home is not here on Earth."

"Mother?" Asher asked, looking over at Karlin, who looked just as confused as he was. "Who's Mother?"

"She's our everything," Cora said dreamily, as though she were a teenager talking about a pop star she was madly in love with. "She's going to save us from extinction, just as she saved the Antelope Creek peoples hundreds of years ago. She has a whole new planet, waiting just for us."

Asher opened his mouth, trying to think of some clarifying question, but it seemed both he and Karlin had been rendered momentarily speechless.

Cora went on.

"Lily doesn't need the drugs to talk to Mother, but the rest of us do. Ayahuasca is pretty good, but DX8 works the best of all. It's a miracle potion, Ms. McKenna. You should be proud of your work in helping to bring it into the world."

Karlin looked horrified, but a second later, her brow furrowed in puzzlement.

"Wait a second. You've been stealing DX8 from my lab, haven't you?"

Cora looked nervous, but Lily's mouth curved into a cruel smile.

"This retreat was an opportunity I couldn't pass up. Not when I knew that the formula for DX8 would have only gotten better since the last time I came and stocked up. Meeting Cora was an extra gift."

Karlin looked like she was going to either throw up or throw punches. Maybe both.

"I still don't understand. Who, exactly, is this Mother person?" Asher cut in quickly.

"I would call her a goddess, but she is too humble to accept such a title," Lily said, her expression softening just as Cora's had at the mention of Mother a few moments before. "I suppose she's an interdimensional being. She cannot manifest herself fully in the everyday world, but across time and cultures, she has always been there."

"How? How does she appear?" Asher demanded.

"For those of us worthy to see, she appears as a large serpent, as green and shimmering as an emerald. She is the most beautiful thing on Earth."

KARLIN

Karlin took a step closer to Axel, recoiling in horror at Lily's words.

"You think the savior of mankind is a giant snake? Seriously?" Axel asked, shaking his head.

She had to agree with his assessment.

From what little she knew of God and the Bible, it was pretty clear that talking to snakes was a bad idea, as was human sacrifice.

And yet, she shouldn't have been surprised. She was familiar with the decades of academic literature on psychedelic drug use, and hallucinations of serpent-like beings were sometimes reported by those who had used the drugs, particularly more potent ones such as ayahuasca and, apparently, DX8.

But she was no longer convinced that the snakes these people saw were mere hallucinations.

Lily ignored Axel's jab. "We were so close to completing the task that Mother laid out for us, but you two were clearly up to something. Always sniffing around, always asking questions. I couldn't risk you finding out too much."

Karlin's mind raced as everything began to come together.

She'd brought Axel in to investigate Senera's misdeeds

and to set herself free, but all the while, a much bigger crime had been happening for years, right there in the shadows.

"You were the one who called the cops on Bajwa, weren't you?" Axel asked.

Lily smiled, clearly pleased by her own cleverness. "I had originally planned to report Ms. McKenna, but then I had second thoughts. Unlike Dr. Bajwa, she was actually working here at the time Amira died, and I was worried that fact might lead the police to dig a little too deep. I didn't think they'd have time to do much before the ritual, but still. Why take the risk?"

"We also couldn't be one hundred percent sure that Bajwa wasn't working with you guys," Cora chimed in. "Mother has a lot of enemies. We had to be careful. In the end, we figured getting all three of you away was the best option."

"But it didn't work," Axel said flatly. "You were too cowardly to kill any of us. I guess it was easier to rope in a conspiracy nut like Cora. Someone who wouldn't resist her own murder."

"I'm not a murderer," Lily snapped. "I would kill only for the greatest good."

Karlin couldn't hold back her speculations any longer. "Amira was part of your cult, wasn't she?"

Lily frowned. "Calling it a cult is so…cliche," she said. "It's a community. We take care of each other."

"We offer people the truth," Cora added. "I had been searching for it my entire life. Until I met Lily and she told me that Mother had chosen me."

"What about Amira?" Karlin snapped, blinking away the tears that were quickly beginning to build. "Did the snake choose her too? Choose for her to kill herself? To leave her husband and daughter behind?"

She felt Axel's hand resting gently on the small of her back, but his touch offered little consolation. Years of guilt and sorrow were bubbling to the surface again, threatening to consume her. She had spent so many years blaming herself, so many years convinced that DX8 alone had been enough to push Amira's mental health beyond its breaking point.

Part of her preferred that story.

At least it made some level of sense.

To consider that the poor woman had been recruited into a violent alien cult was even worse, regardless of whether or not it lessened Karlin's own culpability for her tragic death.

"That was never what Mother, or any of us, wanted," Lily said. For a moment, Karlin could see a flicker of sadness in the woman's eyes, but it was gone in seconds, replaced by the same cold, expressionless mask she'd worn before. "Amira was chosen to be the sacrificial victim, yes. By her blood, Mother would bring us all to the empire of light—including her husband and her little girl."

Axel's jaw tightened, and it was Karlin's turn to place a soothing hand on his forearm. They had no choice but to listen now. Whatever the ugly, terrible truth was, she wanted to know it.

She had to.

"Unfortunately, Amira was weak," Lily continued. "She took part in, shall we say, a preliminary ritual and got cold feet about going through with the final deal."

She remembered that according to Lily, Amira had wanted to talk. To tell her everything. The thought made her sick. Maybe if she'd been paying more attention, the poor woman would have had a chance. Maybe she could have saved her.

But there was no point now dwelling on what could have been. It was far too late for that.

"For what it's worth, I thought we should just let her go and wait for someone else who was willing, but Mother didn't agree. She told me that if Amira took back her willing offering of her blood, I would have to kill her."

"How big of you to disagree with the snake demon," Axel cut in, his muscles tensing beneath Karlin's fingertips.

Lily ignored him.

"By this point, the retreat had ended, and Amira went home. I started to formulate a plan for how I would complete the sacrifice without implicating the community or myself, but I never got the chance. Amira took the third option. She killed herself."

ASHER

Asher reached out a hand to steady Karlin beside him.

Lily's words had stunned everyone into a momentary silence as the full weight of what happened all those years ago began to sink in.

Even Cora looked a little disturbed, and he couldn't help but to wonder just how many of the gritty details she knew about the mess she'd chosen to get herself involved in. He could sympathize with her a little, but then again, if he let himself go very far down that road, he'd be making excuses for Lily, too.

He doubted she'd woken up one day and decided to follow the commands of Mother, either. Someone–probably the Professor–had passed this dark knowledge down to her.

Either way, at the moment, both she and Cora had made their choices.

So had Amira.

As horrific as her death was, and as much as she may have been failed by Senera and by Karlin, she'd been failed even worse by the demon masquerading as a savior and by the people she chose to do her bidding.

All he wanted now was to understand why.

Just as he was going to ask one of the several questions competing in his mind, however, he heard the sound of sirens outside.

Finally, help was coming.

The answers he wanted would have to wait. For the moment, he didn't care.

All he wanted was a warm bed, some food and water, and to know that Karlin was finally safe.

Somewhere behind him, he heard the sound of footsteps. He shifted his position just a little, intending to beckon the first responder over to where they stood, but the half-second distraction was all that it took.

Cora jumped down from the table.

"No!" Karlin screamed, but it was too late.

Asher watched helplessly as the woman picked up the knife from the floor, held it firmly, and plunged it into her chest.

CHAPTER
FORTY-EIGHT

KARLIN

TWO WEEKS LATER

K arlin wrinkled her nose as the lingering fumes of harsh disinfectant filled her nostrils.

She hated that smell, and every hospital seemed to share it.

It always reminded her of the days and weeks after John's overdose, when she woke up every day in a cold sweat, unsure if his brain would be able to recover from the damage he'd inflicted.

Ever since that day, she'd avoided hospitals entirely. Even when her brother had suffered other, more minor overdoses over the years, she'd never made it past the waiting room, where she could keep the exit firmly in sight.

Asher gave her hand a squeeze, and she looked up at

him, offering a quick smile of thanks before she continued walking beside him.

She wasn't over what had happened to her brother.

Not even telling Asher–she was getting used to calling him by his real name now–was enough to take away that trauma completely.

But it helped, and that was enough.

She was here now, refusing to let the memories of her past control her present, and that was something.

Or maybe it just helped that she'd endured enough new traumas to drive most of the old ones deep into the back of her mind.

"To the right, I think," Asher muttered to himself, reading a sign on the wall at the end of the hallway. "This place is a total maze."

"Too manly to ask for directions?" she teased, glad for the opportunity to think of something other than the person they were going to see.

"Obviously," he said, giving her a wink. She couldn't help but to flinch and glance around the hall as he leaned over and kissed her cheek. Though he was no longer undercover, and they had no reason to worry about who saw them together, it was a difficult habit to shake.

They continued on. Now that they were closer to the ICU, it became more obvious that they were, in fact, headed in the right direction.

But with every step, she felt her heart beginning to race a little faster.

"Sweetheart, your hands are sweating," Asher said, pausing for a moment but not letting go. "Are you okay?"

"Yeah, I think so. It's just the smell, I guess," she said, swallowing hard. "It brings back a lot of bad memories. I mean, on top of the current ones."

It was true–it was the smell–but it was also the images that flashed in her mind every time she thought of the woman who lay in bed in the ICU.

The blood that had spread out across the floor of the compound.

The panicked yells of the police officers and paramedics.

The victorious cries of Dana Corbett, who was certain that Mother was about to bring them both to the place she called the empire of light.

Asher pulled her against his chest, stroking her hair.

"I just need to stop thinking about it," she said, her voice muffled against his t-shirt.

Apparently, even when he wasn't undercover, he still dressed like a slightly less grungy garage band drummer. She was surprisingly okay with it, even if she'd never be one of those girls who emulated her man's style.

Not that he was her man.

Not officially, anyway.

That was a conversation that she'd successfully been putting off for weeks now.

"Avoiding your fears won't solve anything," he said gently, pulling back until he was looking down at her, his lips moving dangerously close to her own.

"But a kiss would?" she breathed.

"It's possible. I mean, I don't know about you, but I'm willing to try anything."

Before they could get any closer, however, someone called Asher's name.

Karlin was sure her cheeks were flaming red, but Asher seemed unperturbed as he shook hands with a woman in a white lab coat. She did the same, feeling a twinge of sadness as she took in the doctor's attire.

Would she ever get to dress that way again?

Certainly not at Senera Pharmaceuticals. Dr. Bajwa was currently out on bail while the police investigated the legitimate allegations she and Axel had made against him, but several of the company's executives and members of upper management were still in custody.

It was going to be a long haul, but Karlin had already spoken to the prosecution team, and they had assured her that so long as she was willing to help them bring Senera to justice, she would not face any charges related to her own conduct. Including in the now reopened case of Amira Gorsky's suicide.

But those assurances did little to calm her fears.

It was still very possible that her career in medical research could be over for good.

"Dr. Erica Cliett," the woman said, giving them both a tight smile. "Please, follow me."

Karlin forced her body forward, not wanting to let the woman see how anxious she was. Dr. Cliett was talking, but she struggled to focus on the words.

The memories were suffocating her again, no matter how much she tried to hold them down.

She remembered the pain of performing CPR on John until it felt like she couldn't carry on another second. She remembered all of those nights sleeping in a chair in the hospital because their parents had given up on him...and she remembered Cora.

When she'd taken that knife to herself, they had both reacted on autopilot.

Asher had forced Lily back against a wall so she couldn't run, leaving Karlin to jump in and try to stop the bleeding. When the paramedics finally made it inside, they had taken over, leaving her standing there covered in blood until Asher could safely let Lily go.

It had taken a while.

They'd had to explain everything to the police, and even then, the officers had ended up calling the Forge Brothers Security police liaison in San Antonio, Allie Parker, to confirm Asher was in fact a legitimate private security operator.

And the whole time, Lily had been chanting something unintelligible, probably directed by the demon that she'd allowed to poison her mind.

"Ms. Trejo is stable now," the doctor was saying, snapping Karlin back to reality, "but it's going to have to be a quick visit. We have to run some labs on her in the next little bit, okay?"

Karlin nodded numbly, noticing the local police officer who had been posted outside of the door to Cora's ICU room, standing guard.

"Thank you doctor, officer," Asher said, nodding to them both in turn. "We won't be long."

Offering another quick smile, Dr. Cliett jabbed her hands into the pockets of her lab coat and strode off down the hall.

"Are you ready?" he asked.

Karlin nodded, not trusting herself to speak.

Ready or not, she was going into that room.

———

It was all Karlin could do to suppress a gasp when she entered the room and saw Cora stretched out on the bed.

She looked like a shadow of the woman she had been.

Her formerly shining brown waves looked dry and

dull, and her tanned skin was ashen. Worst of all were her eyes, which were pressed firmly shut.

Her attempt at ritual suicide had almost been successful.

She'd managed to get the knife to strike her heart, but her aim had been off just enough to avoid immediate death. Still, she'd caused catastrophic blood loss and other internal damage, and her medical team had opted to place her in an induced coma in an attempt to promote healing.

They were hopeful that she would retain relatively normal brain function when she woke up, but Karlin knew better than anyone that these things were impossible to guarantee one way or another.

She drew in a deep breath, frozen in the doorway as Asher gave her hand a squeeze.

She'd thought she was prepared for how bad Cora's condition was, but seeing it in person and hearing it secondhand were two very different things.

"If you need to go, I promise, it's okay," he said gently. "We can do this another time."

"No. I want to stay with you," she said, refusing to allow herself to hesitate. "But I still don't really understand why you wanted us to come in the first place."

The question had been simmering in her mind all of last night and this morning, ever since he'd called her from his hotel room in Amarillo and told her he'd finally been given the go-ahead by the hospital for a visit. She'd hoped he'd explain on his own, but her patience had finally worn out.

"I have a few reasons," he said, tugging her forward as he walked closer to Cora's bed, careful to avoid the various wires and IV lines that cluttered the space. "One, I wanted to come and pray for her. The police can't find any living relatives, and though she probably has friends, they struggled to find them all the way down in Los Angeles. Paul told me he wanted to visit, but he had to get back home to Montana before they'd let him. I'm sure Lily–I mean Dana–would have come, but…"

He let the words trail away.

Of course, Dana Corbett was in jail, and probably would be for a very long time.

Karlin gathered as much courage as she could muster and reached out to grasp Cora's hand.

It was cold, but she didn't let go.

"I feel bad for her," she said at last. "She was brought into so much darkness. I just hope that she'll wake up with her mind intact, and if she does, that she'll choose another path."

Asher mumbled his agreement, pressing his hand gently against the small of her back. His touch always managed to send a shiver through her, even here.

"So, what're your other reasons?" she asked.

"The truth," he said simply. "About myself, I guess. I'm trying to come to terms with the fact that my trauma from the war has affected me a lot more than I thought. I don't know what that means for my future yet, but I do know that I'm not going to roll over and let it control me. I didn't want to come here and face these memories today, either, but I knew it would be good for me."

"Well, you're not having a panic attack now," she said, offering him a small smile. "Small victories."

"Exactly."

A comfortable silence fell between them again as they looked over at Cora, listening to the beeping and pumping sounds of the various machines she was hooked up to.

What they had experienced was traumatic, and she was glad that Asher wasn't going to try and laugh it off.

Not that she would let him.

This memory was one they shared, forever binding them. That scared her, but at least it was one dark thing she would never have to face alone.

Assuming Asher wanted to stay in her life, at least.

"You never told me reason number three," Karlin said at last.

"I'm not getting anything past you, am I?"

"Never."

For a moment, he didn't say anything else, and she wondered if he was going to keep his reasons to himself.

She gave Cora's hand a final squeeze before walking over and adjusting a vase of fresh pink flowers that sat on her nightstand. She wondered who could have possibly sent them, but before she could give it any more thought, Asher cleared his throat.

"This might sound kind of silly," he said, his tone guarded.

"Fortunately, that's never stopped you from speaking before."

He closed the distance between them in just a few steps, pressing his lips against hers before she could get away.

"We're in a hospital! We're in an *ICU!*" she said as she pulled back. She had to at least try to keep him in line, even if the dumb grin on her face betrayed her.

"Sorry for the PDA, Cora," Asher said, giving the woman's shoulder a gentle pat. "But you did drug me, so I think you owe me one. Don't tell Dr. Cliett, okay?"

Karlin rolled her eyes.

"Anyway, no changing the subject. What were you going to say?"

"Before you changed the subject by making fun of me?" he teased.

He had a point there.

"I suppose."

But instead of continuing to tease her, Asher's face was serious again.

"I wanted you to see a miracle, Karlin."

She couldn't hide the surprise on her face. Whatever she'd been expecting him to say, that wasn't it.

"This? Cora's in an ICU bed after stabbing herself in the chest. All because she thought some snake alien would take her to a new planet. Not really seeing the miracle. Just a whole lot of crazy."

Asher's eyes were tender as he gazed into her own. "Exactly, and that's the problem. You're looking for these huge miracles that scream in your face, but you're missing the ones that whisper. So many things had to go right for Cora to be alive. For all we know, had we been five minutes later, she and Lily could have completed their ritual killing properly."

She felt a flicker of guilt rising in her chest.

Part of her wanted to argue, but she could see his point. Asher seemed to find God everywhere while she relegated Him to the shadowy moments of life, to be turned to only in extreme desperation.

Maybe she was just blind, so used to seeing things with the eyes of a scientist that she forgot her own bias.

"This isn't the first time this kind of miracle happened to you, either," Asher said, raising an eyebrow. "And I'm not just talking about narrowly escaping that flood."

She pulled away from him a little, crossing her arms

over her chest as the realization slammed into her. She knew where this was going.

Why had it taken so long for her to understand?

"John. When John almost died," she said at last, her voice quiet.

"Yup."

"I hadn't told him I was coming to see him that day. I didn't even really plan it. It just kind of happened. But if I hadn't been there…"

She didn't want to say the words, but Asher finished the sentence for her.

"If you hadn't been there, exactly when you were there, Rome would have died. God was always in control, down to the very last millisecond, timing every minute of that day so that your brother would not only survive, but get a true second chance, with his mind intact."

The thought made her feel strangely sick, but there was no way she could deny it.

The mathematical odds of it all being a coincidence were staggeringly low.

No, they were impossibly low when adding all of the factors together. He shouldn't have lived through being unconscious that long, let alone without brain damage.

It was a miracle.

A miracle she'd never once thanked God for.

"And do you know why He did it?" Asher prompted.

She shook her head, not bothering to wipe away the tears that had begun to slide down her cheeks.

"He did it for the same reason He performs any miracle: He did it so that you would see Him, and that you would turn to Him. He wanted you to live, too."

Asher's words were gentle, but inside, she felt like every part of her was breaking.

God loved her so much, and she hadn't accepted His love.

She hadn't even noticed it.

"I–I rejected the miracle," she stammered, struggling to get the words out through her shame and guilt. "And today I rejected another one."

She was crying freely now. Asher swept her into his arms, pulling her close against his chest, warming her straight through.

"No," he said firmly. "It's not over until you're dead in the ground, Karlin. You can turn to Him at this moment. You can start saying yes. Right here, and right now."

CHAPTER
FORTY-NINE

ASHER

The second that Asher stepped through the lobby doors of the hospital, a gust of freezing wind pummeled him, sending him back a step.

Karlin didn't even flinch.

"I won't miss the worst wind in the United States," he said, taking hold of her hand and gesturing toward where he'd parked his rental car. Another rush of air slid across the open expanse of the hospital parking lot, drowning out any hope of hearing Karlin's reply.

He opened the passenger door for her, holding it tightly so it wouldn't slam shut while she was getting in, and finally, he managed to make it into his own seat.

Turning the key in the ignition, he turned up the heat as high as it would go, deciding at that moment that he would never complain about San Antonio weather again.

Karlin picked up a small stack of old-school mixed CDs that he'd stuck into the center console. Now that the airline

346

had actually returned his luggage, he had something decent to listen to at last.

"You brought all of these with you? Really? No YouTube or Spotify down south?" she teased.

"Nevermind the CDs," he said, laughing as he yanked 'Asher's Top Ten' from her grasp. "I want to talk about the other thing. The real thing."

"What real thing?" she asked innocently, not quite meeting his eyes. "God? Faith?"

"No," he said quickly, shaking his head. "I mean, yes, but–"

"Then what?"

The woman was maddening.

He leaned over until his face was inches away from hers, but this time, he wasn't going to give her the escape route of a kiss. Instead, he took hold of her hands and waited for his eyes to meet hers.

"I want to talk about *this*," he said, his voice coming out in a hushed breath. "Us."

He could tell by the blush rising in her cheeks that she enjoyed his touch, but that didn't fully erase the worry he could see in her bright blue eyes.

"Yeah, I've been thinking about that," she stammered. "You–you've helped me to see so much that I've been missing, and I'm so thankful to have met you. It was–it's been a good time together."

His stomach felt like it had just been filled with rocks. He'd heard words like this before, more than once.

"Hold on. That sounds like what girls say when they dump me. Are you dumping me?"

"I mean, you live all the way in San Antonio," she said, fidgeting beneath the weight of his gaze. "You have a great family, and a whole life there, and I don't know what's going to come next for me. I know I'm going to be stuck here for the foreseeable future. There's the trial for Senera, the trial for Dana...I have to try to keep helping John, somehow, which means I need money, which means I need some kind of well-paying job–"

"All I'm hearing are reasons that you still need *me*, Karlin," he said, cutting her off. "All of the ways that I can help you and be there for you. Did you really think I was going to help you tear everything in your life apart and then just leave you to deal with the aftermath alone?"

She said nothing for several long seconds.

"I don't know. Maybe."

The look in her eyes was enough to shatter his heart.

But before he could wrap his arms around her and assure her he was absolutely not going anywhere, she spoke again.

"I guess I just can't believe that you really want this to be something real. Something lasting. That you want me, when no one else in my life, aside from my brother, ever really has. And then when I think about the distance...I don't know. It's a lot."

He didn't argue with her.

He leaned closer toward her until he could wrap her in his arms, ignoring the bite of pain as one of his plastic CD cases jabbed him in the ribcage. "Of course it's a lot. So what? I want you. I want you, always. And if it costs me something? That's even better. A treasure worth having never comes cheap."

KARLIN

Karlin considered Asher's words as the butterflies in her stomach threatened to lift her away.

Everything he said felt too wonderful to be real, but there was no mistaking his sincerity. Ever since she'd met him, he'd made it clear he cared about her and would do anything for her, even risking his own life to protect her more than once.

She no longer doubted that maybe he really did want her.

But there was one more thing she had to say first. One more thing she had to be sure of, if she was going to find the courage to move forward.

"Asher?"

"Yes, sweetheart?" he said, pulling back just enough for her to be able to look at him face to face.

"It's my turn to sound dumb. There's something I really need to say before I...before I can really believe this is happening for me. Just a few words."

He grinned, his eyes growing mischievous in an instant as he brought his lips dangerously close to her own.

"Say it," he demanded. "Out loud."

Her heart seemed to stop beating.

Clearly he knew what she was trying to confess, and it still didn't stop him from poking fun at her. Not that she could have reasonably expected that he was going to stop driving her insane any time soon.

"Vampire," she said with all of the drama she could muster.

He laughed, still refusing to break eye contact. Clearly, jokes aside, she was not getting out of this.

"You know, you could just say it for me," she said.

"You're the one with a fear to face," he argued. "Besides, you just associated me with Edward Cullen, so we're clearly destined to be together for all eternity. It's a little late to get all shy."

"Hold on. *You* associated you with Edward Cullen!"

He pressed a finger to her lips.

"You argue too much."

"You annoy me too much," she retorted.

"But?"

He paused, waiting.

She drew a shaky breath. There was no way out of the trap she'd set for herself. He was way, way too stubborn.

"But I love you, okay? Goodness! I love you. Even if it's way too soon, and you couldn't possibly love me back yet, and I'm totally ruining everything—"

He moved his finger out of the way for a split second before capturing her mouth in a long, perfect kiss.

By the time he finally pulled back, the fear had melted away, right along with her ability to think straight.

"Not only do I love you," he announced, "but I love you so much that I am liable to do really stupid things if we don't get out of this car and into the cold shower that is Amarillo in November."

She withdrew her fingers from where they'd apparently become entwined around the back of his neck. "I'm sorry, you're right. I wouldn't want to lead you to, you know, do something that might be against your faith. Our faith, I guess. I'm new to this God thing, but–"

Asher grinned. "I was thinking stupid things like 'drive over to a jewelry store and ask you to marry me on the spot,' but your mind went somewhere else."

Karlin felt her jaw dropping open. "Hold on–"

"Sweetheart, it's okay," he said. "I don't blame you. Not with my kissing skills, my body, and my charm. Just like Bella Swan, you are indeed a mere mortal."

She swatted him on the back of the head, and within seconds, they were bickering all over again.

CHAPTER
FIFTY

ASHER

THREE WEEKS LATER

"Yo, big bro!" Asher said as he picked up his ringing cell phone.

He'd been waiting for Gabe to check in. Frankly, he was surprised that it had taken this long. He and Karlin had gotten almost three whole weeks of relative peace, but he knew that real life would start to demand his attention sooner or later.

"How's Amarillo?" his oldest brother asked. Asher could hear the sound of him moving around his office in the background. As far as Gabe saw it, if he was doing only one thing at a time, he was already behind. "Did you finally take a selfie at the Cadillac Ranch? Buy a cow? Start wearing boots?"

"You tease, but I've done two out of three."

Gabe hesitated.

"Not the cow, right?"

He laughed. "No, not the cow. But Karlin says I look fantastic in these cowboy boots."

Karlin was currently at the spa, where he'd insisted on treating her to several pampering treatments, on the condition that he didn't have to actually set foot in the building himself.

To pass the time, he'd decided to hit up a local outdoor store, and was now considering purchasing a ten-gallon hat.

"You're getting way too comfortable up there. It kind of freaks me out. And for the record, buying a fully-loaded pickup truck would be just as dumb as buying a cow. Even if you do decide to stay."

Asher chuckled, but chose to let the comments slide.

The intrusion of real life into his precious time with Karlin was bad enough. The discussion about how long he was planning to stay in Amarillo could wait a few more minutes.

"So, got any updates?" he asked, hoping Gabe would accept the abrupt change of subject.

"A few," Gabe said. "Ben told you he finally worked up the guts to propose to Grace?"

"Obviously. I had to call him five minutes beforehand to make sure he didn't wimp out," Asher said, laughing. "I'm happy for them."

"I would be, except that all this wedding crap is driving me insane already. Do you know how to arrange flowers in a tasteful Christmas-but-not-too-Christmas table setting?"

"Uh, no, why?"

"Because I do now, Asher," Gabe said, his voice almost pleading. "I do. Cameron asked me to help when their florist cancelled, and I told him to pound sand."

"He called in Bristol, didn't he?"

"He called in Bristol. I couldn't say no to her. Not after everything she went through when she started working with us. So yeah. I knew what a poinsettia was, but now I know where to import cymbidium orchids from."

Asher couldn't help but to laugh out loud. It sounded like a typical Forge family nightmare, but it was the kind of nightmare he missed the most.

"When I have been able to escape from that stuff," Gabe continued, "Ben and I have been digging into Dana's past."

"Did you guys figure out the whole Professor thing yet?"

"Yep. Dr. Peter Rorhart was actually pretty brilliant. Got his PhD super young, ended up heading up the history department at Panhandle Plains College. Until he was ousted for preying on female students, that is."

Asher's jaw fell open. "Oh man."

"He wasn't convicted, unfortunately," Gabe said. "Got off on some technicality. But Dana Corbett was apparently one of his victims, groomed by him since she was seventeen, though obviously she refused–and refuses–to see things that way."

"So he started a cult?"

"We've been able to piece together a story that fits pretty well from what we learned from Dana and Cora. When Rorhart was driven out of his teaching job, he started some hippie commune in the desert. It wasn't in the same location, though. Apparently, they moved into their current compound after he disappeared in the early nineties, leaving Dana–who changed her name to Lily Moonchild–in charge."

Asher could hardly believe what he was hearing, but he wasn't exactly surprised, either. This was the weirdest case he'd ever worked on by a long shot.

"Did you ever figure out what the preliminary ritual was that caused Amira Gorsky to try and extricate herself from the group?"

Gabe exhaled loudly. "Their other rituals were sexual in nature, and yes, unfortunately, they included the underage girls that were groomed into the cult."

Asher felt sick to his stomach. It was unbelievable to imagine that this evil had been going on for over twenty years, all without anyone really seeming to notice or care until recently.

How many young girls had turned to hard drugs, alcohol, or other self-destructive behaviors to try and escape the reality of what they'd taken part in?

He could only pray that no one else had followed in Amira's tragic footsteps, but at least the cult had been disbanded now. And hopefully for good.

"Oh, before I forget–were you able to find out why Paul Durant signed up to participate in the DX8 trial?"

Karlin had never found out, and it had been bothering both of them ever since the older man had gone home to Montana.

Gabe sighed. "I did, actually. Kind of broke my heart. Mr. Durant is battling an aggressive cancer. He's not going to live much longer, and despite his Christian faith, he was experiencing intense anxiety about death. I guess he thought a psychedelic experience could help him to face it."

Asher felt like he'd been kicked in the gut. Paul had seemed so calm, like nothing could shake him, and yet, it had all been a facade.

Then again, he knew what that was like. It was easier to put on a happy mask than to admit you were hurting.

"Man, that's terrible. I'll be praying for him."

"Me too, bro. And I'll let you know if we find out anything else important," Gabe said after letting the silence rest between them for several moments. "We're still digging on Senera. We're going to do what we can to help Karlin. I just wish I'd done more sooner. I'm sorry."

His apology sent a jolt of guilt through Asher's heart.

He had so much to apologize for himself, and so much to confess.

And now that the right moment had come, it was absolutely the last thing he wanted to do.

"No, it's…it's okay," he started. "There's actually something I need to talk to you about. I'm sorry I've waited until now."

"Everything okay?" Gabe asked.

"You remember what happened back on South Padre, right? When I screwed up?"

"Yes, somehow, I seem to be able to recall that particular incident pretty well, considering you literally shot a dude by accident."

Asher flinched. Apparently, his big brother was still a little bit mad about that one. Not that he was in any position to get defensive.

"I'm sorry."

Gabe let out a long sigh. "Nah, man, sorry to bring it up again. We all make mistakes."

"That's the thing," Asher said, trying to find the words.

"I knew I was taking a big risk when I took part in that operation. And then I did it again this time."

"What do you mean?"

"When I came back from Afghanistan, I tried to convince you all that Nico's death didn't really affect me. It seemed to work. For a while, I think I even fooled myself."

He allowed himself a second to breathe. He wanted to tell Gabe and the rest of his family the whole ugly truth of what had happened, and just how much he was to blame, but it wasn't the kind of thing he wanted to share over the phone while standing in front of a giant plaster cowboy hat.

"Anyway," he continued, "I started experiencing some symptoms of post-traumatic stress disorder. It didn't seem very serious at first, but it just kept getting worse over time. I should have told you, or at least Ben. Just…I should have told someone."

Gabe's voice was stern. "Uh, yeah you should have. You should have told us so we could help you, Asher. I hate that you've been going through this alone."

Asher couldn't help but to smile at his big brother's mixture of harshness and love. It reminded him so much of their dad, which was probably why the two of them argued so often.

"Thanks, man," he said. "It feels good to get it off my chest, but there's more."

"Try me."

Asher took a deep breath. He'd rehearsed the words in his mind over and over again. All he had to do was get them out.

"My panic attacks have gotten severe enough that I think I'm a risk to both myself and others out in the field.

Because of that, I need to give you my resignation as an operative with Forge Brothers Security."

The other end of the line was silent for so long that he was sure the phone had gone dead.

"Bro, I know I can be tough sometimes, but my main priority is our family. I want everyone to be safe and healthy, including you, and if you think stepping away is what's best, you have my support."

The relief was so intense that he actually felt tears springing to his eyes, which he managed to wipe away a few seconds after one of the sales clerks had already noticed him.

"Er, they're great hats," he said by way of explanation. The guy gave him a funny look before scurrying off toward the gun aisle.

"What?" Gabe asked, but kept talking before he actually had a chance to answer, his voice all business. "Anyway, I assume that probably means you're staying in Amarillo."

"I'm actually not sure," he admitted. "Not long term, anyway. Karlin wouldn't mind a fresh start, and I hate the weather. But for the moment, my focus is on helping her prepare for two trials. I think it's gonna keep us both busy. Ben already knows I'm staying for now, and he was already gonna sell our house so he could move somewhere new with Grace. Either way, Karlin and I will be flying back for the wedding."

"Oh, yeah, there is no world where you're getting out of that," Gabe said quickly. "I'm not putting together all of these flowers by myself, and Reilly and Ben have already called dibs on helping with the much more manly tasks of setting up the marquee and the dance floor."

"I suppose I can live with being the flower boy's assistant for one day."

"I take it you're not going to want a remote job with FBS?" Gabe asked.

Asher laughed. "Me doing paperwork would be more dangerous than me having a panic attack while holding a loaded gun."

"That's true," Gabe agreed. "Well, okay, bro. I guess we'll see what happens. But we're going to miss you."

"I do have one more thing to ask."

Gabe sounded wary. "What? Don't worry, I've already started looking for someone to irradiate your office as we speak."

"Ha-ha," Asher said. "I just need a little favor."

"Just say the word," Gabe said. "I have some mental space for favors now that you're no longer here to mess everything up."

Asher didn't bother to suppress the grin that spread over his face, even as the outdoor store clerk wandered back over in his direction.

There were so many regrets that he would continue to carry, and so many wounds he would never be able to heal.

But this?

This he could fix.

"There's this guy I served with, John Collins, who happens to be Karlin's older brother. I need you to help me find him a PTSD service dog."

———

Thank you so much for reading Forged in Deception!

Did it seem like I was teasing K9s at the end there?

Because I totally was. ;) Gabe's story is coming soon in the next Forge Brothers Security book, *Forged in Shadows*.

Keep reading to find out more about the facts behind the fiction, and to get your free prequel novella!

If you enjoyed this book, please take a moment to leave a brief review — it helps more people to find my stories.

GET YOUR FREE PREQUEL

Find out how Reilly and Lauren met with a FREE novella!

Just head to www.kendrawarden.com/ to sign up for my latest updates and download your copy. :)

AUTHOR'S NOTE

I don't know about you guys, but psychedelics have *always* freaked me out.

Even before my conversion to Christianity back in 2018 (long story—I became a Catholic after years of living a sinful life and ignoring God), I was never tempted to try any 'serious' mind-altering drugs.

The thought of seeing weird shapes, hearing weird noises, and losing track of time sounded extremely scary to me, but that was about as much as I'd thought about it. Even though I'd started seeing more and more talk about the so-called medicinal use of magic mushrooms and the like, psychedelics simply weren't on my radar.

And then I listened to an episode of the Haunted Cosmos podcast entitled *Your D.A.R.E. Officer Was Right!,* and I realized that this topic went much deeper than I ever imagined.

Like Karlin, I'd more or less accepted the assumption that these drugs caused bizarre effects to emerge from *within* the brain, but after listening to the podcast and doing a deep dive into other resources, I have now come to believe that these drugs actually act as a gateway for interaction with honest-to-goodness demonic entities.

Worse, these demonic entities show up again and again in history, and contact with them through these drugs is directly linked with horrors such as human sacrifice. This is not limited to any one place or culture, either.

While I did take a lot of creative liberty with the fictional story of Asher and Karlin, many of the individual elements come from a starting point of truth.

While DX8 is a totally fictional drug, it is loosely based on a compound called dimethyltryptamine, more commonly known as DMT. This compound is commonly ingested by drinking a South American psychoactive brew called ayahuasca.

Just like in the book, there is no current "trip killer" drug that can cut short one's time on DMT or ayahuasca safely. In fact, if Cora used a benzodiazepine to sedate Asher in real life, it could have been extremely dangerous!

While the character of Mother is probably the most highly-dramatized part of the story, there is a commonly reported entity known as "Mother Ayahuasca" mentioned by hundreds if not thousands of users of the drug. Like Mother in the story, this entity is often—though not always—described as a serpent.

Another fun fact: while I thought that I mentioned vomiting way too much in this story, I was actually wildly understating it. In reality, many psychedelic drugs (including ayahuasca) commonly cause severe vomiting, and sometimes this can go on for *hours*.

Like you needed another reason to stay away. Gross.

Psychedelic psychosis, like what happened to Destiny in the story, is also a real phenomenon, though I did of course dramatize her experience. Fortunately, in real life, most traditional/shamanic practitioners who help others to use drugs like ayahuasca advise against mixing them with conditions like schizophrenia.

That said, one of the most disturbing things about writing this story was learning just how much real life research is going into using psychedelics (often psilocybin, commonly known as 'magic mushrooms') to treat mental illnesses such as anxiety, depression, and even PTSD.

If you want to learn more about this topic, I highly recommend starting with the psychedelic drug episode of the Haunted Cosmos podcast mentioned above, which you can find on Youtube or any podcast platform.

Secondly, there is a great book on this topic by a Christian author that focuses primarily on the connection between psychedelic drug use, demonic entities, and human sacrifice. It's called *Return of the Dragon* by Lewis Ungit.

A final, related resource I would like to offer is the article *Lost in Thought* by David Kortava. It tells the tragic story of a woman named Megan Vogt who committed suicide after experiencing a meditation-induced psychotic break. Many of these New Age practices are connected, and we must be very cautious.

I firmly believe that the use of psychedelic drugs is an ongoing issue that Christians need to be praying about and educating ourselves on, and that it will only become more common moving forward.

Demons are real. We don't need to be afraid, but we do need to be prudent and courageous in Christ.

"Be sober, be watchful. Your adversary the devil prowls around like a roaring lion, seeking some one to devour." (1 Peter 5:8)

Blessings,

Kendra